Bertrand Russell's

The Problems of Philosophy

The complete text

Along with relevant selections from various philosophers
selected and edited by

J. Addington

ISBN 978-1-257-94988-5

Table of Contents

Preface

This volume is something of an experiment, and perhaps requires explanation. Bertrand Russell was arguably the greatest logician since Aristotle, a major figure in 20th century philosophy, and a Nobel laureate in literature besides, so it hardly seems as if his "The Problems of Philosophy" stands in need of improvement. Indeed, his book alone is perhaps the best introduction to philosophy ever written, being both broad and deep, while being accessible to the newcomer to philosophy.

However, having taught this book at the introductory level, I found it useful to provide my students with selections of the material to which Russell alludes. This book is the result. Each chapter of Russell's book is accompanied by a selection from a philosopher that is relevant to the discussion at that point. The selections are somewhat idiosyncratic, but I believe they improve the educational experience.

In six chapters, Russell refers to particular philosophers by name, and addresses their particular arguments. In these cases I tried to choose the selections that he presumably had in mind. Where he does not name a particular philosopher, but speaks more broadly on some topic, I took some liberties with the selections, choosing works which, while perhaps not directly relevant to his argument, serve, I think, to illustrate the concept at hand.

I made no attempt to Americanize or even modernize the spelling in any of the pieces. The first and last chapters are unaccompanied, as I thought it appropriate to give Russell the first and last word.

J. Addington 2011

CHAPTER I.

APPEARANCE AND REALITY

Is there any knowledge in the world which is so certain that no reasonable man could doubt it? This question, which at first sight might not seem difficult, is really one of the most difficult that can be asked. When we have realized the obstacles in the way of a straightforward and confident answer, we shall be well launched on the study of philosophy--for philosophy is merely the attempt to answer such ultimate questions, not carelessly and dogmatically, as we do in ordinary life and even in the sciences, but critically, after exploring all that makes such questions puzzling, and after realizing all the vagueness and confusion that underlie our ordinary ideas.

In daily life, we assume as certain many things which, on a closer scrutiny, are found to be so full of apparent contradictions that only a great amount of thought enables us to know what it is that we really may believe. In the search for certainty, it is natural to begin with our present experiences, and in some sense, no doubt, knowledge is to be derived from them. But any statement as to what it is that our immediate experiences make us know is very likely to be wrong. It seems to me that I am now sitting in a chair, at a table of a certain shape, on which I see sheets of paper with writing or print. By turning my head I see out of the window buildings and clouds and the sun. I believe that the sun is about ninety-three million miles from the earth; that it is a hot globe many times bigger than the earth; that, owing to the earth's rotation, it rises every morning, and will continue to do so for an indefinite time in the future. I believe that, if any other normal person comes into my room, he will see the same chairs and tables and books and papers as I see, and that the table which I see is the same as the table which I feel pressing against my arm.

All this seems to be so evident as to be hardly worth stating, except in answer to a man who doubts whether I know anything. Yet all this may be reasonably doubted, and all of it requires much careful discussion before we can be sure that we have stated it in a form that is wholly true.

To make our difficulties plain, let us concentrate attention on the table. To the eye it is oblong, brown and shiny, to the touch it is smooth and cool and hard; when I tap it, it gives out a wooden sound. Any one else who sees and feels and hears the table will agree with this description, so that it might seem as if no difficulty would arise; but as soon as we try to be more precise our troubles begin. Although I believe that the table is 'really' of the same colour all over, the parts that reflect the light look much brighter than the other parts, and some parts look white because of reflected light. I know that, if I move, the parts that reflect the light will be different, so that the apparent distribution of colours on the table will change. It follows that if several people are looking at the table at the same moment, no two of them will see exactly the same distribution of colours, because no two can see it from exactly the same point of view, and any change in the point of view makes some change in the way the light is reflected.

For most practical purposes these differences are unimportant, but to the painter they are all-important: the painter has to unlearn the habit of thinking that things seem to have the colour which common sense says they 'really' have, and to learn the habit of seeing things as they appear. Here we have already the beginning of one of the distinctions that cause most trouble in philosophy--the distinction between 'appearance' and 'reality', between what things seem to be and what they are. The painter wants to know what things seem to be, the practical man and the philosopher want to know what they are; but the philosopher's wish to know this is stronger than the practical man's, and is more troubled by knowledge as to the difficulties of answering the question.

To return to the table. It is evident from what we have found, that there is no colour which pre-eminently appears to be *the* colour of the table, or even of any one particular part of the table--it appears to be of different colours from different points of view, and there is no reason for regarding some of these as more really its colour than others. And we know that even from a given point of view the colour will seem different by artificial light, or to a colour-blind man, or to a man wearing blue spectacles, while in the dark there will be no colour at all, though to touch and hearing the table will be unchanged. This colour is not something which is inherent in the table, but something depending upon the table and the spectator and the way the light falls on the table. When, in ordinary life, we speak of *the* colour of the table, we only mean the sort of colour which it will seem to have to a normal spectator from an ordinary point of view under usual conditions of light. But the other colours which appear under other conditions have just as good a right to be considered real; and therefore, to avoid favouritism, we are compelled to deny that, in itself, the table has any one particular colour.

The same thing applies to the texture. With the naked eye one can see the grain, but otherwise the table looks smooth and even. If we looked at it through a microscope, we should see roughnesses and hills and valleys, and all sorts of differences that are imperceptible to the naked eye. Which of these is the 'real' table? We are naturally tempted to say that what we see through the microscope is more real, but that in turn would be changed by a still more powerful microscope. If, then, we cannot trust what we see with the naked eye, why should we trust what we see through a microscope? Thus, again, the confidence in our senses with which we began deserts us.

The shape of the table is no better. We are all in the habit of judging as to the 'real' shapes of things, and we do this so unreflectingly that we come to think we actually see the real shapes. But, in fact, as we all have to learn if we try to draw, a given thing looks different in shape from every different point of view. If our table is 'really' rectangular, it will look, from almost all points of view, as if it had two acute angles and two obtuse angles. If opposite sides are parallel, they will look as if they converged to a point away from the spectator; if they are of equal length, they will look as if the nearer side were longer. All these things are not commonly noticed in looking at a table, because experience has taught us to construct the 'real' shape from the apparent shape, and the 'real' shape is what interests us as practical men. But the 'real' shape is not what we see; it is something inferred from what we see. And what we see is constantly changing in shape as we move about the room; so that here again the senses seem not to give us the truth about the table itself, but only about the appearance of the table.

Similar difficulties arise when we consider the sense of touch. It is true that the table always gives us a sensation of hardness, and we feel that it resists pressure. But the sensation we obtain depends upon how hard we press the table and also upon what part of the body we press with; thus the various sensations due to various pressures or various parts of the body cannot be supposed to reveal *directly* any definite property of the table, but at most to be *signs* of some property which perhaps *causes* all the sensations, but is not actually apparent in any of them. And the same applies still more obviously to the sounds which can be elicited by rapping the table.

Thus it becomes evident that the real table, if there is one, is not the same as what we immediately experience by sight or touch or hearing. The real table, if there is one, is not *immediately* known to us at all, but must be an inference from what is immediately known. Hence, two very difficult questions at once arise; namely, (1) Is there a real table at all? (2) If so, what sort of object can it be?

It will help us in considering these questions to have a few simple terms of which the meaning is definite and clear. Let us give the name of 'sense-data' to the things that are immediately known in sensation: such things as colours, sounds, smells, hardnesses, roughnesses, and so on. We shall give the name 'sensation' to the experience of being immediately aware of these things. Thus, whenever we see a colour, we have a sensation *of* the colour, but the colour itself is a sense-datum, not a sensation. The colour is that *of* which we are immediately aware, and the awareness itself is the sensation. It is plain that if we are to know anything about the table, it must be by means of the sense-data--brown colour, oblong shape, smoothness, etc.--which we associate with the table; but, for the reasons which have been given, we cannot say that the table is the sense-data, or even that the sense-data are directly properties of the table. Thus a problem arises as to the relation of the sense-data to the real table, supposing there is such a thing.

The real table, if it exists, we will call a 'physical object'. Thus we have to consider the relation of sense-data to physical objects. The collection of all physical objects is called 'matter'. Thus our two questions may be re-stated as follows: (1) Is there any such thing as matter? (2) If so, what is its nature?

The philosopher who first brought prominently forward the reasons for regarding the immediate objects of our senses as not existing independently of us was Bishop Berkeley (1685-1753). His *Three Dialogues between Hylas and Philonous, in Opposition to Sceptics and Atheists*, undertake to prove that there is no such thing as matter at all, and that the world consists of nothing but minds and their ideas. Hylas has hitherto believed in matter, but he is no match for Philonous, who mercilessly drives him into contradictions and paradoxes, and makes his own denial of matter seem, in the end, as if it were almost common sense. The arguments employed are of very different value: some are important and sound, others are confused or quibbling. But Berkeley retains the merit of having shown that the existence of matter is capable of being denied without absurdity, and that if there are any things that exist independently of us they cannot be the immediate objects of our sensations. There are two different questions involved when we ask whether matter exists, and it is important to keep them clear. We commonly mean by 'matter' something which is opposed to 'mind', something which we think of as occupying space and as radically incapable of any sort of thought or consciousness. It is chiefly in this sense that Berkeley denies matter; that is to say, he does not deny that the sense-data which we commonly take as signs of the existence of the table are really signs of the existence of *something* independent of us, but he does deny that this something is non-mental, that it is neither mind nor ideas entertained by some mind. He admits that there must be something which continues to exist when we go out of the room or shut our eyes, and that what we call seeing the table does really give us reason for believing in something which persists even when we are not seeing it. But he thinks that this something cannot be radically different in nature from what we see, and cannot be independent of seeing altogether, though it must be independent of *our* seeing. He is thus led to regard the 'real' table as an idea in the mind of God. Such an idea has the required permanence and independence of ourselves, without being--as matter would otherwise be--something quite unknowable, in the sense that we can only infer it, and can never be directly and immediately aware of it.

Other philosophers since Berkeley have also held that, although the table does not depend for its existence upon being seen by me, it does depend upon being seen (or otherwise apprehended in sensation) by *some* mind--not necessarily the mind of God, but more often the whole collective mind of the universe. This they hold, as Berkeley does, chiefly because they think there can be nothing real--or at any rate nothing known to be real except minds and their thoughts and feelings. We might state the argument by which they support their view in some such way as this: 'Whatever can be thought of is an idea in the mind of the person thinking of it; therefore nothing can be thought of except ideas in minds; therefore anything else is inconceivable, and what is inconceivable cannot exist.'

Such an argument, in my opinion, is fallacious; and of course those who advance it do not put it so shortly or so crudely. But whether valid or not, the argument has been very widely advanced in one form or another; and very many philosophers, perhaps a majority, have held that there is nothing real except minds and their ideas. Such philosophers are called 'idealists'. When they come to explaining matter, they either say, like Berkeley, that matter is really nothing but a collection of ideas,or they say, like Leibniz (1646-1716), that what appears as matter is really a collection of more or less rudimentary minds.

But these philosophers, though they deny matter as opposed to mind, nevertheless, in another sense, admit matter. It will be remembered that we asked two questions; namely, (1) Is there a real table at all? (2) If so, what sort of object can it be? Now both Berkeley and Leibniz admit that there is a real table, but Berkeley says it is certain ideas in the mind of God, and Leibniz says it is a colony of souls. Thus both of them answer our first question in the affirmative, and only diverge from the views of ordinary mortals in their answer to our second question. In fact, almost all philosophers seem to be agreed that there is a real table: they almost all agree that, however much our sense-data--colour, shape, smoothness, etc.--may depend upon us, yet their occurrence is a sign of something existing independently of us, something differing, perhaps, completely from our sense-data, and yet to be regarded as causing those sense-data whenever we are in a suitable relation to the real table. Now obviously this point in which the philosophers are agreed--the view that there *is* a real table, whatever its nature may be--is vitally important, and it will be worth while to consider what reasons there are for accepting this view before we go on to the further question as to the nature of the real table. Our next chapter, therefore, will be concerned with the reasons for supposing that there is a real table at all.

Before we go farther it will be well to consider for a moment what it is that we have discovered so far. It has appeared that, if we take any common object of the sort that is supposed to be known by the senses, what the senses *immediately* tell us is not the truth about the object as it is apart from us, but only the truth about certain sense-data which, so far as we can see, depend upon the relations between us and the object. Thus what we directly see and feel is merely 'appearance', which we believe to be a sign of some 'reality' behind. But if the reality is not what appears, have we any means of knowing whether there is any reality at all? And if so, have we any means of finding out what it is like?

Such questions are bewildering, and it is difficult to know that even the strangest hypotheses may not be true. Thus our familiar table, which has roused but the slightest thoughts in us hitherto, has become a problem full of surprising possibilities. The one thing we know about it is that it is not what it seems. Beyond this modest result, so far, we have the most complete liberty of conjecture. Leibniz tells us it is a community of souls: Berkeley tells us it is an idea in the mind of God; sober science, scarcely less wonderful, tells us it is a vast collection of electric charges in violent motion.

Among these surprising possibilities, doubt suggests that perhaps there is no table at all. Philosophy, if it cannot *answer* so many questions as we could wish, has at least the power of *asking* questions which increase the interest of the world, and show the strangeness and wonder lying just below the surface even in the commonest things of daily life.

CHAPTER II.

THE EXISTENCE OF MATTER

In this chapter we have to ask ourselves whether, in any sense at all, there is such a thing as matter. Is there a table which has a certain intrinsic nature, and continues to exist when I am not looking, or is the table merely a product of my imagination, a dream-table in a very prolonged dream? This question is of the greatest importance. For if we cannot be sure of the independent existence of objects, we cannot be sure of the independent existence of other people's bodies, and therefore still less of other people's minds, since we have no grounds for believing in their minds except such as are derived from observing their bodies. Thus if we cannot be sure of the independent existence of objects, we shall be left alone in a desert--it may be that the whole outer world is nothing but a dream, and that we alone exist. This is an uncomfortable possibility; but although it cannot be strictly proved to be false, there is not the slightest reason to suppose that it is true. In this chapter we have to see why this is the case. Before we embark upon doubtful matters, let us try to find some more or less fixed point from which to start. Although we are doubting the physical existence of the table, we are not doubting the existence of the sense-data which made us think there was a table; we are not doubting that, while we look, a certain colour and shape appear to us, and while we press, a certain sensation of hardness is experienced by us. All this, which is psychological, we are not calling in question. In fact, whatever else may be doubtful, some at least of our immediate experiences seem absolutely certain.

Descartes (1596-1650), the founder of modern philosophy, invented a method which may still be used with profit--the method of systematic doubt. He determined that he would believe nothing which he did not see quite clearly and distinctly to be true. Whatever he could bring himself to doubt, he would doubt, until he saw reason for not doubting it. By applying this method he gradually became convinced that the only existence of which he could be *quite* certain was his own. He imagined a deceitful demon, who presented unreal things to his senses in a perpetual phantasmagoria; it might be very improbable that such a demon existed, but still it was possible, and therefore doubt concerning things perceived by the senses was possible.

But doubt concerning his own existence was not possible, for if he did not exist, no demon could deceive him. If he doubted, he must exist; if he had any experiences whatever, he must exist. Thus his own existence was an absolute certainty to him. 'I think, therefore I am,' he said (*Cogito ergo sum*); and on the basis of this certainty he set to work to build up again the world of knowledge which his doubt had laid in ruins. By inventing the method of doubt, and by showing that subjective things are the most certain, Descartes performed a great service to philosophy, and one which makes him still useful to all students of the subject.

But some care is needed in using Descartes' argument. 'I think, therefore I am' says rather more than is strictly certain. It might seem as though we were quite sure of being the same person to-day as we were yesterday, and this is no doubt true in some sense. But the real Self is as hard to arrive at as the real table, and does not seem to have that absolute, convincing certainty that belongs to particular experiences. When I look at my table and see a certain brown colour, what is quite certain at once is not '*I* am seeing a brown colour', but rather, 'a brown colour is being seen'. This of course involves something (or somebody) which (or who) sees the brown colour; but it does not of itself involve that more or less permanent person whom we call 'I'. So far as immediate certainty goes, it might be that the something which sees the brown colour is quite momentary, and not the same as the something which has some different experience the next moment.

Thus it is our particular thoughts and feelings that have primitive certainty. And this applies to dreams and hallucinations as well as to normal perceptions: when we dream or see a ghost, we certainly do have the sensations we think we have, but for various reasons it is held that no physical object corresponds to these sensations. Thus the certainty of our knowledge of our own experiences does not have to be limited in any way to allow for exceptional cases. Here, therefore, we have, for what it is worth, a solid basis from which to begin our pursuit of knowledge. The problem we have to consider is this: Granted that we are certain of our own sense-data, have we any reason for regarding them as signs of the existence of something else, which we can call the physical object? When we have enumerated all the sense-data which we should naturally regard as connected with the table, have we said all there is to say about the table, or is there still something else--something not a sense-datum, something which persists when we go out of the room? Common sense unhesitatingly answers that there is. What can be bought and sold and pushed about and have a cloth laid on it, and so on, cannot be a *mere* collection of sense-data. If the cloth completely hides the table, we shall derive no sense-data from the table, and therefore, if the table were merely sense-data, it would have ceased to exist, and the cloth would be suspended in empty air, resting, by a miracle, in the place where the table formerly was. This seems plainly absurd; but whoever wishes to become a philosopher must learn not to be frightened by absurdities.

One great reason why it is felt that we must secure a physical object in addition to the sense-data, is that we want the same object for different people. When ten people are sitting round a dinner-table, it seems preposterous to maintain that they are not seeing the same tablecloth, the same knives and forks and spoons and glasses. But the sense-data are private to each separate person; what is immediately present to the sight of one is not immediately present to the sight of another: they all see things from slightly different points of view, and therefore see them slightly differently. Thus, if there are to be public neutral objects, which can be in some sense known to many different people, there must be something over and above the private and particular sense-data which appear to various people. What reason, then, have we for believing that there are such public neutral objects?

The first answer that naturally occurs to one is that, although different people may see the table slightly differently, still they all see more or less similar things when they look at the table, and the variations in what they see follow the laws of perspective and reflection of light, so that it is easy to arrive at a permanent object underlying all the different people's sense-data. I bought my table from the former occupant of my room; I could not buy *his* sense-data, which died when he went away, but I could and did buy the confident expectation of more or less similar sense-data. Thus it is the fact that different people have similar sense-data, and that one person in a given place at different times has similar sense-data, which makes us suppose that over and above the sense-data there is a permanent public object which underlies or causes the sense-data of various people at various times.

Now in so far as the above considerations depend upon supposing that there are other people besides ourselves, they beg the very question at issue. Other people are represented to me by certain sense-data, such as the sight of them or the sound of their voices, and if I had no reason to believe that there were physical objects independent of my sense-data, I should have no reason to believe that other people exist except as part of my dream. Thus, when we are trying to show that there must be objects independent of our own sense-data, we cannot appeal to the testimony of other people, since this testimony itself consists of sense-data, and does not reveal other people's experiences unless our own sense-data are signs of things existing independently of us. We must therefore, if possible, find, in our own purely private experiences, characteristics which show, or tend to show, that there are in the world things other than ourselves and our private experiences. In one sense it must be admitted that we can never prove the existence of things other than ourselves and our experiences. No logical absurdity results from the hypothesis that the world consists of myself and my thoughts and feelings and sensations, and that everything else is mere fancy. In dreams a very complicated world may seem to be present, and yet on waking we find it was a delusion; that is to say, we find that the sense-data in the dream do not appear to have corresponded with such physical objects as we should naturally infer from our sense-data. (It is true that, when the physical world is assumed, it is possible to find physical causes for the sense-data in dreams: a door banging, for instance, may cause us to dream of a naval engagement. But although, in this case, there is a physical cause for the sense-data, there is not a physical object corresponding to the sense-data in the way in which an actual naval battle would correspond.) There is no logical impossibility in the supposition that the whole of life is a dream, in which we ourselves create all the objects that come before us. But although this is not logically impossible, there is no reason whatever to suppose that it is true; and it is, in fact, a less simple hypothesis, viewed as a means of accounting for the facts of our own life, than the common-sense hypothesis that there really are objects independent of us, whose action on us causes our sensations.

The way in which simplicity comes in from supposing that there really are physical objects is easily seen. If the cat appears at one moment in one part of the room, and at another in another part, it is natural to suppose that it has moved from the one to the other, passing over a series of intermediate positions. But if it is merely a set of sense-data, it cannot have ever been in any place where I did not see it; thus we shall have to suppose that it did not exist at all while I was not looking, but suddenly sprang into being in a new place. If the cat exists whether I see it or not, we can understand from our own experience how it gets hungry between one meal and the next; but if it does not exist when I am not seeing it, it seems odd that appetite should grow during non-existence as fast as during existence. And if the cat consists only of sense-data, it cannot be hungry, since no hunger but my own can be a sense-datum to me. Thus the behaviour of the sense-data which represent the cat to me, though it seems quite natural when regarded as an expression of hunger, becomes utterly inexplicable when regarded as mere movements and changes of patches of colour, which are as incapable of hunger as a triangle is of playing football.

But the difficulty in the case of the cat is nothing compared to the difficulty in the case of human beings. When human beings speak —that is, when we hear certain noises which we associate with ideas, and simultaneously see certain motions of lips and expressions of face—it is very difficult to suppose that what we hear is not the expression of a thought, as we know it would be if we emitted the same sounds. Of course similar things happen in dreams, where we are mistaken as to the existence of other people. But dreams are more or less suggested by what we call waking life, and are capable of being more or less accounted for on scientific principles if we assume that there really is a physical world. Thus every principle of simplicity urges us to adopt the natural view, that there really are objects other than ourselves and our sense-data which have an existence not dependent upon our perceiving them. Of course it is not by argument that we originally come by our belief in an independent external world. We find this belief ready in ourselves as soon as we begin to reflect: it is what may be called an *instinctive* belief. We should never have been led to question this belief but for the fact that, at any rate in the case of sight, it seems as if the sense-datum itself were instinctively believed to be the independent object, whereas argument shows that the object cannot be identical with the sense-datum. This discovery, however--which is not at all paradoxical in the case of taste and smell and sound, and only slightly so in the case of touch--leaves undiminished our instinctive belief that there *are* objects *corresponding* to our sense-data. Since this belief does not lead to any difficulties, but on the contrary tends to simplify and systematize our account of our experiences, there seems no good reason for rejecting it. We may therefore admit--though with a slight doubt derived from dreams--that the external world does really exist, and is not wholly dependent for its existence upon our continuing to perceive it.

The argument which has led us to this conclusion is doubtless less strong than we could wish, but it is typical of many philosophical arguments, and it is therefore worth while to consider briefly its general character and validity. All knowledge, we find, must be built up upon our instinctive beliefs, and if these are rejected, nothing is left. But among our instinctive beliefs some are much stronger than others, while many have, by habit and association, become entangled with other beliefs, not really instinctive, but falsely supposed to be part of what is believed instinctively.

Philosophy should show us the hierarchy of our instinctive beliefs, beginning with those we hold most strongly, and presenting each as much isolated and as free from irrelevant additions as possible. It should take care to show that, in the form in which they are finally set forth, our instinctive beliefs do not clash, but form a harmonious system. There can never be any reason for rejecting one instinctive belief except that it clashes with others; thus, if they are found to harmonize, the whole system becomes worthy of acceptance.

It is of course *possible* that all or any of our beliefs may be mistaken, and therefore all ought to be held with at least some slight element of doubt. But we cannot have *reason* to reject a belief except on the ground of some other belief. Hence, by organizing our instinctive beliefs and their consequences, by considering which among them is most possible, if necessary, to modify or abandon, we can arrive, on the basis of accepting as our sole data what we instinctively believe, at an orderly systematic organization of our knowledge, in which, though the *possibility* of error remains, its likelihood is diminished by the interrelation of the parts and by the critical scrutiny which has preceded acquiescence.

This function, at least, philosophy can perform. Most philosophers, rightly or wrongly, believe that philosophy can do much more than this--that it can give us knowledge, not otherwise attainable, concerning the universe as a whole, and concerning the nature of ultimate reality. Whether this be the case or not, the more modest function we have spoken of can certainly be performed by philosophy, and certainly suffices, for those who have once begun to doubt the adequacy of common sense, to justify the arduous and difficult labours that philosophical problems involve.

Rene Descartes (1596- 1650) is widely considered to be the first "modern" philosopher. His thought represents a break with Medieval philosophy, both in substance and method. It is not an exaggeration to say that he set the course for the next few centuries of philosophical speculation, since the problems he raised and wrestled with consume the attention of professional philosophers to this day.

Indeed, the question with which Russell begins this book, "Is there any knowledge in the world which is so certain that no reasonable man could doubt it?" is the very question with which Descartes begins his own ruminations with. His answer is that the one thing he can be sure of is that he exists, and that 'he' refers to his mind, an immaterial thing that thinks. He is less sure that matter exists, even the matter of his own body. He then devotes much of his energy to proving that we can, after all, have real knowledge of the material world. Descartes is a Rationalist; he claims that we cannot rely on our senses for certain knowledge, but rather on the purely logical or intellectual powers of the mind. His conclusions in this regard are controversial, and have since provided the grist for many a philosophical mill.

Renee Descartes

from

Discourse on Method, Part IV

I am in doubt as to the propriety of making my first meditations in the place above mentioned matter of discourse; for these are so metaphysical, and so uncommon, as not, perhaps, to be acceptable to every one. And yet, that it may be determined whether the foundations that I have laid are sufficiently secure, I find myself in a measure constrained to advert to them. I had long before remarked that, in relation to practice, it is sometimes necessary to adopt, as if above doubt, opinions which we discern to be highly uncertain, as has been already said; but as I then desired to give my attention solely to the search after truth, I thought that a procedure exactly the opposite was called for, and that I ought to reject as absolutely false all opinions in regard to which I could suppose the least ground for doubt, in order to ascertain whether after that there remained aught in my belief that was wholly indubitable. Accordingly, seeing that our senses sometimes deceive us, I was willing to suppose that there existed nothing really such as they presented to us; and because some men err in reasoning, and fall into paralogisms, even on the simplest matters of geometry, I, convinced that I was as open to error as any other, rejected as false all the reasonings I had hitherto taken for demonstrations; and finally, when I considered that the very same thoughts (presentations) which we experience when awake may also be experienced when we are asleep, while there is at that time not one of them true, I supposed that all the objects (presentations) that had ever entered into my mind when awake, had in them no more truth than the illusions of my dreams. But immediately upon this I observed that, whilst I thus wished to think that all was false, it was absolutely necessary that I, who thus thought, should be somewhat; and as I observed that this truth, I think, therefore I am (COGITO ERGO SUM), was so certain and of such evidence that no ground of doubt, however extravagant, could be alleged by the sceptics capable of shaking it, I concluded that I might, without scruple, accept it as the first principle of the philosophy of which I was in search.

In the next place, I attentively examined what I was and as I observed that I could suppose that I had no body, and that there was no world nor any place in which I might be; but that I could not therefore suppose that I was not; and that, on the contrary, from the very circumstance that I thought to doubt of the truth of other things, it most clearly and certainly followed that I was; while, on the other hand, if I had only ceased to think, although all the other objects which I had ever imagined had been in reality existent, I would have had no reason to believe that I existed; I thence concluded that I was a substance whose whole essence or nature consists only in thinking, and which, that it may exist, has need of no place, nor is dependent on any material thing; so that "I," that is to say, the mind by which I am what I am, is wholly distinct from the body, and is even more easily known than the latter, and is such, that although the latter were not, it would still continue to be all that it is.

After this I inquired in general into what is essential to the truth and certainty of a proposition; for since I had discovered one which I knew to be true, I thought that I must likewise be able to discover the ground of this certitude. And as I observed that in the words I think, therefore I am, there is nothing at all which gives me assurance of their truth beyond this, that I see very clearly that in order to think it is necessary to exist, I concluded that I might take, as a general rule, the principle, that all the things which we very clearly and distinctly conceive are true, only observing, however, that there is some difficulty in rightly determining the objects which we distinctly conceive.

In the next place, from reflecting on the circumstance that I doubted, and that consequently my being was not wholly perfect (for I clearly saw that it was a greater perfection to know than to doubt), I was led to inquire whence I had learned to think of something more perfect than myself; and I clearly recognized that I must hold this notion from some nature which in reality was more perfect. As for the thoughts of many other objects external to me, as of the sky, the earth, light, heat, and a thousand more, I was less at a loss to know whence these came; for since I remarked in them nothing which seemed to render them superior to myself, I could believe that, if these were true, they were dependencies on my own nature, in so far as it possessed a certain perfection, and, if they were false, that I held them from nothing, that is to say, that they were in me because of a certain imperfection of my nature. But this could not be the case with-the idea of a nature more perfect than myself; for to receive it from nothing was a thing manifestly impossible; and, because it is not less repugnant that the more perfect should be an effect of, and dependence on the less perfect, than that something should proceed from nothing, it was equally impossible that I could hold it from myself: accordingly, it but remained that it had been placed in me by a nature which was in reality more perfect than mine, and which even possessed within itself all the perfections of which I could form any idea; that is to say, in a single word, which was God. And to this I added that, since I knew some perfections which I did not possess, I was not the only being in existence (I will here, with your permission, freely use the terms of the schools); but, on the contrary, that there was of necessity some other more perfect Being upon whom I was dependent, and from whom I had received all that I possessed; for if I had existed alone, and independently of every other being, so as to have had from myself all the perfection, however little, which I actually possessed, I should have been able, for the same reason, to have had from myself the whole remainder of perfection, of the want of which I was conscious, and thus could of myself have become infinite, eternal, immutable, omniscient, all-powerful, and, in fine, have possessed all the perfections which I could recognize in God. For in order to know the nature of God (whose existence has been established by the preceding reasonings), as far as my own nature permitted, I had only to consider in reference to all the properties of which I found in my mind some idea, whether their possession was a mark of perfection; and I was assured that no one which indicated any imperfection was in him, and that none of the rest was awanting. Thus I perceived that doubt, inconstancy, sadness, and such like, could not be found in God, since I myself would have been happy to be free from them. Besides, I had ideas of many sensible and corporeal things; for although I might suppose that I was dreaming, and that all which I saw or imagined was false, I could not, nevertheless, deny that the ideas were in reality in my thoughts. But, because I had already very clearly recognized in myself that the intelligent nature is distinct from the corporeal, and as I observed that all composition is an evidence of dependency, and that a state of dependency is manifestly a state of imperfection, I therefore determined that it could not be a perfection in God to be compounded of these two natures and that consequently he was not so compounded; but that if there were any bodies in the world, or even any intelligences, or other natures that were not wholly perfect, their existence depended on his power in such a way that they could not subsist without him for a single moment.

I was disposed straightway to search for other truths and when I had represented to myself the object of the geometers, which I conceived to be a continuous body or a space indefinitely extended in length, breadth, and height or depth, divisible into divers parts which admit of different figures and sizes, and of being moved or transposed in all manner of ways (for all this the geometers suppose to be in the object they contemplate), I went over some of their simplest demonstrations. And, in the first place, I observed, that the great certitude which by common consent is accorded to these demonstrations, is founded solely upon this, that they are clearly conceived in accordance with the rules I have already laid down In the next place, I perceived that there was nothing at all in these demonstrations which could assure me of the existence of their object: thus, for example, supposing a triangle to be given, I distinctly perceived that its three angles were necessarily equal to two right angles, but I did not on that account perceive anything which could assure me that any triangle existed: while, on the contrary, recurring to the examination of the idea of a Perfect Being, I found that the existence of the Being was comprised in the idea in the same way that the equality of its three angles to two right angles is comprised in the idea of a triangle, or as in the idea of a sphere, the equidistance of all points on its surface from the center, or even still more clearly; and that consequently it is at least as certain that God, who is this Perfect Being, is, or exists, as any demonstration of geometry can be.

But the reason which leads many to persuade them selves that there is a difficulty in knowing this truth, and even also in knowing what their mind really is, is that they never raise their thoughts above sensible objects, and are so accustomed to consider nothing except by way of imagination, which is a mode of thinking limited to material objects, that all that is not imaginable seems to them not intelligible. The truth of this is sufficiently manifest from the single circumstance, that the philosophers of the schools accept as a maxim that there is nothing in the understanding which was not previously in the senses, in which however it is certain that the ideas of God and of the soul have never been; and it appears to me that they who make use of their imagination to comprehend these ideas do exactly the some thing as if, in order to hear sounds or smell odors, they strove to avail themselves of their eyes; unless indeed that there is this difference, that the sense of sight does not afford us an inferior assurance to those of smell or hearing; in place of which, neither our imagination nor our senses can give us assurance of anything unless our understanding intervene.

Finally, if there be still persons who are not sufficiently persuaded of the existence of God and of the soul, by the reasons I have adduced, I am desirous that they should know that all the other propositions, of the truth of which they deem themselves perhaps more assured, as that we have a body, and that there exist stars and an earth, and such like, are less certain; for, although we have a moral assurance of these things, which is so strong that there is an appearance of extravagance in doubting of their existence, yet at the same time no one, unless his intellect is impaired, can deny, when the question relates to a metaphysical certitude, that there is sufficient reason to exclude entire assurance, in the observation that when asleep we can in the same way imagine ourselves possessed of another body and that we see other stars and another earth, when there is nothing of the kind. For how do we know that the thoughts which occur in dreaming are false rather than those other which we experience when awake, since the former are often not less vivid and distinct than the latter? And though men of the highest genius study this question as long as they please, I do not believe that they will be able to give any reason which can be sufficient to remove this doubt, unless they presuppose the existence of God. For, in the first place even the principle which I have already taken as a rule, viz., that all the things which we clearly and distinctly conceive are true, is certain only because God is or exists and because he is a Perfect Being, and because all that we possess is derived from him: whence it follows that our ideas or notions, which to the extent of their clearness and distinctness are real, and proceed from God, must to that extent be true. Accordingly, whereas we not infrequently have ideas or notions in which some falsity is contained, this can only be the case with such as are to some extent confused and obscure, and in this proceed from nothing (participate of negation), that is, exist in us thus confused because we are not wholly perfect. And it is evident that it is not less repugnant that falsity or imperfection, in so far as it is imperfection, should proceed from God, than that truth or perfection should proceed from nothing. But if we did not know that all which we possess of real and true proceeds from a Perfect and Infinite Being, however clear and distinct our ideas might be, we should have no ground on that account for the assurance that they possessed the perfection of being true.

But after the knowledge of God and of the soul has rendered us certain of this rule, we can easily understand that the truth of the thoughts we experience when awake, ought not in the slightest degree to be called in question on account of the illusions of our dreams. For if it happened that an individual, even when asleep, had some very distinct idea, as, for example, if a geometer should discover some new demonstration, the circumstance of his being asleep would not militate against its truth; and as for the most ordinary error of our dreams, which consists in their representing to us various objects in the same way as our external senses, this is not prejudicial, since it leads us very properly to suspect the truth of the ideas of sense; for we are not infrequently deceived in the same manner when awake; as when persons in the jaundice see all objects yellow, or when the stars or bodies at a great distance appear to us much smaller than they are. For, in fine, whether awake or asleep, we ought never to allow ourselves to be persuaded of the truth of anything unless on the evidence of our reason. And it must be noted that I say of our reason, and not of our imagination or of our senses: thus, for example, although we very clearly see the sun, we ought not therefore to determine that it is only of the size which our sense of sight presents; and we may very distinctly imagine the head of a lion joined to the body of a goat, without being therefore shut up to the conclusion that a chimaera exists; for it is not a dictate of reason that what we thus see or imagine is in reality existent; but it plainly tells us that all our ideas or notions contain in them some truth; for otherwise it could not be that God, who is wholly perfect and veracious, should have placed them in us. And because our reasonings are never so clear or so complete during sleep as when we are awake, although sometimes the acts of our imagination are then as lively and distinct, if not more so than in our waking moments, reason further dictates that, since all our thoughts cannot be true because of our partial imperfection, those possessing truth must infallibly be found in the experience of our waking moments rather than in that of our dreams.

CHAPTER III.

THE NATURE OF MATTER

In the preceding chapter we agreed, though without being able to find demonstrative reasons, that it is rational to believe that our sense-data--for example, those which we regard as associated with my table--are really signs of the existence of something independent of us and our perceptions. That is to say, over and above the sensations of colour, hardness, noise, and so on, which make up the appearance of the table to me, I assume that there is something else, of which these things are appearances. The colour ceases to exist if I shut my eyes, the sensation of hardness ceases to exist if I remove my arm from contact with the table, the sound ceases to exist if I cease to rap the table with my knuckles. But I do not believe that when all these things cease the table ceases. On the contrary, I believe that it is because the table exists continuously that all these sense-data will reappear when I open my eyes, replace my arm, and begin again to rap with my knuckles. The question we have to consider in this chapter is: What is the nature of this real table, which persists independently of my perception of it?

To this question physical science gives an answer, somewhat incomplete it is true, and in part still very hypothetical, but yet deserving of respect so far as it goes. Physical science, more or less unconsciously, has drifted into the view that all natural phenomena ought to be reduced to motions. Light and heat and sound are all due to wave-motions, which travel from the body emitting them to the person who sees light or feels heat or hears sound. That which has the wave-motion is either aether or 'gross matter', but in either case is what the philosopher would call matter. The only properties which science assigns to it are position in space, and the power of motion according to the laws of motion. Science does not deny that it *may* have other properties; but if so, such other properties are not useful to the man of science, and in no way assist him in explaining the phenomena.

It is sometimes said that 'light *is* a form of wave-motion', but this is misleading, for the light which we immediately see, which we know directly by means of our senses, is *not* a form of wave-motion, but something quite different--something which we all know if we are not blind, though we cannot describe it so as to convey our knowledge to a man who is blind. A wave-motion, on the contrary, could quite well be described to a blind man, since he can acquire a knowledge of space by the sense of touch; and he can experience a wave-motion by a sea voyage almost as well as we can. But this, which a blind man can understand, is not what we mean by *light*: we mean by *light* just that which a blind man can never understand, and which we can never describe to him. Now this something, which all of us who are not blind know, is not, according to science, really to be found in the outer world: it is something caused by the action of certain waves upon the eyes and nerves and brain of the person who sees the light. When it is said that light *is* waves, what is really meant is that waves are the physical cause of our sensations of light. But light itself, the thing which seeing people experience and blind people do not, is not supposed by science to form any part of the world that is independent of us and our senses. And very similar remarks would apply to other kinds of sensations. It is not only colours and sounds and so on that are absent from the scientific world of matter, but also *space* as we get it through sight or touch. It is essential to science that its matter should be in *a* space, but the space in which it is cannot be exactly the space we see or feel. To begin with, space as we see it is not the same as space as we get it by the sense of touch; it is only by experience in infancy that we learn how to touch things we see, or how to get a sight of things which we feel touching us. But the space of science is neutral as between touch and sight; thus it cannot be either the space of touch or the space of sight.

Again, different people see the same object as of different shapes, according to their point of view. A circular coin, for example, though we should always *judge* it to be circular, will *look* oval unless we are straight in front of it. When we judge that it *is* circular, we are judging that it has a real shape which is not its apparent shape, but belongs to it intrinsically apart from its appearance. But this real shape, which is what concerns science, must be in a real space, not the same as anybody's *apparent* space. The real space is public, the apparent space is private to the percipient. In different people's *private* spaces the same object seems to have different shapes; thus the real space, in which it has its real shape, must be different from the private spaces. The space of science, therefore, though *connected* with the spaces we see and feel, is not identical with them, and the manner of its connexion requires investigation.

We agreed provisionally that physical objects cannot be quite like our sense-data, but may be regarded as *causing* our sensations. These physical objects are in the space of science, which we may call 'physical' space. It is important to notice that, if our sensations are to be caused by physical objects, there must be a physical space containing these objects and our sense-organs and nerves and brain. We get a sensation of touch from an object when we are in contact with it; that is to say, when some part of our body occupies a place in physical space quite close to the space occupied by the object. We see an object (roughly speaking) when no opaque body is between the object and our eyes in physical space. Similarly, we only hear or smell or taste an object when we are sufficiently near to it, or when it touches the tongue, or has some suitable position in physical space relatively to our body. We cannot begin to state what different sensations we shall derive from a given object under different circumstances unless we regard the object and our body as both in one physical space, for it is mainly the relative positions of the object and our body that determine what sensations we shall derive from the object.

Now our sense-data are situated in our private spaces, either the space of sight or the space of touch or such vaguer spaces as other senses may give us. If, as science and common sense assume, there is one public all-embracing physical space in which physical objects are, the relative positions of physical objects in physical space must more or less correspond to the relative positions of sense-data in our private spaces. There is no difficulty in supposing this to be the case. If we see on a road one house nearer to us than another, our other senses will bear out the view that it is nearer; for example, it will be reached sooner if we walk along the road. Other people will agree that the house which looks nearer to us is nearer; the ordnance map will take the same view; and thus everything points to a spatial relation between the houses corresponding to the relation between the sense-data which we see when we look at the houses. Thus we may assume that there is a physical space in which physical objects have spatial relations corresponding to those which the corresponding sense-data have in our private spaces. It is this physical space which is dealt with in geometry and assumed in physics and astronomy. Assuming that there is physical space, and that it does thus correspond to private spaces, what can we know about it? We can know *only* what is required in order to secure the correspondence. That is to say, we can know nothing of what it is like in itself, but we can know the sort of arrangement of physical objects which results from their spatial relations. We can know, for example, that the earth and moon and sun are in one straight line during an eclipse, though we cannot know what a physical straight line is in itself, as we know the look of a straight line in our visual space. Thus we come to know much more about the *relations* of distances in physical space than about the distances themselves; we may know that one distance is greater than another, or that it is along the same straight line as the other, but we cannot have that immediate acquaintance with physical distances that we have with distances in our private spaces, or with colours or sounds or other sense-data. We can know all those things about physical space which a man born blind might know through other people about the space of sight; but the kind of things which a man born blind could never know about the space of sight we also cannot know about physical space. We can know the properties of the relations required to preserve the correspondence with sense-data, but we cannot know the nature of the terms between which the relations hold.

With regard to time, our *feeling* of duration or of the lapse of time is notoriously an unsafe guide as to the time that has elapsed by the clock. Times when we are bored or suffering pain pass slowly, times when we are agreeably occupied pass quickly, and times when we are sleeping pass almost as if they did not exist. Thus, in so far as time is constituted by duration, there is the same necessity for distinguishing a public and a private time as there was in the case of space. But in so far as time consists in an *order* of before and after, there is no need to make such a distinction; the time-order which events seem to have is, so far as we can see, the same as the time-order which they do have. At any rate no reason can be given for supposing that the two orders are not the same. The same is usually true of space: if a regiment of men are marching along a road, the shape of the regiment will look different from different points of view, but the men will appear arranged in the same order from all points of view. Hence we regard the order as true also in physical space, whereas the shape is only supposed to correspond to the physical space so far as is required for the preservation of the order.

In saying that the time-order which events seem to have is the same as the time-order which they really have, it is necessary to guard against a possible misunderstanding. It must not be supposed that the various states of different physical objects have the same time-order as the sense-data which constitute the perceptions of those objects. Considered as physical objects, the thunder and lightning are simultaneous; that is to say, the lightning is simultaneous with the disturbance of the air in the place where the disturbance begins, namely, where the lightning is. But the sense-datum which we call hearing the thunder does not take place until the disturbance of the air has travelled as far as to where we are. Similarly, it takes about eight minutes for the sun's light to reach us; thus, when we see the sun we are seeing the sun of eight minutes ago. So far as our sense-data afford evidence as to the physical sun they afford evidence as to the physical sun of eight minutes ago; if the physical sun had ceased to exist within the last eight minutes, that would make no difference to the sense-data which we call 'seeing the sun'. This affords a fresh illustration of the necessity of distinguishing between sense-data and physical objects. What we have found as regards space is much the same as what we find in relation to the correspondence of the sense-data with their physical counterparts. If one object looks blue and another red, we may reasonably presume that there is some corresponding difference between the physical objects; if two objects both look blue, we may presume a corresponding similarity. But we cannot hope to be acquainted directly with the quality in the physical object which makes it look blue or red. Science tells us that this quality is a certain sort of wave-motion, and this sounds familiar, because we think of wave-motions in the space we see. But the wave-motions must really be in physical space, with which we have no direct acquaintance; thus the real wave-motions have not that familiarity which we might have supposed them to have. And what holds for colours is closely similar to what holds for other sense-data. Thus we find that, although the *relations* of physical objects have all sorts of knowable properties, derived from their correspondence with the relations of sense-data, the physical objects themselves remain unknown in their intrinsic nature, so far at least as can be discovered by means of the senses. The question remains whether there is any other method of discovering the intrinsic nature of physical objects.

The most natural, though not ultimately the most defensible, hypothesis to adopt in the first instance, at any rate as regards visual sense-data, would be that, though physical objects cannot, for the reasons we have been considering, be *exactly* like sense-data, yet they may be more or less like. According to this view, physical objects will, for example, really have colours, and we might, by good luck, see an object as of the colour it really is. The colour which an object seems to have at any given moment will in general be very similar, though not quite the same, from many different points of view; we might thus suppose the 'real' colour to be a sort of medium colour, intermediate between thc various shades which appear from the different points of view.

Such a theory is perhaps not capable of being definitely refuted, but it can be shown to be groundless. To begin with, it is plain that the colour we see depends only upon the nature of the light-waves that strike the eye, and is therefore modified by the medium intervening between us and the object, as well as by the manner in which light is reflected from the object in the direction of the eye. The intervening air alters colours unless it is perfectly clear, and any strong reflection will alter them completely. Thus the colour we see is a result of the ray as it reaches the eye, and not simply a property of the object from which the ray comes. Hence, also, provided certain waves reach the eye, we shall see a certain colour, whether the object from which the waves start has any colour or not. Thus it is quite gratuitous to suppose that physical objects have colours, and therefore there is no justification for making such a supposition. Exactly similar arguments will apply to other sense-data.

It remains to ask whether there are any general philosophical arguments enabling us to say that, if matter is real, it must be of such and such a nature. As explained above, very many philosophers, perhaps most, have held that whatever is real must be in some sense mental, or at any rate that whatever we can know anything about must be in some sense mental. Such philosophers are called 'idealists'. Idealists tell us that what appears as matter is really something mental; namely, either (as Leibniz held) more or less rudimentary minds, or (as Berkeley contended) ideas in the minds which, as we should commonly say, 'perceive' the matter. Thus idealists deny the existence of matter as something intrinsically different from mind, though they do not deny that our sense-data are signs of something which exists independently of our private sensations. In the following chapter we shall consider briefly the reasons--in my opinion fallacious--which idealists advance in favour of their theory.

Baron d'Holbach (1723 – 1789) was a French-German philosopher who was a strong proponent of philosophical materialism. He was a prominent figure of the Enlightenment whose ideas were widely known, and argued over.

D'Holbach differed quite sharply from Descartes. Descartes argued that all of our perceptions could be the product of our minds; after all, there is always the possibility that we are dreaming. Therefore our knowledge of matter was imperfect. D'Holbach, to the contrary argues forcefully that all of our perceptions, indeed all of our mental activity, can be explained in terms of the motion and interaction of matter. We don;t need to imagine a disembodied and immaterial "mind" to account for our ability to think and reason.

This passage, from d'Holbach's "The System of Nature" is a good representative of materialist thought. It is a much more radical form of materialism than the kind that Russell ultimately argues for, as we shall see.

Baron D'Holbach

from

A System of Nature CHAP. III.

Of Matter.—Of its various Combinations.—Of its diversified Motion, or of the Course of Nature.

We know nothing of the elements of bodies, but we know some of their properties or qualities; and we distinguish their various matter by the effect or change produced on our senses; that is to say, by the variety of motion their presence excites in us. In consequence, we discover in them, extent, mobility, divisibility, solidity, gravity, and inert force. From these general and primitive properties flow a number of others, such as density, figure, colour, ponderosity, &c. Thus, relatively to us, matter is all that affects our senses in any manner whatever; the various properties we attribute to matter, by which we discriminate its diversity, are founded on the different impressions we receive on the changes they produce in us.

A satisfactory definition of matter has not yet been given. Man, deceived and led astray by his prejudices, formed but vague, superficial, and imperfect notions concerning it. He looked upon it as an unique being, gross and passive, incapable of either moving by itself, of forming combinations, or of producing any thing by its own energies. Instead of this unintelligible jargon, he ought to have contemplated it as a *genus* of beings, of which the individuals, although they might possess some common properties, such as extent, divisibility, figure, &c. should not, however, be all ranked in the same class, nor comprised under the same general denomination.

An example will serve more fully to explain what we have asserted, throw its correctness into light, and facilitate the application. The properties common to all matter, are extent, divisibility, impenetrability, figure, mobility, or the property of being moved in mass. FIRE, beside these general properties, common to all matter, enjoys also the peculiar property of being put into activity by a motion that produces on our organs of feeling the sensation of heat; and by another, that communicates to our visual organs the sensation of light. Iron, in common with matter in general, has extent and figure; is divisible, and moveable in mass: if fire be combined with it in a certain proportion, the iron acquires two new properties; namely, those of exciting in us similar sensations of heat and light, which were excited by the element of fire, but which the iron had not, before its combination with the igneous matter. These distinguishing properties are inseparable from matter, and the phenomena that result, may, in the strictest sense of the word, be said to result necessarily.

If we contemplate a little the paths of Nature—if, for a time, we trace the beings in this Nature, under the different states through which, by reason of their properties, they are compelled to pass; we shall discover, that it is to motion, and motion only, that is to be ascribed all the changes, all the combinations, all the forms, in short, all the various modifications of matter. That it is by motion every thing that exists is produced, experiences change, expands, and is destroyed. It is motion that alters the aspect of beings; that adds to, or takes away from their properties; which obliges each of them, by a consequence of its nature, after having occupied a certain rank or order, to quit it, to occupy another, and to contribute to the generation, maintenance, and decomposition of other beings, totally different in their bulk, rank, and essence.

In what experimental philosophers have styled the THREE ORDERS OF NATURE, that is to say, the *mineral*, the *vegetable*, and *animal* worlds, they have established, by the aid of motion, a transmigration, an exchange, a continual circulation in the particles of matter. Nature has occasion in one place, for those particles which, for a time, she has placed in another. These particles, after having, by particular combinations, constituted beings endued with peculiar essences, with specific properties, with determinate modes of action, dissolve and separate with more or less facility; and combining in a new manner, they form new beings. The attentive observer sees this law execute itself, in a manner more or less prominent, through all the beings by which he is surrounded. He sees nature full of *erratic germs*, some of which expand themselves, whilst others wait until motion has placed them in their proper situation, in suitable wombs or matrices, in the necessary circumstances, to unfold, to increase, to render them more perceptible by the addition of other substances of matter analogous to their primitive being. In all this we see nothing but the effect of motion, necessarily guided, modified, accelerated or slackened, strengthened or weakened, by reason of the various properties that beings successively acquire and lose; which, every moment, infallibly produces alterations in bodies more or less marked. Indeed, these bodies cannot be, strictly speaking, the same in any two successive moments of their existence; they must, every instant, either acquire or lose: in short, they are obliged to undergo continual variations in their essences, in their properties, in their energies, in their masses, in their qualities, in their mode of existence.

Animals, after they have been expanded in, and brought out of, the wombs that are suitable to the elements of their machine, enlarge, strengthen, acquire new properties, new energies, new faculties; either by deriving nourishment from plants analogous to their being, or by devouring other animals whose substance is suitable to their preservation; that is to say, to repair the continual deperdition or loss of some portion of their own substance, that is disengaging itself every instant. These same animals are nourished, preserved, strengthened, and enlarged, by the aid of air, water, earth, and fire. Deprived of air, or of the fluid that surrounds them, that presses on them, that penetrates them, that gives them their elasticity, they presently cease to live. Water, combined with this air, enters into their whole mechanism of which it facilitates the motion. Earth serves them for a basis, by giving solidity to their texture: it is conveyed by air and water, which carry it to those parts of the body with which it can combine. Fire itself, disguised and enveloped under an infinity of forms, continually received into the animal, procures him heat, continues him in life, renders him capable of exercising his functions. The aliments, charged with these various principles, entering into the stomach, re-establish the nervous system, and restore, by their activity, and the elements which compose them, the machine which begins to languish, to be depressed, by the loss it has sustained. Forthwith the animal experiences a change in his whole system; he has more energy, more activity; he feels more courage; displays more gaiety; he acts, he moves, he thinks, after a different manner; all his faculties are exercised with more ease. This igneous matter, so congenial to generation—so restorative in its effect—so necessary to life, was the JUPITER of the ancients: from all that has preceded, it is clear, that what are called the elements, or primitive parts of matter, variously combined, are, by the agency of motion, continually united to, and assimilated with, the substance of animals— that they visibly modify their being—have an evident influence over their actions, that is to say, upon the motion they undergo, whether visible or concealed.

The same elements, which under certain circumstances serve to nourish, to strengthen, to maintain the animal, become, under others, the principles of his weakness, the instruments of his dissolution—of his death: they work his destruction, whenever they are not in that just proportion which renders them proper to maintain his existence: thus, when water becomes too abundant in the body of the animal, it enervates him, it relaxes the fibres, and impedes the necessary action of the other elements: thus, fire admitted in excess, excites in him disorderly motion destructive of his machine: thus, air, charged with principles not analogous to his mechanism, brings upon him dangerous diseases and contagion. In fine, the aliments modified after certain modes, in the room of nourishing, destroy the animal, and conduce to his ruin: the animal is preserved no longer than these substances are analogous to his system. They ruin him when they want that just equilibrium that renders them suitable to maintain his existence.

Plants that serve to nourish and restore animals are themselves nourished by earth; they expand on its bosom, enlarge and strengthen at its expense, continually receiving into their texture, by their roots and their pores, water, air, and igneous matter: water visibly reanimates them whenever their vegetation or genus of life languishes; it conveys to them those analogous principles by which they are enabled to reach perfection: air is requisite to their expansion, and furnishes them with water, earth, and the igneous matter with which it is charged. By these means they receive more or less of the inflammable matter; the different proportions of these principles, their numerous combinations, from whence result an infinity of properties, a variety of forms, constitute the various families and classes into which botanists have distributed plants: it is thus we see the cedar and the hyssop develop their growth; the one rises to the clouds, the other creep humbly on the earth. Thus, by degrees, from an acorn springs the majestic oak, accumulating, with time, its numerous branches, and overshadowing us with its foliage. Thus, a grain of corn, after having drawn its own nourishment from the juices of the earth, serves, in its turn, for the nourishment of man, into whose system it conveys the elements or principles by which it has been itself expanded, combined, and modified in such a manner, as to render this vegetable proper to assimilate and unite with the human frame; that is to say, with the fluids and solids of which it is composed.

The same elements, the same principles, are found in the formation of minerals, as well as in their decomposition, whether natural or artificial. We find that earth, diversely modified, wrought, and combined, serves to increase their bulk, and give them more or less density and gravity. Air and water contribute to make their particles cohere; the igneous matter, or inflammable principle, tinges them with colour, and sometimes plainly indicates its presence, by the brilliant scintillation which motion elicits from them. These stones and metals, these bodies, so compact and solid, are disunited, are destroyed, by the agency of air, water, and fire; which the most ordinary analysis is sufficient to prove, as well as a multitude of experience, to which our eyes are the daily evidence.

Animals, plants, and minerals, after a lapse of time, give back to Nature; that is to say, to the general mass of things, to the universal magazine, the elements, or principles, which they have borrowed: The earth retakes that portion of the body of which it formed the basis and the solidity; the air charges itself with these parts, that are, analogous to it, and with those particles which are light and subtle; water carries off that which is suitable to liquescency; fire, bursting its chains, disengages itself, and rushes into new combinations with other bodies.

The elementary particles of the animal, being thus dissolved, disunited, and dispersed; assume new activity, and form new combinations: thus, they serve to nourish, to preserve, or destroy new beings; among others, plants, which arrived at their maturity, nourish and preserve new animals; these in their turn yielding to the same fate as the first.

Such is the constant, the invariable course, of Nature; such is the eternal circle of mutation, which all that exists is obliged to describe. It is thus motion generates, preserves for a time, and successively, destroys, one part of the universe by the other; whilst the sum of existence remains eternally the same. Nature, by its combinations, produces suns, which place themselves in the centre of so many systems: she forms planets, which, by their peculiar essence, gravitate and describe their revolutions round these suns: by degrees the motion is changed altogether, and becomes eccentric: perhaps the day may arrive when these wondrous masses will disperse, of which man, in the short space of his existence, can only have a faint and transient glimpse.

It is clear, then, that the continual motion inherent in matter, changes and destroys all beings; every instant depriving them of some of their properties, to substitute others: it is motion, which, in thus changing their actual essence, changes also their order, their direction, their tendency, and the laws which regulate their mode of acting and being: from the stone formed in the bowels of the earth, by the intimate combination and close coherence of similar and analogous particles, to the sun, that vast reservoir of igneous particles, which sheds torrents of light over the firmament; from the benumbed oyster, to the thoughtful and active man; we see an uninterrupted progression, a perpetual chain of motion and combination; from which is produced, beings that only differ from each other by the variety of their elementary matter—by the numerous combinations of these elements, from whence springs modes of action and existence, diversified to infinity. In generation, in nutrition, in preservation, we see nothing more than matter, variously combined, of which each has its peculiar motion, regulated by fixed and determinate laws, which oblige them to submit to necessary changes. We shall find, in the formation, in the growth, in the instantaneous life, of animals, vegetables, and minerals, nothing but matter; which combining, accumulating, aggregating, and expanding by degrees, forms beings, who are either feeling, living, vegetating, or else destitute of these faculties; which, having existed some time under one particular form, are obliged to contribute by their ruin to the production of other forms. Thus, to speak strictly, nothing in Nature is either born, or dies, according to the common acceptation of those terms. This truth was felt by many of the ancient philosophers. PLATO says, that according to tradition, "the living were born of the dead, the same as the dead did come of the living; and that this is the constant routine of Nature." He adds from himself, "who knows, if to live, be not to die; and if to die, be not to live?" This was the doctrine of PYTHAGORAS, a man of great talent and no less note. EMPEDOCLES asserts, "there is neither birth nor death, for any mortal; but only a combination, and a separation of that which was combined, and that this is what amongst men they call birth, and death." Again he remarks, "those are infants, or short-sighted persons, with very contracted understandings, who imagine any thing is born, which did not exist before, or that any thing can die or perish totally."

CHAPTER IV.

IDEALISM

The word 'idealism' is used by different philosophers in somewhat different senses. We shall understand by it the doctrine that whatever exists, or at any rate whatever can be known to exist, must be in some sense mental. This doctrine, which is very widely held among philosophers, has several forms, and is advocated on several different grounds. The doctrine is so widely held, and so interesting in itself, that even the briefest survey of philosophy must give some account of it.

Those who are unaccustomed to philosophical speculation may be inclined to dismiss such a doctrine as obviously absurd. There is no doubt that common sense regards tables and chairs and the sun and moon and material objects generally as something radically different from minds and the contents of minds, and as having an existence which might continue if minds ceased. We think of matter as having existed long before there were any minds, and it is hard to think of it as a mere product of mental activity. But whether true or false, idealism is not to be dismissed as obviously absurd.

We have seen that, even if physical objects do have an independent existence, they must differ very widely from sense-data, and can only have a *correspondence* with sense-data, in the same sort of way in which a catalogue has a correspondence with the things catalogued. Hence common sense leaves us completely in the dark as to the true intrinsic nature of physical objects, and if there were good reason to regard them as mental, we could not legitimately reject this opinion merely because it strikes us as strange. The truth about physical objects *must* be strange. It may be unattainable, but if any philosopher believes that he has attained it, the fact that what he offers as the truth is strange ought not to be made a ground of objection to his opinion.

The grounds on which idealism is advocated are generally grounds derived from the theory of knowledge, that is to say, from a discussion of the conditions which things must satisfy in order that we may be able to know them. The first serious attempt to establish idealism on such grounds was that of Bishop Berkeley. He proved first, by arguments which were largely valid, that our sense-data cannot be supposed to have an existence independent of us, but must be, in part at least, 'in' the mind, in the sense that their existence would not continue if there were no seeing or hearing or touching or smelling or tasting. So far, his contention was almost certainly valid, even if some of his arguments were not so. But he went on to argue that sense-data were the only things of whose existence our perceptions could assure us; and that to be known is to be 'in' a mind, and therefore to be mental. Hence he concluded that nothing can ever be known except what is in some mind, and that whatever is known without being in my mind must be in some other mind. In order to understand his argument, it is necessary to understand his use of the word 'idea'. He gives the name 'idea' to anything which is *immediately* known, as, for example, sense-data are known. Thus a particular colour which we see is an idea; so is a voice which we hear, and so on. But the term is not wholly confined to sense-data. There will also be things remembered or imagined, for with such things also we have immediate acquaintance at the moment of remembering or imagining. All such immediate data he calls 'ideas'.

He then proceeds to consider common objects, such as a tree, for instance. He shows that all we know immediately when we 'perceive' the tree consists of ideas in his sense of the word, and he argues that there is not the slightest ground for supposing that there is anything real about the tree except what is perceived. Its being, he says, consists in being perceived: in the Latin of the schoolmen its '*esse*' is '*percipi*'. He fully admits that the tree must continue to exist even when we shut our eyes or when no human being is near it. But this continued existence, he says, is due to the fact that God continues to perceive it; the 'real' tree, which corresponds to what we called the physical object, consists of ideas in the mind of God, ideas more or less like those we have when we see the tree, but differing in the fact that they are permanent in God's mind so long as the tree continues to exist. All our perceptions, according to him, consist in a partial participation in God's perceptions, and it is because of this participation that different people see more or less the same tree. Thus apart from minds and their ideas there is nothing in the world, nor is it possible that anything else should ever be known, since whatever is known is necessarily an idea.

There are in this argument a good many fallacies which have been important in the history of philosophy, and which it will be as well to bring to light. In the first place, there is a confusion engendered by the use of the word 'idea'. We think of an idea as essentially something in somebody's mind, and thus when we are told that a tree consists entirely of ideas, it is natural to suppose that, if so, the tree must be entirely in minds. But the notion of being 'in' the mind is ambiguous. We speak of bearing a person in mind, not meaning that the person is in our minds, but that a thought of him is in our minds. When a man says that some business he had to arrange went clean out of his mind, he does not mean to imply that the business itself was ever in his mind, but only that a thought of the business was formerly in his mind, but afterwards ceased to be in his mind. And so when Berkeley says that the tree must be in our minds if we can know it, all that he really has a right to say is that a thought of the tree must be in our minds. To argue that the tree itself must be in our minds is like arguing that a person whom we bear in mind is himself in our minds. This confusion may seem too gross to have been really committed by any competent philosopher, but various attendant circumstances rendered it possible. In order to see how it was possible, we must go more deeply into the question as to the nature of ideas. Before taking up the general question of the nature of ideas, we must disentangle two entirely separate questions which arise concerning sense-data and physical objects.

We saw that, for various reasons of detail, Berkeley was right in treating the sense-data which constitute our perception of the tree as more or less subjective, in the sense that they depend upon us as much as upon the tree, and would not exist if the tree were not being perceived. But this is an entirely different point from the one by which Berkeley seeks to prove that whatever can be immediately known must be in a mind. For this purpose arguments of detail as to the dependence of sense-data upon us are useless. It is necessary to prove, generally, that by being known, things are shown to be mental. This is what Berkeley believes himself to have done. It is this question, and not our previous question as to the difference between sense-data and the physical object, that must now concern us.

Taking the word 'idea' in Berkeley's sense, there are two quite distinct things to be considered whenever an idea is before the mind. There is on the one hand the thing of which we are aware--say the colour of my table--and on the other hand the actual awareness itself, the mental act of apprehending the thing. The mental act is undoubtedly mental, but is there any reason to suppose that the thing apprehended is in any sense mental? Our previous arguments concerning the colour did not prove it to be mental; they only proved that its existence depends upon the relation of our sense organs to the physical object--in our case, the table. That is to say, they proved that a certain colour will exist, in a certain light, if a normal eye is placed at a certain point relatively to the table. They did not prove that the colour is in the mind of the percipient.

Berkeley's view, that obviously the colour must be in the mind, seems to depend for its plausibility upon confusing the thing apprehended with the act of apprehension. Either of these might be called an 'idea'; probably either would have been called an idea by Berkeley. The act is undoubtedly in the mind; hence, when we are thinking of the act, we readily assent to the view that ideas must be in the mind. Then, forgetting that this was only true when ideas were taken as acts of apprehension, we transfer the proposition that 'ideas are in the mind' to ideas in the other sense, i.e. to the things apprehended by our acts of apprehension. Thus, by an unconscious equivocation, we arrive at the conclusion that whatever we can apprehend must be in our minds. This seems to be the true analysis of Berkeley's argument, and the ultimate fallacy upon which it rests.

This question of the distinction between act and object in our apprehending of things is vitally important, since our whole power of acquiring knowledge is bound up with it. The faculty of being acquainted with things other than itself is the main characteristic of a mind. Acquaintance with objects essentially consists in a relation between the mind and something other than the mind; it is this that constitutes the mind's power of knowing things. If we say that the things known must be in the mind, we are either unduly limiting the mind's power of knowing, or we are uttering a mere tautology. We are uttering a mere tautology if we mean by '*in* the mind' the same as by '*before* the mind', i.e. if we mean merely being apprehended by the mind. But if we mean this, we shall have to admit that what, *in this sense*, is in the mind, may nevertheless be not mental. Thus when we realize the nature of knowledge, Berkeley's argument is seen to be wrong in substance as well as in form, and his grounds for supposing that 'ideas'--i.e. the objects apprehended--must be mental, are found to have no validity whatever. Hence his grounds in favour of idealism may be dismissed. It remains to see whether there are any other grounds. It is often said, as though it were a self-evident truism, that we cannot know that anything exists which we do not know. It is inferred that whatever can in any way be relevant to our experience must be at least capable of being known by us; whence it follows that if matter were essentially something with which we could not become acquainted, matter would be something which we could not know to exist, and which could have for us no importance whatever. It is generally also implied, for reasons which remain obscure, that what can have no importance for us cannot be real, and that therefore matter, if it is not composed of minds or of mental ideas, is impossible and a mere chimaera.

To go into this argument fully at our present stage would be impossible, since it raises points requiring a considerable preliminary discussion; but certain reasons for rejecting the argument may be noticed at once. To begin at the end: there is no reason why what cannot have any *practical* importance for us should not be real. It is true that, if *theoretical* importance is included, everything real is of *some* importance to us, since, as persons desirous of knowing the truth about the universe, we have some interest in everything that the universe contains. But if this sort of interest is included, it is not the case that matter has no importance for us, provided it exists even if we cannot know that it exists. We can, obviously, suspect that it may exist, and wonder whether it does; hence it is connected with our desire for knowledge, and has the importance of either satisfying or thwarting this desire. Again, it is by no means a truism, and is in fact false, that we cannot know that anything exists which we do not know. The word 'know' is here used in two different senses. (1) In its first use it is applicable to the sort of knowledge which is opposed to error, the sense in which what we know is *true*, the sense which applies to our beliefs and convictions, i.e. to what are called *judgements*. In this sense of the word we know *that* something is the case. This sort of knowledge may be described as knowledge of *truths*. (2) In the second use of the word 'know' above, the word applies to our knowledge of *things*, which we may call *acquaintance*. This is the sense in which we know sense data. (The distinction involved is roughly that between *savoir* and *connaitre* in French, or between *wissen* and *kennen* in German.)

Thus the statement which seemed like a truism becomes, when re-stated, the following: 'We can never truly judge that something with which we are not acquainted exists.' This is by no means a truism, but on the contrary a palpable falsehood. I have not the honour to be acquainted with the Emperor of China, but I truly judge that he exists. It may be said, of course, that I judge this because of other people's acquaintance with him. This, however, would be an irrelevant retort, since, if the principle were true, I could not know that any one else is acquainted with him. But further: there is no reason why I should not know of the existence of something with which nobody is acquainted. This point is important, and demands elucidation.

If I am acquainted with a thing which exists, my acquaintance gives me the knowledge that it exists. But it is not true that, conversely, whenever I can know that a thing of a certain sort exists, I or some one else must be acquainted with the thing. What happens, in cases where I have true judgement without acquaintance, is that the thing is known to me by *description*, and that, in virtue of some general principle, the existence of a thing answering to this description can be inferred from the existence of something with which I am acquainted. In order to understand this point fully, it will be well first to deal with the difference between knowledge by acquaintance and knowledge by description, and then to consider what knowledge of general principles, if any, has the same kind of certainty as our knowledge of the existence of our own experiences. These subjects will be dealt with in the following chapters.

George Berkeley (1685 – 1753) was an Anglican Bishop as well as a philosopher. His philosophy, which he called "immaterialism,"but which has come to be known as "Idealism," has had wide reaching influence, being something like philosophical orthodoxy for a century or more after his death. Russell himself made his philosophical reputation by arguing against the British Idealists which dominated English philosophy at the turn of the last century.

Berkeley begins where Descartes did, with a focus on our perception of the world, but to the question "How can we be sure that the matter that we seem to perceive actually exists?" he gives a very different answer, namely "It doesn't exist. The only things that exists are sensible qualities." This is a radical conclusion, but it is difficult to prove it wrong. It is safe to say, I think, that Russell's primary motivation for writing "The Problems of Philosophy" is to do juts that: to prove Berkeley wrong, and show that something, namely matter, exists independently of our perception of it.

George Berkeley

from

Three Dialogues Between Hylas and Philonous, The First Dialogue

PHILONOUS. What mean you by Sensible Things?

HYL. Those things which are perceived by the senses. Can you imagine that I mean anything else?

PHIL. Pardon me, Hylas, if I am desirous clearly to apprehend your notions, since this may much shorten our inquiry. Suffer me then to ask you this farther question. Are those things only perceived by the senses which are perceived immediately? Or, may those things properly be said to be SENSIBLE which are perceived mediately, or not without the intervention of others?

HYL. I do not sufficiently understand you.

PHIL. In reading a book, what I immediately perceive are the letters; but mediately, or by means of these, are suggested to my mind the notions of God, virtue, truth, &c. Now, that the letters are truly sensible things, or perceived by sense, there is no doubt: but I would know whether you take the things suggested by them to be so too.

HYL. No, certainly: it were absurd to think GOD or VIRTUE sensible things; though they may be signified and suggested to the mind by sensible marks, with which they have an arbitrary connexion.

PHIL. It seems then, that by SENSIBLE THINGS you mean those only which can be perceived IMMEDIATELY by sense?

HYL. Right.

PHIL. Doth it not follow from this, that though I see one part of the sky red, and another blue, and that my reason doth thence evidently conclude there must be some cause of that diversity of colours, yet that cause cannot be said to be a sensible thing, or perceived by the sense of seeing?

HYL. It doth.

PHIL. In like manner, though I hear variety of sounds, yet I cannot be said to hear the causes of those sounds?

HYL. You cannot.

PHIL. And when by my touch I perceive a thing to be hot and heavy, I cannot say, with any truth or propriety, that I feel the cause of its heat or weight?

HYL. To prevent any more questions of this kind, I tell you once for all, that by SENSIBLE THINGS I mean those only which are perceived by sense; and that in truth the senses perceive nothing which they do not perceive IMMEDIATELY: for they make no inferences. The deducing therefore of causes or occasions from effects and appearances, which alone are perceived by sense, entirely relates to reason.

PHIL. This point then is agreed between us—That SENSIBLE THINGS ARE THOSE ONLY WHICH are IMMEDIATELY

PERCEIVED BY SENSE. You will farther inform me, whether we immediately perceive by sight anything beside light, and colours, and figures; or by hearing, anything but sounds; by the palate, anything beside tastes; by the smell, beside odours; or by the touch, more than tangible qualities.

HYL. We do not.

PHIL. It seems, therefore, that if you take away all sensible qualities, there remains nothing sensible?

HYL. I grant it.

PHIL. Sensible things therefore are nothing else but so many sensible qualities, or combinations of sensible qualities?

HYL. Nothing else.

PHIL. HEAT then is a sensible thing?

HYL. Certainly.

PHIL. Doth the REALITY of sensible things consist in being perceived? or, is it something distinct from their being perceived, and that bears no relation to the mind?

HYL. To EXIST is one thing, and to be PERCEIVED is another.

PHIL. I speak with regard to sensible things only. And of these I ask, whether by their real existence you mean a subsistence exterior to the mind, and distinct from their being perceived?

HYL. I mean a real absolute being, distinct from, and without any relation to, their being perceived.

PHIL. Heat therefore, if it be allowed a real being, must exist without the mind?

HYL. It must.

PHIL. Tell me, Hylas, is this real existence equally compatible to all degrees of heat, which we perceive; or is there any reason why we should attribute it to some, and deny it to others? And if there be, pray let me know that reason.

HYL. Whatever degree of heat we perceive by sense, we may be sure the same exists in the object that occasions it.

PHIL. What! the greatest as well as the least?

HYL. *I* tell you, the reason is plainly the same in respect of both. They are both perceived by sense; nay, the greater degree of heat is more sensibly perceived; and consequently, if there is any difference, we are more certain of its real existence than we can be of the reality of a lesser degree.

PHIL. But is not the most vehement and intense degree of heat a very great pain?

HYL. No one can deny it.

PHIL. And is any unperceiving thing capable of pain or pleasure?

HYL. No, certainly.

PHIL. Is your material substance a senseless being, or a being endowed with sense and perception?

HYL. It is senseless without doubt.

PHIL. It cannot therefore be the subject of pain?

HYL. By no means.

PHIL. Nor consequently of the greatest heat perceived by sense, since you acknowledge this to be no small pain?

HYL. I grant it.

PHIL. What shall we say then of your external object; is it a material Substance, or no?

HYL. It is a material substance with the sensible qualities inhering in it.

PHIL. How then can a great heat exist in it, since you own it cannot in a material substance? I desire you would clear this point.

HYL. Hold, Philonous, I fear I was out in yielding intense heat to be a pain. It should seem rather, that pain is something distinct from heat, and the consequence or effect of it.

PHIL. Upon putting your hand near the fire, do you perceive one simple uniform sensation, or two distinct sensations?

HYL. But one simple sensation.

PHIL. Is not the heat immediately perceived?

HYL. It is.

PHIL. And the pain?

HYL. True.

PHIL. Seeing therefore they are both immediately perceived at the same time, and the fire affects you only with one simple or uncompounded idea, it follows that this same simple idea is both the intense heat immediately perceived, and the pain; and, consequently, that the intense heat immediately perceived is nothing distinct from a particular sort of pain.

HYL. It seems so.

PHIL. Again, try in your thoughts, Hylas, if you can conceive a vehement sensation to be without pain or pleasure.

HYL. I cannot.

PHIL. Or can you frame to yourself an idea of sensible pain or pleasure in general, abstracted from every particular idea of heat, cold, tastes, smells? &c.

HYL. I do not find that I can.

PHIL. Doth it not therefore follow, that sensible pain is nothing distinct from those sensations or ideas, in an intense degree?

HYL. It is undeniable; and, to speak the truth, I begin to suspect a very great heat cannot exist but in a mind perceiving it.

PHIL. What! are you then in that sceptical state of suspense, between affirming and denying?

HYL. I think I may be positive in the point. A very violent and painful heat cannot exist without the mind.

PHIL. It hath not therefore according to you, any REAL being?

HYL. I own it.

PHIL. Is it therefore certain, that there is no body in nature really hot?

HYL. I have not denied there is any real heat in bodies. I only say, there is no such thing as an intense real heat.

PHIL. But, did you not say before that all degrees of heat were equally real; or, if there was any difference, that the greater were more undoubtedly real than the lesser?

HYL. True: but it was because I did not then consider the ground there is for distinguishing between them, which I now plainly see. And it is this: because intense heat is nothing else but a particular kind of painful sensation; and pain cannot exist but in a perceiving being; it follows that no intense heat can really exist in an unperceiving corporeal substance. But this is no reason why we should deny heat in an inferior degree to exist in such a substance.

PHIL. But how shall we be able to discern those degrees of heat which exist only in the mind from those which exist without it?

HYL. That is no difficult matter. You know the least pain cannot exist unperceived; whatever, therefore, degree of heat is a pain exists only in the mind. But, as for all other degrees of heat, nothing obliges us to think the same of them.

PHIL. I think you granted before that no unperceiving being was capable of pleasure, any more than of pain.

HYL. I did.

PHIL. And is not warmth, or a more gentle degree of heat than what causes uneasiness, a pleasure?

HYL. What then?

PHIL. Consequently, it cannot exist without the mind in an unperceiving substance, or body.

HYL. So it seems.

PHIL. Since, therefore, as well those degrees of heat that are not painful, as those that are, can exist only in a thinking substance; may we not conclude that external bodies are absolutely incapable of any degree of heat whatsoever?

HYL. On second thoughts, I do not think it so evident that warmth is a pleasure as that a great degree of heat is a pain.

PHIL. *I* do not pretend that warmth is as great a pleasure as heat is a pain. But, if you grant it to be even a small pleasure, it serves to make good my conclusion.

HYL. I could rather call it an INDOLENCE. It seems to be nothing more than a privation of both pain and pleasure. And that such a quality or state as this may agree to an unthinking substance, I hope you will not deny.

PHIL. If you are resolved to maintain that warmth, or a gentle degree of heat, is no pleasure, I know not how to convince you otherwise than by appealing to your own sense. But what think you of cold?

HYL. The same that I do of heat. An intense degree of cold is a pain; for to feel a very great cold, is to perceive a great uneasiness: it cannot therefore exist without the mind; but a lesser degree of cold may, as well as a lesser degree of heat.

PHIL. Those bodies, therefore, upon whose application to our own, we perceive a moderate degree of heat, must be concluded to have a moderate degree of heat or warmth in them; and those, upon whose application we feel a like degree of cold, must be thought to have cold in them.

HYL. They must.

PHIL. Can any doctrine be true that necessarily leads a man into an absurdity?

HYL. Without doubt it cannot.

PHIL. Is it not an absurdity to think that the same thing should be at the same time both cold and warm?

HYL. It is.

PHIL. Suppose now one of your hands hot, and the other cold, and that they are both at once put into the same vessel of water, in an intermediate state; will not the water seem cold to one hand, and warm to the other?

HYL. It will.

PHIL. Ought we not therefore, by your principles, to conclude it is really both cold and warm at the same time, that is, according to your own concession, to believe an absurdity?

HYL. I confess it seems so.

PHIL. Consequently, the principles themselves are false, since you have granted that no true principle leads to an absurdity.

HYL. But, after all, can anything be more absurd than to say, THERE IS NO HEAT IN THE FIRE?

PHIL. To make the point still clearer; tell me whether, in two cases exactly alike, we ought not to make the same judgment?

HYL. We ought.

PHIL. When a pin pricks your finger, doth it not rend and divide the fibres of your flesh?

HYL. It doth.

PHIL. And when a coal burns your finger, doth it any more?

HYL. It doth not.

PHIL. Since, therefore, you neither judge the sensation itself occasioned by the pin, nor anything like it to be in the pin; you should not, conformably to what you have now granted, judge the sensation occasioned by the fire, or anything like it, to be in the fire.

HYL. Well, since it must be so, I am content to yield this point, and acknowledge that heat and cold are only sensations existing in our minds. But there still remain qualities enough to secure the reality of external things.

* * *

PHIL. You are still then of opinion that EXTENSION and FIGURES are inherent in external unthinking substances?

HYL. I am.

PHIL. But what if the same arguments which are brought against Secondary Qualities will hold good against these also?

HYL. Why then I shall be obliged to think, they too exist only in the mind.

PHIL. Is it your opinion the very figure and extension which you perceive by sense exist in the outward object or material substance? HYL. It is.

PHIL. Have all other animals as good grounds to think the same of the figure and extension which they see and feel?

HYL. Without doubt, if they have any thought at all.

PHIL. Answer me, Hylas. Think you the senses were bestowed upon all animals for their preservation and well-being in life? or were they given to men alone for this end?

HYL. I make no question but they have the same use in all other animals.

PHIL. If so, is it not necessary they should be enabled by them to perceive their own limbs, and those bodies which are capable of harming them?

HYL. Certainly.

PHIL. A mite therefore must be supposed to see his own foot, and things equal or even less than it, as bodies of some considerable dimension; though at the same time they appear to you scarce discernible, or at best as so many visible points?

HYL. I cannot deny it.

PHIL. And to creatures less than the mite they will seem yet larger?

HYL. They will.

PHIL. Insomuch that what you can hardly discern will to another extremely minute animal appear as some huge mountain?

HYL. All this I grant.

PHIL. Can one and the same thing be at the same time in itself of different dimensions?

HYL. That were absurd to imagine.

PHIL. But, from what you have laid down it follows that both the extension by you perceived, and that perceived by the mite itself, as likewise all those perceived by lesser animals, are each of them the true extension of the mite's foot; that is to say, by your own principles you are led into an absurdity.

HYL. There seems to be some difficulty in the point.

PHIL. Again, have you not acknowledged that no real inherent property of any object can be changed without some change in the thing itself?

HYL. I have.

PHIL. But, as we approach to or recede from an object, the visible extension varies, being at one distance ten or a hundred times greater than another. Doth it not therefore follow from hence likewise that it is not really inherent in the object?

HYL. I own I am at a loss what to think.

CHAPTER V.

KNOWLEDGE BY ACQUAINTANCE AND KNOWLEDGE BY DESCRIPTION

In the preceding chapter we saw that there are two sorts of knowledge: knowledge of things, and knowledge of truths. In this chapter we shall be concerned exclusively with knowledge of things, of which in turn we shall have to distinguish two kinds. Knowledge of things, when it is of the kind we call knowledge by *acquaintance*, is essentially simpler than any knowledge of truths, and logically independent of knowledge of truths, though it would be rash to assume that human beings ever, in fact, have acquaintance with things without at the same time knowing some truth about them. Knowledge of things by *description*, on the contrary, always involves, as we shall find in the course of the present chapter, some knowledge of truths as its source and ground. But first of all we must make clear what we mean by 'acquaintance' and what we mean by 'description'.

We shall say that we have *acquaintance* with anything of which we are directly aware, without the intermediary of any process of inference or any knowledge of truths. Thus in the presence of my table I am acquainted with the sense-data that make up the appearance of my table--its colour, shape, hardness, smoothness, etc.; all these are things of which I am immediately conscious when I am seeing and touching my table. The particular shade of colour that I am seeing may have many things said about it--I may say that it is brown, that it is rather dark, and so on. But such statements, though they make me know truths about the colour, do not make me know the colour itself any better than I did before so far as concerns knowledge of the colour itself, as opposed to knowledge of truths about it, I know the colour perfectly and completely when I see it, and no further knowledge of it itself is even theoretically possible. Thus the sense-data which make up the appearance of my table are things with which I have acquaintance, things immediately known to me just as they are. My knowledge of the table as a physical object, on the contrary, is not direct knowledge. Such as it is, it is obtained through acquaintance with the sense-data that make up the appearance of the table. We have seen that it is possible, without absurdity, to doubt whether there is a table at all, whereas it is not possible to doubt the sense-data. My knowledge of the table is of the kind which we shall call 'knowledge by description'. The table is 'the physical object which causes such-and-such sense-data'. This describes the table by means of the sense-data. In order to know anything at all about the table, we must know truths connecting it with things with which we have acquaintance: we must know that 'such-and-such sense-data are caused by a physical object'. There is no state of mind in which we are directly aware of the table; all our knowledge of the table is really knowledge of truths, and the actual thing which is the table is not, strictly speaking, known to us at all. We know a description, and we know that there is just one object to which this description applies, though the object itself is not directly known to us. In such a case, we say that our knowledge of the object is knowledge by description.

All our knowledge, both knowledge of things and knowledge of truths, rests upon acquaintance as its foundation. It is therefore important to consider what kinds of things there are with which we have acquaintance.

Sense-data, as we have already seen, are among the things with which we are acquainted; in fact, they supply the most obvious and striking example of knowledge by acquaintance. But if they were the sole example, our knowledge would be very much more restricted than it is. We should only know what is now present to our senses: we could not know anything about the past--not even that there was a past--nor could we know any truths about our sense-data, for all knowledge of truths, as we shall show, demands acquaintance with things which are of an essentially different character from sense-data, the things which are sometimes called 'abstract ideas', but which we shall call 'universals'. We have therefore to consider acquaintance with other things besides sense-data if we are to obtain any tolerably adequate analysis of our knowledge.

The first extension beyond sense-data to be considered is acquaintance by *memory*. It is obvious that we often remember what we have seen or heard or had otherwise present to our senses, and that in such cases we are still immediately aware of what we remember, in spite of the fact that it appears as past and not as present. This immediate knowledge by memory is the source of all our knowledge concerning the past: without it, there could be no knowledge of the past by inference, since we should never know that there was anything past to be inferred.

The next extension to be considered is acquaintance by *introspection*. We are not only aware of things, but we are often aware of being aware of them. When I see the sun, I am often aware of my seeing the sun; thus 'my seeing the sun' is an object with which I have acquaintance. When I desire food, I may be aware of my desire for food; thus 'my desiring food' is an object with which I am acquainted. Similarly we may be aware of our feeling pleasure or pain, and generally of the events which happen in our minds. This kind of acquaintance, which may be called self-consciousness, is the source of all our knowledge of mental things. It is obvious that it is only what goes on in our own minds that can be thus known immediately. What goes on in the minds of others is known to us through our perception of their bodies, that is, through the sense-data in us which are associated with their bodies. But for our acquaintance with the contents of our own minds, we should be unable to imagine the minds of others, and therefore we could never arrive at the knowledge that they have minds. It seems natural to suppose that self-consciousness is one of the things that distinguish men from animals: animals, we may suppose, though they have acquaintance with sense-data, never become aware of this acquaintance. I do not mean that they *doubt* whether they exist, but that they have never become conscious of the fact that they have sensations and feelings, nor therefore of the fact that they, the subjects of their sensations and feelings, exist. We have spoken of acquaintance with the contents of our minds as *self*-consciousness, but it is not, of course, consciousness of our *self*: it is consciousness of particular thoughts and feelings. The question whether we are also acquainted with our bare selves, as opposed to particular thoughts and feelings, is a very difficult one, upon which it would be rash to speak positively. When we try to look into ourselves we always seem to come upon some particular thought or feeling, and not upon the 'I' which has the thought or feeling. Nevertheless there are some reasons for thinking that we are acquainted with the 'I', though the acquaintance is hard to disentangle from other things. To make clear what sort of reason there is, let us consider for a moment what our acquaintance with particular thoughts really involves.

When I am acquainted with 'my seeing the sun', it seems plain that I am acquainted with two different things in relation to each other. On the one hand there is the sense-datum which represents the sun to me, on the other hand there is that which sees this sense-datum. All acquaintance, such as my acquaintance with the sense-datum which represents the sun, seems obviously a relation between the person acquainted and the object with which the person is acquainted. When a case of acquaintance is one with which I can be acquainted (as I am acquainted with my acquaintance with the sense-datum representing the sun), it is plain that the person acquainted is myself. Thus, when I am acquainted with my seeing the sun, the whole fact with which I am acquainted is 'Self-acquainted-with-sense-datum'.

Further, we know the truth 'I am acquainted with this sense-datum'. It is hard to see how we could know this truth, or even understand what is meant by it, unless we were acquainted with something which we call 'I'. It does not seem necessary to suppose that we are acquainted with a more or less permanent person, the same to-day as yesterday, but it does seem as though we must be acquainted with that thing, whatever its nature, which sees the sun and has acquaintance with sense-data. Thus, in some sense it would seem we must be acquainted with our Selves as opposed to our particular experiences. But the question is difficult, and complicated arguments can be adduced on either side. Hence, although acquaintance with ourselves seems *probably* to occur, it is not wise to assert that it undoubtedly does occur.

We may therefore sum up as follows what has been said concerning acquaintance with things that exist. We have acquaintance in sensation with the data of the outer senses, and in introspection with the data of what may be called the inner sense--thoughts, feelings, desires, etc.; we have acquaintance in memory with things which have been data either of the outer senses or of the inner sense. Further, it is probable, though not certain, that we have acquaintance with Self, as that which is aware of things or has desires towards things.

In addition to our acquaintance with particular existing things, we also have acquaintance with what we shall call *universals*, that is to say, general ideas, such as *whiteness*, *diversity*, *brotherhood*, and so on. Every complete sentence must contain at least one word which stands for a universal, since all verbs have a meaning which is universal. We shall return to universals later on, in Chapter IX; for the present, it is only necessary to guard against the supposition that whatever we can be acquainted with must be something particular and existent. Awareness of universals is called *conceiving*, and a universal of which we are aware is called a *concept*. It will be seen that among the objects with which we are acquainted are not included physical objects (as opposed to sense-data), nor other people's minds. These things are known to us by what I call 'knowledge by description', which we must now consider.

By a 'description' I mean any phrase of the form 'a so-and-so' or 'the so-and-so'. A phrase of the form 'a so-and-so' I shall call an 'ambiguous' description; a phrase of the form 'the so-and-so' (in the singular) I shall call a 'definite' description. Thus 'a man' is an ambiguous description, and 'the man with the iron mask' is a definite description. There are various problems connected with ambiguous descriptions, but I pass them by, since they do not directly concern the matter we are discussing, which is the nature of our knowledge concerning objects in cases where we know that there is an object answering to a definite description, though we are not acquainted with any such object. This is a matter which is concerned exclusively with definite descriptions. I shall therefore, in the sequel, speak simply of 'descriptions' when I mean 'definite descriptions'. Thus a description will mean any phrase of the form 'the so-and-so' in the singular.

We shall say that an object is 'known by description' when we know that it is 'the so-and-so', i.e. when we know that there is one object, and no more, having a certain property; and it will generally be implied that we do not have knowledge of the same object by acquaintance. We know that the man with the iron mask existed, and many propositions are known about him; but we do not know who he was. We know that the candidate who gets the most votes will be elected, and in this case we are very likely also acquainted (in the only sense in which one can be acquainted with some one else) with the man who is, in fact, the candidate who will get most votes; but we do not know which of the candidates he is, i.e. we do not know any proposition of the form 'A is the candidate who will get most votes' where A is one of the candidates by name. We shall say that we have 'merely descriptive knowledge' of the so-and-so when, although we know that the so-and-so exists, and although we may possibly be acquainted with the object which is, in fact, the so-and-so, yet we do not know any proposition '*a* is the so-and-so', where *a* is something with which we are acquainted. When we say 'the so-and-so exists', we mean that there is just one object which is the so-and-so. The proposition '*a* is the so-and-so' means that *a* has the property so-and-so, and nothing else has. 'Mr. A. is the

Unionist candidate for this constituency' means 'Mr. A. is a Unionist candidate for this constituency, and no one else is'. 'The Unionist candidate for this constituency exists' means 'some one is a Unionist candidate for this constituency, and no one else is'. Thus, when we are acquainted with an object which is the so-and-so, we know that the so-and-so exists; but we may know that the so-and-so exists when we are not acquainted with any object which we know to be the so-and-so, and even when we are not acquainted with any object which, in fact, is the so-and-so. Common words, even proper names, are usually really descriptions. That is to say, the thought in the mind of a person using a proper name correctly can generally only be expressed explicitly if we replace the proper name by a description. Moreover, the description required to express the thought will vary for different people, or for the same person at different times. The only thing constant (so long as the name is rightly used) is the object to which the name applies. But so long as this remains constant, the particular description involved usually makes no difference to the truth or falsehood of the proposition in which the name appears.

Let us take some illustrations. Suppose some statement made about Bismarck. Assuming that there is such a thing as direct acquaintance with oneself, Bismarck himself might have used his name directly to designate the particular person with whom he was acquainted. In this case, if he made a judgement about himself, he himself might be a constituent of the judgement. Here the proper name has the direct use which it always wishes to have, as simply standing for a certain object, and not for a description of the object. But if a person who knew Bismarck made a judgement about him, the case is different. What this person was acquainted with were certain sense-data which he connected (rightly, we will suppose) with Bismarck's body. His body, as a physical object, and still more his mind, were only known as the body and the mind connected with these sense-data. That is, they were known by description. It is, of course, very much a matter of chance which characteristics of a man's appearance will come into a friend's mind when he thinks of him;

thus the description actually in the friend's mind is accidental. The essential point is that he knows that the various descriptions all apply to the same entity, in spite of not being acquainted with the entity in question.

When we, who did not know Bismarck, make a judgement about him, the description in our minds will probably be some more or less vague mass of historical knowledge--far more, in most cases, than is required to identify him. But, for the sake of illustration, let us assume that we think of him as 'the first Chancellor of the German Empire'. Here all the words are abstract except 'German'. The word 'German' will, again, have different meanings for different people. To some it will recall travels in Germany, to some the look of Germany on the map, and so on. But if we are to obtain a description which we know to be applicable, we shall be compelled, at some point, to bring in a reference to a particular with which we are acquainted. Such reference is involved in any mention of past, present, and future (as opposed to definite dates), or of here and there, or of what others have told us. Thus it would seem that, in some way or other, a description known to be applicable to a particular must involve some reference to a particular with which we are acquainted, if our knowledge about the thing described is not to be merely what follows *logically* from the description. For example, 'the most long-lived of men' is a description involving only universals, which must apply to some man, but we can make no judgements concerning this man which involve knowledge about him beyond what the description gives. If, however, we say, 'The first Chancellor of the German Empire was an astute diplomatist', we can only be assured of the truth of our judgement in virtue of something with which we are acquainted--usually a testimony heard or read. Apart from the information we convey to others, apart from the fact about the actual Bismarck, which gives importance to our judgement, the thought we really have contains the one or more particulars involved, and otherwise consists wholly of concepts. All names of places--London, England, Europe, the Earth, the Solar System--similarly involve, when used, descriptions which start from some one or more particulars with which we are acquainted. I suspect that even the Universe, as considered by metaphysics, involves such a connexion with particulars. In logic, on the contrary, where we are concerned not merely with what does exist, but with whatever might or could exist or be, no reference to actual particulars is involved.

It would seem that, when we make a statement about something only known by description, we often *intend* to make our statement, not in the form involving the description, but about the actual thing described. That is to say, when we say anything about Bismarck, we should like, if we could, to make the judgement which Bismarck alone can make, namely, the judgement of which he himself is a constituent. In this we are necessarily defeated, since the actual Bismarck is unknown to us. But we know that there is an object B, called Bismarck, and that B was an astute diplomatist. We can thus *describe* the proposition we should like to affirm, namely, 'B was an astute diplomatist', where B is the object which was Bismarck. If we are describing Bismarck as 'the first Chancellor of the German Empire', the proposition we should like to affirm may be described as 'the proposition asserting, concerning the actual object which was the first Chancellor of the German Empire, that this object was an astute diplomatist'. What enables us to communicate in spite of the varying descriptions we employ is that we know there is a true proposition concerning the actual Bismarck, and that however we may vary the description (so long as the description is correct) the proposition described is still the same. This proposition, which is described and is known to be true, is what interests us; but we are not acquainted with the proposition itself, and do not know it, though we know it is true.

It will be seen that there are various stages in the removal from acquaintance with particulars: there is Bismarck to people who knew him; Bismarck to those who only know of him through history; the man with the iron mask; the longest-lived of men. These are progressively further removed from acquaintance with particulars; the first comes as near to acquaintance as is possible in regard to another person; in the second, we shall still be said to know 'who Bismarck was'; in the third, we do not know who was the man with the iron mask, though we can know many propositions about him which are not logically deducible from the fact that he wore an iron mask; in the fourth, finally, we know nothing beyond what is logically deducible from the definition of the man. There is a similar hierarchy in the region of universals. Many universals, like many particulars, are only known to us by description. But here, as in the case of particulars, knowledge concerning what is known by description is ultimately reducible to knowledge concerning what is known by acquaintance.

The fundamental principle in the analysis of propositions containing descriptions is this: *Every proposition which we can understand must be composed wholly of constituents with which we are acquainted.* We shall not at this stage attempt to answer all the objections which may be urged against this fundamental principle. For the present, we shall merely point out that, in some way or other, it must be possible to meet these objections, for it is scarcely conceivable that we can make a judgement or entertain a supposition without knowing what it is that we are judging or supposing about. We must attach *some* meaning to the words we use, if we are to speak significantly and not utter mere noise; and the meaning we attach to our words must be something with which we are acquainted. Thus when, for example, we make a statement about Julius Caesar, it is plain that Julius Caesar himself is not before our minds, since we are not acquainted with him. We have in mind some description of Julius Caesar: 'the man who was assassinated on the Ides of March', 'the founder of the Roman Empire', or, perhaps, merely 'the man whose name was *Julius Caesar*'. (In this last description, *Julius Caesar* is a noise or shape with which we are acquainted.) Thus our statement does not mean quite what it seems to mean, but means something involving, instead of Julius Caesar, some description of him which is composed wholly of particulars and universals with which we are acquainted.

The chief importance of knowledge by description is that it enables us to pass beyond the limits of our private experience. In spite of the fact that we can only know truths which are wholly composed of terms which we have experienced in acquaintance, we can yet have knowledge by description of things which we have never experienced. In view of the very narrow range of our immediate experience, this result is vital, and until it is understood, much of our knowledge must remain mysterious and therefore doubtful.

Ludwig Wittgenstein (1889 – 1951) was a student of Russell's who in many respects came to overshadow his mentor. Considered by many the most important philosopher of the 20th century, he published very little in his own lifetime, but corresponded with many of the important figures of modern logic, including Russell. The Tratatus Logico-Philosophicus, for which Russell provided an introduction when it was published in England, was presented as a doctoral dissertation at Cambridge.

The style of the Tractatus is problematic: highly technical in places, brief and aphoristic, almost cryptic in others. It is not intended as a work of popular philosophy, as is "The Problems of Philosophy." However, one can see that the same ideas are being contemplated in each work. In particular the distinction that Russell makes much of, between "Knowledge of things" and "Knowledge of Truths" is obviously related (although perhaps not exactly the same as) the distinction Wittgenstein draws between things that can be said and things that can only be shown. The distinction Wittgenstein draws between "things" and "facts" also seems to mirror Russell's distinction.

It is also worth comparing this passage to Russell's discussion in Chapter XII, to see two very different theories of the proposition, and two views of what makes a proposition "true."

Ludwig Wittgenstein

from

Tractatus Logico-Philospohicus, 1 - 3.141

1 The world is everything that is the case.

1.1 The world is the totality of facts, not of things.

1.11 The world is determined by the facts, and by these being al l the facts.

1.12 For the totality of facts determines both what is the case, and also all that is not the case.

1.13 The facts in logical space are the world.

1.2 The world divides into facts.

1.21 Any one can either be the case or not be the case, and everything else remain the same.

2 What is the case, the fact, is the existence of atomic facts.

2.01 An atomic fact is a combination of objects (entities, things).

2.011 It is essential to a thing that it can be a constituent part of an atomic fact.

2.012 In logic nothing is accidental: if a thing can occur in an atomic fact the possibility of that atomic fact must already be prejudged in the thing.

2.0121 It would, so to speak, appear as an accident, when to a thing that could exist alone on its own account, subsequently a state of affairs could be made to fit. If things can occur in atomic facts, this possibility must already lie in them. (A logical entity cannot be merely possible. Logic treats of every possibility, and all possibilities are its facts.) Just as we cannot think of spatial objects at all apart from space, or temporal objects apart from time, so we cannot think of any object apart from the possibility of its connexion with other things. If I can think of an object in the context of an atomic fact, I cannot think of it apart from the possibility of this context.

2.0122 The thing is independent, in so far as it can occur in all possible circumstances, but this form of independence is a form of connexion with the atomic fact, a form of dependence. (It is impossible for words to occur in two different ways, alone and in the proposition.)

2.0123 If I know an object, then I also know all the possibilities of its occurrence in atomic facts. (Every such possibility must lie in the nature of the object.) A new possibility cannot subsequently be found.

2.01231 In order to know an object, I must know not its external but all its internal qualities.

2.0124 If all objects are given, then thereby are all possible atomic facts also given.

2.013 Every thing is, as it were, in a space of possible atomic facts. I can think of this space as empty, but not of the thing without the space.

2.0131 A spatial object must lie in infinite space. (A point in space is a place for an argument.) A speck in a visual field need not be red, but it must have a colour; it has, so to speak, a colour space round it. A tone must have a pitch, the object of the sense of touch a hardness, etc.

2.014 objects contain the possibility of all states of affairs.

2.0141 The possibility of its occurrence in atomic facts is the form of the object.

2.02 The object is simple.

2.0201 Every statement about complexes can be analysed into a statement about their constituent parts, and into those propositions which completely describe the complexes.

2.021 objects form the substance of the world. Therefore they cannot be compound.

2.0211 If the world had no substance, then whether a proposition had sense would depend on whether another proposition was true.

2.0212 It would then be impossible to form a picture of the world (true or false).

2.022 It is clear that however different from the real one an imagined world may be, it must have something—a form—in common with the real world.

2.023 This fixed form consists of the objects.

2.0231 The substance of the world can only determine a form and not any material properties. For these are first presented by the propositions—first formed by the configuration of the objects.

2.0232 Roughly speaking: objects are colourless.

2.0233 Two objects of the same logical form are—apart from their external properties—only differentiated from one another in that they are different.

2.02331 Either a thing has properties which no other has, and then one can distinguish it straight away from the others by a description and refer to it; or, on the other hand, there are several things which have the totality of their properties in common, and then it is quite impossible to point to any one of them. For if a thing is not distinguished by anything, I cannot distinguish it—for otherwise it would be distinguished.

2.024 Substance is what exists independently of what is the case.

2.025 It is form and content.

2.0251 Space, time and colour (colouredness) are forms of objects.

2.026 Only if there are objects can there be a fixed form of the world.

2.027 The fixed, the existent and the object are one.

2.0271 The object is the fixed, the existent; the configuration is the changing, the variable.

2.0272 The configuration of the objects forms the atomic fact.

2.03 In the atomic fact objects hang one in another, like the members of a chain.

2.031 In the atomic fact the objects are combined in a definite way.

2.032 The way in which objects hang together in the atomic fact is the structure of the atomic fact.

2.033 The form is the possibility of the structure.

2.034 The structure of the fact consists of the structures of the atomic facts.

2.04 The totality of existent atomic facts is the world.

2.05 The totality of existent atomic facts also determines which atomic facts do not exist.

2.06 The existence and non-existence of atomic facts is the reality. (The existence of atomic facts we also call a positive fact, their non-existence a negative fact.)

2.061 Atomic facts are independent of one another.

2.062 From the existence or non-existence of an atomic fact we cannot infer the existence or non-existence of another.

2.063 The total reality is the world.

2.1 We make to ourselves pictures of facts.

2.11 The picture presents the facts in logical space, the existence and non-existence of atomic facts.

2.12 The picture is a model of reality.

2.13 To the objects correspond in the picture the elements of the picture.

2.131 The elements of the picture stand, in the picture, for the objects.

2.14 The picture consists in the fact that its elements are combined with one another in a definite way.

2.141 The picture is a fact.

2.15 That the elements of the picture are combined with one another in a definite way, represents that the things are so combined with one another. This connexion of the elements of the picture is called its structure, and the possibility of this structure is called the form of representation of the picture.

2.151 The form of representation is the possibility that the things are combined with one another as are the elements of the picture.

2.1511 Thus the picture is linked with reality; it reaches up to it.

2.1512 It is like a scale applied to reality.

2.15121 Only the outermost points of the dividing lines touch the object to be measured.

2.1513 According to this view the representing relation which makes it a picture, also belongs to the picture.

2.1514 The representing relation consists of the co-ordinations of the elements of the picture and the things.

2.1515 These co-ordinations are as it were the feelers of its elements with which the picture touches reality.

2.16 In order to be a picture a fact must have something in common with what it pictures.

2.161 In the picture and the pictured there must be something identical in order that the one can be a picture of the other at all.

2.17 What the picture must have in common with reality in order to be able to represent it after its manner—rightly or falsely—is its form of representation.

2.171 The picture can represent every reality whose form it has. The spatial picture, everything spatial, the coloured, everything coloured, etc.

2.172 The picture, however, cannot represent its form of representation; it shows it forth.

2.173 The picture represents its object from without (its standpoint is its form of representation), therefore the picture represents its object rightly or falsely.

2.174 But the picture cannot place itself outside of its form of representation.

2.18 What every picture, of whatever form, must have in common with reality in order to be able to represent it at all—rightly or falsely—is the logical form, that is, the form of reality.

2.181 If the form of representation is the logical form, then the picture is called a logical picture.

2.182 Every picture is also a logical picture. (On the other hand, for example, not every picture is spatial.)

2.19 The logical picture can depict the world.

2.2 The picture has the logical form of representation in common with what it pictures.

2.201 The picture depicts reality by representing a possibility of the existence and non-existence of atomic facts.

2.202 The picture represents a possible state of affairs in logical space.

2.203 The picture contains the possibility of the state of affairs which it represents.

2.21 The picture agrees with reality or not; it is right or wrong, true or false.

2.22 The picture represents what it represents, independently of its truth or falsehood, through the form of representation.

2.221 What the picture represents is its sense.

2.222 In the agreement or disagreement of its sense with reality, its truth or falsity consists.

2.223 In order to discover whether the picture is true or false we must compare it with reality.

2.224 It cannot be discovered from the picture alone whether it is true or false.

2.225 There is no picture which is a priori true.

3 The logical picture of the facts is the thought.

3.001 "An atomic fact is thinkable"—means: we can imagine it.

3.01 The totality of true thoughts is a picture of the world.

3.02 The thought contains the possibility of the state of affairs which it thinks. What is thinkable is also possible.

3.03 We cannot think anything unlogical, for otherwise we should have to think unlogically.

3.031 It used to be said that God could create everything, except what was contrary to the laws of logic. The truth is, we could not say of an "unlogical" world how it would look.

3.032 To present in language anything which "contradicts logic" is as impossible as in geometry to present by its co-ordinates a figure which contradicts the laws of space; or to give the co-ordinates of a point which does not exist.

3.0321 We could present spatially an atomic fact which contradicted the laws of physics, but not one which contradicted the laws of geometry.

3.04 An a priori true thought would be one whose possibility guaranteed its truth.

3.05 We could only know a priori that a thought is true if its truth was to be recognized from the thought itself (without an object of comparison).

3.1 In the proposition the thought is expressed perceptibly through the senses.

3.11 We use the sensibly perceptible sign (sound or written sign, etc.) of the proposition as a projection of the possible state of affairs. The method of projection is the thinking of the sense of the proposition.

3.12 The sign through which we express the thought I call the propositional sign. And the proposition is the propositional sign in its projective relation to the world.

3.13 To the proposition belongs everything which belongs to the projection; but not what is projected. Therefore the possibility of what is projected but not this itself. In the proposition, therefore, its sense is not yet contained, but the possibility of expressing it. ("The content of the proposition" means the content of the significant proposition.) In the proposition the form of its sense is contained, but not its content.

3.14 The propositional sign consists in the fact that its elements, the words, are combined in it in a definite way. The propositional sign is a fact.

3.141 The proposition is not a mixture of words (just as the musical theme is not a mixture of tones). The proposition is articulate.

CHAPTER VI.

ON INDUCTION

In almost all our previous discussions we have been concerned in the attempt to get clear as to our data in the way of knowledge of existence. What things are there in the universe whose existence is known to us owing to our being acquainted with them? So far, our answer has been that we are acquainted with our sense-data, and, probably, with ourselves. These we know to exist. And past sense-data which are remembered are known to have existed in the past. This knowledge supplies our data.

But if we are to be able to draw inferences from these data--if we are to know of the existence of matter, of other people, of the past before our individual memory begins, or of the future, we must know general principles of some kind by means of which such inferences can be drawn. It must be known to us that the existence of some one sort of thing, A, is a sign of the existence of some other sort of thing, B, either at the same time as A or at some earlier or later time, as, for example, thunder is a sign of the earlier existence of lightning. If this were not known to us, we could never extend our knowledge beyond the sphere of our private experience; and this sphere, as we have seen, is exceedingly limited. The question we have now to consider is whether such an extension is possible, and if so, how it is effected. Let us take as an illustration a matter about which none of us, in fact, feel the slightest doubt. We are all convinced that the sun will rise to-morrow. Why? Is this belief a mere blind outcome of past experience, or can it be justified as a reasonable belief? It is not easy to find a test by which to judge whether a belief of this kind is reasonable or not, but we can at least ascertain what sort of general beliefs would suffice, if true, to justify the judgement that the sun will rise to-morrow, and the many other similar judgements upon which our actions are based.

It is obvious that if we are asked why we believe that the sun will rise to-morrow, we shall naturally answer 'Because it always has risen every day'. We have a firm belief that it will rise in the future, because it has risen in the past. If we are challenged as to why we believe that it will continue to rise as heretofore, we may appeal to the laws of motion: the earth, we shall say, is a freely rotating body, and such bodies do not cease to rotate unless something interferes from outside, and there is nothing outside to interfere with the earth between now and to-morrow. Of course it might be doubted whether we are quite certain that there is nothing outside to interfere, but this is not the interesting doubt. The interesting doubt is as to whether the laws of motion will remain in operation until to-morrow. If this doubt is raised, we find ourselves in the same position as when the doubt about the sunrise was first raised. The *only* reason for believing that the laws of motion will remain in operation is that they have operated hitherto, so far as our knowledge of the past enables us to judge. It is true that we have a greater body of evidence from the past in favour of the laws of motion than we have in favour of the sunrise, because the sunrise is merely a particular case of fulfillment of the laws of motion, and there are countless other particular cases. But the real question is: Do *any* number of cases of a law being fulfilled in the past afford evidence that it will be fulfilled in the future? If not, it becomes plain that we have no ground whatever for expecting the sun to rise to-morrow, or for expecting the bread we shall eat at our next meal not to poison us, or for any of the other scarcely conscious expectations that control our daily lives. It is to be observed that all such expectations are only *probable*; thus we have not to seek for a proof that they *must* be fulfilled, but only for some reason in favour of the view that they are *likely* to be fulfilled.

Now in dealing with this question we must, to begin with, make an important distinction, without which we should soon become involved in hopeless confusions. Experience has shown us that, hitherto, the frequent repetition of some uniform succession or coexistence has been a *cause* of our expecting the same succession or coexistence on the next occasion. Food that has a certain appearance generally has a certain taste, and it is a severe shock to our expectations when the familiar appearance is found to be associated with an unusual taste. Things which we see become associated, by habit, with certain tactile sensations which we expect if we touch them; one of the horrors of a ghost (in many ghost-stories) is that it fails to give us any sensations of touch. Uneducated people who go abroad for the first time are so surprised as to be incredulous when they find their native language not understood. And this kind of association is not confined to men; in animals also it is very strong. A horse which has been often driven along a certain road resists the attempt to drive him in a different direction. Domestic animals expect food when they see the person who usually feeds them. We know that all these rather crude expectations of uniformity are liable to be misleading. The man who has fed the chicken every day throughout its life at last wrings its neck instead, showing that more refined views as to the uniformity of nature would have been useful to the chicken.

But in spite of the misleadingness of such expectations, they nevertheless exist. The mere fact that something has happened a certain number of times causes animals and men to expect that it will happen again. Thus our instincts certainly cause us to believe that the sun will rise to-morrow, but we may be in no better a position than the chicken which unexpectedly has its neck wrung. We have therefore to distinguish the fact that past uniformities *cause* expectations as to the future, from the question whether there is any reasonable ground for giving weight to such expectations after the question of their validity has been raised.

The problem we have to discuss is whether there is any reason for believing in what is called 'the uniformity of nature'. The belief in the uniformity of nature is the belief that everything that has happened or will happen is an instance of some general law to which there are no exceptions. The crude expectations which we have been considering are all subject to exceptions, and therefore liable to disappoint those who entertain them. But science habitually assumes, at least as a working hypothesis, that general rules which have exceptions can be replaced by general rules which have no exceptions. 'Unsupported bodies in air fall' is a general rule to which balloons and aeroplanes are exceptions. But the laws of motion and the law of gravitation, which account for the fact that most bodies fall, also account for the fact that balloons and aeroplanes can rise; thus the laws of motion and the law of gravitation are not subject to these exceptions.

The belief that the sun will rise to-morrow might be falsified if the earth came suddenly into contact with a large body which destroyed its rotation; but the laws of motion and the law of gravitation would not be infringed by such an event. The business of science is to find uniformities, such as the laws of motion and the law of gravitation, to which, so far as our experience extends, there are no exceptions. In this search science has been remarkably successful, and it may be conceded that such uniformities have held hitherto. This brings us back to the question: Have we any reason, assuming that they have always held in the past, to suppose that they will hold in the future?

It has been argued that we have reason to know that the future will resemble the past, because what was the future has constantly become the past, and has always been found to resemble the past, so that we really have experience of the future, namely of times which were formerly future, which we may call past futures. But such an argument really begs the very question at issue. We have experience of past futures, but not of future futures, and the question is: Will future futures resemble past futures? This question is not to be answered by an argument which starts from past futures alone. We have therefore still to seek for some principle which shall enable us to know that the future will follow the same laws as the past. The reference to the future in this question is not essential. The same question arises when we apply the laws that work in our experience to past things of which we have no experience--as, for example, in geology, or in theories as to the origin of the Solar System. The question we really have to ask is: 'When two things have been found to be often associated, and no instance is known of the one occurring without the other, does the occurrence of one of the two, in a fresh instance, give any good ground for expecting the other?' On our answer to this question must depend the validity of the whole of our expectations as to the future, the whole of the results obtained by induction, and in fact practically all the beliefs upon which our daily life is based.

It must be conceded, to begin with, that the fact that two things have been found often together and never apart does not, by itself, suffice to *prove* demonstratively that they will be found together in the next case we examine. The most we can hope is that the oftener things are found together, the more probable it becomes that they will be found together another time, and that, if they have been found together often enough, the probability will amount *almost* to certainty. It can never quite reach certainty, because we know that in spite of frequent repetitions there sometimes is a failure at the last, as in the case of the chicken whose neck is wrung. Thus probability is all we ought to seek.

It might be urged, as against the view we are advocating, that we know all natural phenomena to be subject to the reign of law, and that sometimes, on the basis of observation, we can see that only one law can possibly fit the facts of the case. Now to this view there are two answers. The first is that, even if *some* law which has no exceptions applies to our case, we can never, in practice, be sure that we have discovered that law and not one to which there are exceptions. The second is that the reign of law would seem to be itself only probable, and that our belief that it will hold in the future, or in unexamined cases in the past, is itself based upon the very principle we are examining.

The principle we are examining may be called the *principle of induction*, and its two parts may be stated as follows:

> (a) When a thing of a certain sort A has been found to be associated with a thing of a certain other sort B, and has never been found dissociated from a thing of the sort B, the greater the number of cases in which A and B have been associated, the greater is the probability that they will be associated in a fresh case in which one of them is known to be present;

> (b) Under the same circumstances, a sufficient number of cases of association will make the probability of a fresh association nearly a certainty, and will make it approach certainty without limit.

As just stated, the principle applies only to the verification of our expectation in a single fresh instance. But we want also to know that there is a probability in favour of the general law that things of the sort A are *always* associated with things of the sort B, provided a sufficient number of cases of association are known, and no cases of failure of association are known. The probability of the general law is obviously less than the probability of the particular case, since if the general law is true, the particular case must also be true, whereas the particular case may be true without the general law being true. Nevertheless the probability of the general law is increased by repetitions, just as the probability of the particular case is. We may therefore repeat the two parts of our principle as regards the general law, thus:

> (a) The greater the number of cases in which a thing of the sort A has been found associated with a thing of the sort B, the more probable it is (if no cases of failure of association are known) that A is always associated with B;

> b) Under the same circumstances, a sufficient number of cases of the association of A with B will make it nearly certain that A is always associated with B, and will make this general law approach certainty without limit.

It should be noted that probability is always relative to certain data. In our case, the data are merely the known cases of coexistence of A and B. There may be other data, which *might* be taken into account, which would gravely alter the probability. For example, a man who had seen a great many white swans might argue, by our principle, that on the data it was *probable* that all swans were white, and this might be a perfectly sound argument. The argument is not disproved by the fact that some swans are black, because a thing may very well happen in spite of the fact that some data render it improbable. In the case of the swans, a man might know that colour is a very variable characteristic in many species of animals, and that, therefore, an induction as to colour is peculiarly liable to error. But this knowledge would be a fresh datum, by no means proving that the probability relatively to our previous data had been wrongly estimated. The fact, therefore, that things often fail to fulfill our expectations is no evidence that our expectations will not *probably* be fulfilled in a given case or a given class of cases. Thus our inductive principle is at any rate not capable of being disproved by an appeal to experience.

The inductive principle, however, is equally incapable of being *proved* by an appeal to experience. Experience might conceivably confirm the inductive principle as regards the cases that have been already examined; but as regards unexamined cases, it is the inductive principle alone that can justify any inference from what has been examined to what has not been examined. All arguments which, on the basis of experience, argue as to the future or the unexperienced parts of the past or present, assume the inductive principle; hence we can never use experience to prove the inductive principle without begging the question. Thus we must either accept the inductive principle on the ground of its intrinsic evidence, or forgo all justification of our expectations about the future. If the principle is unsound, we have no reason to expect the sun to rise to-morrow, to expect bread to be more nourishing than a stone, or to expect that if we throw ourselves off the roof we shall fall. When we see what looks like our best friend approaching us, we shall have no reason to suppose that his body is not inhabited by the mind of our worst enemy or of some total stranger. All our conduct is based upon associations which have worked in the past, and which we therefore regard as likely to work in the future; and this likelihood is dependent for its validity upon the inductive principle. The general principles of science, such as the belief in the reign of law, and the belief that every event must have a cause, are as completely dependent upon the inductive principle as are the beliefs of daily life All such general principles are believed because mankind have found innumerable instances of their truth and no instances of their falsehood. But this affords no evidence for their truth in the future, unless the inductive principle is assumed.

Thus all knowledge which, on a basis of experience tells us something about what is not experienced, is based upon a belief which experience can neither confirm nor confute, yet which, at least in its more concrete applications, appears to be as firmly rooted in us as many of the facts of experience. The existence and justification of such beliefs--for the inductive principle, as we shall see, is not the only example--raises some of the most difficult and most debated problems of philosophy. We will, in the next chapter, consider briefly what may be said to account for such knowledge, and what is its scope and its degree of certainty.

David Hume (1711 – 1776) is perhaps the most radical representative of philosophical skepticism. To Russell's question "Is there any knowledge in the world which is so certain that no reasonable man could doubt it?" Hume answers "No," or at least "Very little." If we limit our knowledge to what we get from our senses (as Berkeley tells us we must) then there is really very little that we can know for sure. Our beliefs about the future, in particular, do not qualify as certain knowledge. Our belief that the sun will rise tomorrow (the standard example here) is based on our memory that the sun rose yesterday, combined with the assumption that the future will be like the past. What justifies this assumption? This is the question Hume raises.

Hume centers his discussion on the concepts of Cause and Effect, and concludes that, however strong our belief in these are, they are not justified by our experience, or by anything else. This calls into question the very possibility of science, which relies on our ability to form general laws from a finite set of observations; that is to apply what is called the Principle of Induction.

Rusell's treatment of this problem is inspired by Hume.

David Hume

from

An Enquiry Concerning Human Understanding, Section IV

20. All the objects of human reason or enquiry may naturally be divided into two kinds, to wit, *Relations of Ideas*, and *Matters of Fact*. Of the first kind are the sciences of Geometry, Algebra, and Arithmetic; and in short, every affirmation which is either intuitively or demonstratively certain. *That the square of the hypothenuse is equal to the square of the two sides*, is a proposition which expresses a relation between these figures. *That three times five is equal to the half of thirty*, expresses a relation between these numbers. Propositions of this kind are discoverable by the mere operation of thought, without dependence on what is anywhere existent in the universe. Though there never were a circle or triangle in nature, the truths demonstrated by Euclid would for ever retain their certainty and evidence.

21. Matters of fact, which are the second objects of human reason, are not ascertained in the same manner; nor is our evidence of their truth, however great, of a like nature with the foregoing. The contrary of every matter of fact is still possible; because it can never imply a contradiction, and is conceived by the mind with the same facility and distinctness, as if ever so conformable to reality. *That the sun will not rise to-morrow* is no less intelligible a proposition, and implies no more contradiction than the affirmation, *that it will rise*. We should in vain, therefore, attempt to demonstrate its falsehood. Were it demonstratively false, it would imply a contradiction, and could never be distinctly conceived by the mind.

It may, therefore, be a subject worthy of curiosity, to enquire what is the nature of that evidence which assures us of any real existence and matter of fact, beyond the present testimony of our senses, or the records of our memory. This part of philosophy, it is observable, has been little cultivated, either by the ancients or moderns; and therefore our doubts and errors, in the prosecution of so important an enquiry, may be the more excusable; while we march through such difficult paths without any guide or direction. They may even prove useful, by exciting curiosity, and destroying that implicit faith and security, which is the bane of all reasoning and free enquiry. The discovery of defects in the common philosophy, if any such there be, will not, I presume, be a discouragement, but rather an incitement, as is usual, to attempt something more full and satisfactory than has yet been proposed to the public.

22. All reasonings concerning matter of fact seem to be founded on the relation of *Cause and Effect.* By means of that relation alone we can go beyond the evidence of our memory and senses. If you were to ask a man, why he believes any matter of fact, which is absent; for instance, that his friend is in the country, or in France; he would give you a reason; and this reason would be some other fact; as a letter received from him, or the knowledge of his former resolutions and promises. A man finding a watch or any other machine in a desert island, would conclude that there had once been men in that island. All our reasonings concerning fact are of the same nature. And here it is constantly supposed that there is a connexion between the present fact and that which is inferred from it. Were there nothing to bind them together, the inference would be entirely precarious. The hearing of an articulate voice and rational discourse in the dark assures us of the presence of some person: Why? because these are the effects of the human make and fabric, and closely connected with it. If we anatomize all the other reasonings of this nature, we shall find that they are founded on the relation of cause and effect, and that this relation is either near or remote, direct or collateral. Heat and light are collateral effects of fire, and the one effect may justly be inferred from the other.

23. If we would satisfy ourselves, therefore, concerning the nature of that evidence, which assures us of matters of fact, we must enquire how we arrive at the knowledge of cause and effect.

I shall venture to affirm, as a general proposition, which admits of no exception, that the knowledge of this relation is not, in any instance, attained by reasonings *a priori*; but arises entirely from experience, when we find that any particular objects are constantly conjoined with each other. Let an object be presented to a man of ever so strong natural reason and abilities; if that object be entirely new to him, he will not be able, by the most accurate examination of its sensible qualities, to discover any of its causes or effects. Adam, though his rational faculties be supposed, at the very first, entirely perfect, could not have inferred from the fluidity and transparency of water that it would suffocate him, or from the light and warmth of fire that it would consume him. No object ever discovers, by the qualities which appear to the senses, either the causes which produced it, or the effects which will arise from it; nor can our reason, unassisted by experience, ever draw any inference concerning real existence and matter of fact.

24. This proposition, *that causes and effects are discoverable, not by reason but by experience*, will readily be admitted with regard to such objects, as we remember to have once been altogether unknown to us; since we must be conscious of the utter inability, which we then lay under, of foretelling what would arise from them. Present two smooth pieces of marble to a man who has no tincture of natural philosophy; he will never discover that they will adhere together in such a manner as to require great force to separate them in a direct line, while they make so small a resistance to a lateral pressure. Such events, as bear little analogy to the common course of nature, are also readily confessed to be known only by experience; nor does any man imagine that the explosion of gunpowder, or the attraction of a loadstone, could ever be discovered by arguments *a priori*. In like manner, when an effect is supposed to depend upon an intricate machinery or secret

structure of parts, we make no difficulty in attributing all our knowledge of it to experience. Who will assert that he can give the ultimate reason, why milk or bread is proper nourishment for a man, not for a lion or a tiger?

But the same truth may not appear, at first sight, to have the same evidence with regard to events, which have become familiar to us from our first appearance in the world, which bear a close analogy to the whole course of nature, and which are supposed to depend on the simple qualities of objects, without any secret structure of parts. We are apt to imagine that we could discover these effects by the mere operation of our reason, without experience. We fancy, that were we brought on a sudden into this world, we could at first have inferred that one Billiard-ball would communicate motion to another upon impulse; and that we needed not to have waited for the event, in order to pronounce with certainty concerning it. Such is the influence of custom, that, where it is strongest, it not only covers our natural ignorance, but even conceals itself, and seems not to take place, merely because it is found in the highest degree.

25. But to convince us that all the laws of nature, and all the operations of bodies without exception, are known only by experience, the following reflections may, perhaps, suffice. Were any object presented to us, and were we required to pronounce concerning the effect, which will result from it, without consulting past observation; after what manner, I beseech you, must the mind proceed in this operation? It must invent or imagine some event, which it ascribes to the object as its effect; and it is plain that this invention must be entirely arbitrary. The mind can never possibly find the effect in the supposed cause, by the most accurate scrutiny and examination. For the effect is totally different from the cause, and consequently can never be discovered in it. Motion in the second Billiard-ball is a quite distinct event from motion in the first; nor is there anything in the one to suggest the smallest hint of the other. A stone or piece of metal raised into the air, and left without any support,

immediately falls: but to consider the matter *a priori*, is there anything we discover in this situation which can beget the idea of a downward, rather than an upward, or any other motion, in the stone or metal? And as the first imagination or invention of a particular effect, in all natural operations, is arbitrary, where we consult not experience; so must we also esteem the supposed tie or connexion between the cause and effect, which binds them together, and renders it impossible that any other effect could result from the operation of that cause. When I see, for instance, a Billiard-ball moving in a straight line towards another; even suppose motion in the second ball should by accident be suggested to me, as the result of their contact or impulse; may I not conceive, that a hundred different events might as well follow from that cause? May not both these balls remain at absolute rest? May not the first ball return in a straight line, or leap off from the second in any line or direction? All these suppositions are consistent and conceivable. Why then should we give the preference to one, which is no more consistent or conceivable than the rest? All our reasonings *a priori* will never be able to show us any foundation for this preference.

In a word, then, every effect is a distinct event from its cause. It could not, therefore, be discovered in the cause, and the first invention or conception of it, *a priori*, must be entirely arbitrary. And even after it is suggested, the conjunction of it with the cause must appear equally arbitrary; since there are always many other effects, which, to reason, must seem fully as consistent and natural. In vain, therefore, should we pretend to determine any single event, or infer any cause or effect, without the assistance of observation and experience.

26. Hence we may discover the reason why no philosopher, who is rational and modest, has ever pretended to assign the ultimate cause of any natural operation, or to show distinctly the action of that power, which produces any single effect in the universe. It is confessed, that the utmost effort of human reason is to reduce the principles, productive of natural phenomena, to a greater

simplicity, and to resolve the many particular effects into a few general causes, by means of reasonings from analogy, experience, and observation. But as to the causes of these general causes, we should in vain attempt their discovery; nor shall we ever be able to satisfy ourselves, by any particular explication of them. These ultimate springs and principles are totally shut up from human curiosity and enquiry. Elasticity, gravity, cohesion of parts, communication of motion by impulse; these are probably the ultimate causes and principles which we shall ever discover in nature; and we may esteem ourselves sufficiently happy, if, by accurate enquiry and reasoning, we can trace up the particular phenomena to, or near to, these general principles. The most perfect philosophy of the natural kind only staves off our ignorance a little longer: as perhaps the most perfect philosophy of the moral or metaphysical kind serves only to discover larger portions of it. Thus the observation of human blindness and weakness is the result of all philosophy, and meets us at every turn, in spite of our endeavours to elude or avoid it.

27. Nor is geometry, when taken into the assistance of natural philosophy, ever able to remedy this defect, or lead us into the knowledge of ultimate causes, by all that accuracy of reasoning for which it is so justly celebrated. Every part of mixed mathematics proceeds upon the supposition that certain laws are established by nature in her operations; and abstract reasonings are employed, either to assist experience in the discovery of these laws, or to determine their influence in particular instances, where it depends upon any precise degree of distance and quantity. Thus, it is a law of motion, discovered by experience, that the moment or force of any body in motion is in the compound ratio or proportion of its solid contents and its velocity; and consequently, that a small force may remove the greatest obstacle or raise the greatest weight, if, by any contrivance or machinery, we can increase the velocity of that force, so as to make it an overmatch for its antagonist. Geometry assists us in the application of this law, by giving us the just dimensions of all the parts and figures which can enter into any species of machine; but still the discovery of the law itself is

owing merely to experience, and all the abstract reasonings in the world could never lead us one step towards the knowledge of it. When we reason *a priori*, and consider merely any object or cause, as it appears to the mind, independent of all observation, it never could suggest to us the notion of any distinct object, such as its effect; much less, show us the inseparable and inviolable connexion between them. A man must be very sagacious who could discover by reasoning that crystal is the effect of heat, and ice of cold, without being previously acquainted with the operation of these qualities.

PART II.

28. But we have not yet attained any tolerable satisfaction with regard to the question first proposed. Each solution still gives rise to a new question as difficult as the foregoing, and leads us on to farther enquiries. When it is asked, *What is the nature of all our reasonings concerning matter of fact?* the proper answer seems to be, that they are founded on the relation of cause and effect. When again it is asked, *What is the foundation of all our reasonings and conclusions concerning that relation?* it may be replied in one word, Experience. But if we still carry on our sifting humour, and ask, *What is the foundation of all conclusions from experience?* this implies a new question, which may be of more difficult solution and explication. Philosophers, that give themselves airs of superior wisdom and sufficiency, have a hard task when they encounter persons of inquisitive dispositions, who push them from every corner to which they retreat, and who are sure at last to bring them to some dangerous dilemma. The best expedient to prevent this confusion, is to be modest in our pretensions; and even to discover the difficulty ourselves before it is objected to us. By this means, we may make a kind of merit of our very ignorance.

I shall content myself, in this section, with an easy task, and shall pretend only to give a negative answer to the question here proposed. I say then, that, even after we have experience of the operations of cause and effect, our conclusions from that experience are *not* founded on reasoning, or any process of the understanding. This answer we must endeavour both to explain and to defend.

29. It must certainly be allowed, that nature has kept us at a great distance from all her secrets, and has afforded us only the knowledge of a few superficial qualities of objects; while she conceals from us those powers and principles on which the influence of those objects entirely depends. Our senses inform us of the colour, weight, and consistence of bread; but neither sense nor reason can ever inform us of those qualities which fit it for the nourishment and support of a human body. Sight or feeling conveys an idea of the actual motion of bodies; but as to that wonderful force or power, which would carry on a moving body for ever in a continued change of place, and which bodies never lose but by communicating it to others; of this we cannot form the most distant conception. But notwithstanding this ignorance of natural powers6 and principles, we always presume, when we see like sensible qualities, that they have like secret powers, and expect that effects, similar to those which we have experienced, will follow from them. If a body of like colour and consistence with that bread, which we have formerly eat, be presented to us, we make no scruple of repeating the experiment, and foresee, with certainty, like nourishment and support. Now this is a process of the mind or thought, of which I would willingly know the foundation. It is allowed on all hands that there is no known connexion between the sensible qualities and the secret powers; and consequently, that the mind is not led to form such a conclusion concerning their constant and regular conjunction, by anything which it knows of their nature. As to past *Experience*, it can be allowed to give *direct* and *certain* information of those precise objects only, and that precise period of time, which fell under its cognizance: but why this experience should be extended to future times, and to other objects, which for aught we know, may be only in appearance similar; this is the main question on which I would insist. The bread, which I formerly eat, nourished me; that is, a body of such sensible qualities was, at that time, endued with such secret powers: but does it follow, that other bread must also nourish me at another time, and that like sensible

qualities must always be attended with like secret powers? The consequence seems nowise necessary. At least, it must be acknowledged that there is here a consequence drawn by the mind; that there is a certain step taken; a process of thought, and an inference, which wants to be explained. These two propositions are far from being the same, *I have found that such an object has always been attended with such an effect*, and *I foresee, that other objects, which are, in appearance, similar, will be attended with similar effects*. I shall allow, if you please, that the one proposition may justly be inferred from the other: I know, in fact, that it always is inferred. But if you insist that the inference is made by a chain of reasoning, I desire you to produce that reasoning. The connexion between these propositions is not intuitive. There is required a medium, which may enable the mind to draw such an inference, if indeed it be drawn by reasoning and argument. What that medium is, I must confess, passes my comprehension; and it is incumbent on those to produce it, who assert that it really exists, and is the origin of all our conclusions concerning matter of fact.

30. This negative argument must certainly, in process of time, become altogether convincing, if many penetrating and able philosophers shall turn their enquiries this way and no one be ever able to discover any connecting proposition or intermediate step, which supports the understanding in this conclusion. But as the question is yet new, every reader may not trust so far to his own penetration, as to conclude, because an argument escapes his enquiry, that therefore it does not really exist. For this reason it may be requisite to venture upon a more difficult task; and enumerating all the branches of human knowledge, endeavour to show that none of them can afford such an argument.

All reasonings may be divided into two kinds, namely, demonstrative reasoning, or that concerning relations of ideas, and moral reasoning, or that concerning matter of fact and existence. That there are no demonstrative arguments in the case seems evident; since it implies no contradiction that the course of nature may change, and that an object, seemingly like those which we have experienced, may be attended with different or contrary effects. May I not clearly and distinctly conceive that a body, falling from the clouds, and which, in all other respects, resembles snow, has yet the taste of salt or feeling of fire? Is there any more intelligible proposition than to affirm, that all the trees will flourish in December and January, and decay in May and June? Now whatever is intelligible, and can be distinctly conceived, implies no contradiction, and can never be proved false by any demonstrative argument or abstract reasoning *priori*.

If we be, therefore, engaged by arguments to put trust in past experience, and make it the standard of our future judgement, these arguments must be probable only, or such as regard matter of fact and real existence, according to the division above mentioned. But that there is no argument of this kind, must appear, if our explication of that species of reasoning be admitted as solid and satisfactory. We have said that all arguments concerning existence are founded on the relation of cause and effect; that our knowledge of that relation is derived entirely from experience; and that all our experimental conclusions proceed upon the supposition that the future will be conformable to the past. To endeavour, therefore, the proof of this last supposition by probable arguments, or arguments regarding existence, must be evidently going in a circle, and taking that for granted, which is the very point in question.

31. In reality, all arguments from experience are founded on the similarity which we discover among natural objects, and by which we are induced to expect effects similar to those which we have found to follow from such objects. And though none but a fool or madman will ever pretend to dispute the authority of experience, or to reject that great guide of human life, it may surely be allowed a philosopher to have so much curiosity at least as to examine the principle of human nature, which gives this mighty authority to experience, and makes us draw advantage from that similarity which nature has placed among different objects. From causes which appear *similar* we expect similar effects. This is the

sum of all our experimental conclusions. Now it seems evident that, if this conclusion were formed by reason, it would be as perfect at first, and upon one instance, as after ever so long a course of experience. But the case is far otherwise. Nothing so like as eggs; yet no one, on account of this appearing similarity, expects the same taste and relish in all of them. It is only after a long course of uniform experiments in any kind, that we attain a firm reliance and security with regard to a particular event. Now where is that process of reasoning which, from one instance, draws a conclusion, so different from that which it infers from a hundred instances that are nowise different from that single one? This question I propose as much for the sake of information, as with an intention of raising difficulties. I cannot find, I cannot imagine any such reasoning. But I keep my mind still open to instruction, if any one will vouchsafe to bestow it on me.

32. Should it be said that, from a number of uniform experiments, we *infer* a connexion between the sensible qualities and the secret powers; this, I must confess, seems the same difficulty, couched in different terms. The question still recurs, on what process of argument this *inference* is founded? Where is the medium, the interposing ideas, which join propositions so very wide of each other? It is confessed that the colour, consistence, and other sensible qualities of bread appear not, of themselves, to have any connexion with the secret powers of nourishment and support. For otherwise we could infer these secret powers from the first appearance of these sensible qualities, without the aid of experience; contrary to the sentiment of all philosophers, and contrary to plain matter of fact. Here, then, is our natural state of ignorance with regard to the powers and influence of all objects. How is this remedied by experience? It only shows us a number of uniform effects, resulting from certain objects, and teaches us that those particular objects, at that particular time, were endowed with such powers and forces. When a new object, endowed with similar sensible qualities, is produced, we expect similar powers and forces, and look for a like effect. From a body of like colour and consistence with bread we expect like nourishment and support. But this surely is a step or progress of

the mind, which wants to be explained. When a man says, *I have found, in all past instances, such sensible qualities conjoined with such secret powers*: And when he says, *Similar sensible qualities will always be conjoined with similar secret powers*, he is not guilty of a tautology, nor are these propositions in any respect the same. You say that the one proposition is an inference from the other. But you must confess that the inference is not intuitive; neither is it demonstrative: Of what nature is it, then? To say it is experimental, is begging the question. For all inferences from experience suppose, as their foundation, that the future will resemble the past, and that similar powers will be conjoined with similar sensible qualities. If there be any suspicion that the course of nature may change, and that the past may be no rule for the future, all experience becomes useless, and can give rise to no inference or conclusion. It is impossible, therefore, that any arguments from experience can prove this resemblance of the past to the future; since all these arguments are founded on the supposition of that resemblance. Let the course of things be allowed hitherto ever so regular; that alone, without some new argument or inference, proves not that, for the future, it will continue so. In vain do you pretend to have learned the nature of bodies from your past experience. Their secret nature, and consequently all their effects and influence, may change, without any change in their sensible qualities. This happens sometimes, and with regard to some objects: Why may it not happen always, and with regard to all objects? What logic, what process of argument secures you against this supposition? My practice, you say, refutes my doubts. But you mistake the purport of my question. As an agent, I am quite satisfied in the point; but as a philosopher, who has some share of curiosity, I will not say scepticism, I want to learn the foundation of this inference. No reading, no enquiry has yet been able to remove my difficulty, or give me satisfaction in a matter of such importance. Can I do better than propose the difficulty to the public, even though, perhaps, I have small hopes of obtaining a solution? We shall at least, by this means, be sensible of our ignorance, if we do not augment our knowledge.

33. I must confess that a man is guilty of unpardonable arrogance who concludes, because an argument has escaped his own investigation, that therefore it does not really exist. I must also confess that, though all the learned, for several ages, should have employed themselves in fruitless search upon any subject, it may still, perhaps, be rash to conclude positively that the subject must, therefore, pass all human comprehension. Even though we examine all the sources of our knowledge, and conclude them unfit for such a subject, there may still remain a suspicion, that the enumeration is not complete, or the examination not accurate. But with regard to the present subject, there are some considerations which seem to remove all this accusation of arrogance or suspicion of mistake.

It is certain that the most ignorant and stupid peasants—nay infants, nay even brute beasts—improve by experience, and learn the qualities of natural objects, by observing the effects which result from them. When a child has felt the sensation of pain from touching the flame of a candle, he will be careful not to put his hand near any candle; but will expect a similar effect from a cause which is similar in its sensible qualities and appearance. If you assert, therefore, that the understanding of the child is led into this conclusion by any process of argument or ratiocination, I may justly require you to produce that argument; nor have you any pretence to refuse so equitable a demand. You cannot say that the argument is abstruse, and may possibly escape your enquiry; since you confess that it is obvious to the capacity of a mere infant. If you hesitate, therefore, a moment, or if, after reflection, you produce any intricate or profound argument, you, in a manner, give up the question, and confess that it is not reasoning which engages us to suppose the past resembling the future, and to expect similar effects from causes which are, to appearance, similar. This is the proposition which I intended to enforce in the present section. If I be right, I pretend not to have made any mighty discovery. And if I be wrong, I must acknowledge myself to be indeed a very backward scholar; since I cannot now discover an argument which, it seems, was perfectly familiar to me long before I was out of my cradle.

CHAPTER VII.

ON OUR KNOWLEDGE OF GENERAL PRINCIPLES

We saw in the preceding chapter that the principle of induction, while necessary to the validity of all arguments based on experience, is itself not capable of being proved by experience, and yet is unhesitatingly believed by every one, at least in all its concrete applications. In these characteristics the principle of induction does not stand alone. There are a number of other principles which cannot be proved or disproved by experience, but are used in arguments which start from what is experienced.

Some of these principles have even greater evidence than the principle of induction, and the knowledge of them has the same degree of certainty as the knowledge of the existence of sense-data. They constitute the means of drawing inferences from what is given in sensation; and if what we infer is to be true, it is just as necessary that our principles of inference should be true as it is that our data should be true. The principles of inference are apt to be overlooked because of their very obviousness--the assumption involved is assented to without our realizing that it is an assumption. But it is very important to realize the use of principles of inference, if a correct theory of knowledge is to be obtained; for our knowledge of them raises interesting and difficult questions.

In all our knowledge of general principles, what actually happens is that first of all we realize some particular application of the principle, and then we realize that the particularity is irrelevant, and that there is a generality which may equally truly be affirmed. This is of course familiar in such matters as teaching arithmetic: 'two and two are four' is first learnt in the case of some particular pair of couples, and then in some other particular case, and so on, until at last it becomes possible to see that it is true of any pair of couples. The same thing happens with logical principles. Suppose two men are discussing what day of the month it is. One of them says, 'At least you will admit that *if* yesterday was the 15th to-day must be the 16th.' 'Yes', says the other, 'I admit that.' 'And you know', the first continues, 'that yesterday was the 15th, because you dined with Jones, and your diary will tell you that was on the 15th.' 'Yes', says the second; 'therefore to-day *is* the 16th.' Now such an argument is not hard to follow; and if it is granted that its premisses are true in fact, no one will deny that the conclusion must also be true. But it depends for its truth upon an instance of a general logical principle. The logical principle is as follows: 'Suppose it known that *if* this is true, then that is true. Suppose it also known that this *is* true, then it follows that that is true.' When it is the case that if this is true, that is true, we shall say that this 'implies' that, and that that 'follows from' this. Thus our principle states that if this implies that, and this is true, then that is true. In other words, 'anything implied by a true proposition is true', or 'whatever follows from a true proposition is true'.

This principle is really involved--at least, concrete instances of it are involved--in all demonstrations. Whenever one thing which we believe is used to prove something else, which we consequently believe, this principle is relevant. If any one asks: 'Why should I accept the results of valid arguments based on true premisses?' we can only answer by appealing to our principle. In fact, the truth of the principle is impossible to doubt, and its obviousness is so great that at first sight it seems almost trivial. Such principles, however, are not trivial to the philosopher, for they show that we may have indubitable knowledge which is in no way derived from objects of sense.

The above principle is merely one of a certain number of self-evident logical principles. Some at least of these principles must be granted before any argument or proof becomes possible. When some of them have been granted, others can be proved, though these others, so long as they are simple, are just as obvious as the principles taken for granted. For no very good reason, three of these principles have been singled out by tradition under the name of 'Laws of Thought'. They are as follows:

(1) *The law of identity*: 'Whatever is, is.'

(2) *The law of contradiction*: 'Nothing can both be and not be.'

(3) *The law of excluded middle*: 'Everything must either be or not be.'

These three laws are samples of self-evident logical principles, but are not really more fundamental or more self-evident than various other similar principles: for instance, the one we considered just now, which states that what follows from a true premiss is true. The name 'laws of thought' is also misleading, for what is important is not the fact that we think in accordance with these laws, but the fact that things behave in accordance with them; in other words, the fact that when we think in accordance with them we think *truly*. But this is a large question, to which we must return at a later stage.

In addition to the logical principles which enable us to prove from a given premiss that something is *certainly* true, there are other logical principles which enable us to prove, from a given premiss, that there is a greater or less probability that something is true. An example of such principles--perhaps the most important example is the inductive principle, which we considered in the preceding chapter. One of the great historic controversies in philosophy is the controversy between the two schools called respectively 'empiricists' and 'rationalists'. The empiricists--who are best represented by the British philosophers, Locke, Berkeley, and Hume--maintained that all our knowledge is derived from experience; the rationalists--who are represented by the

Continental philosophers of the seventeenth century, especially Descartes and Leibniz--maintained that, in addition to what we know by experience, there are certain 'innate ideas' and 'innate principles', which we know independently of experience. It has now become possible to decide with some confidence as to the truth or falsehood of these opposing schools. It must be admitted, for the reasons already stated, that logical principles are known to us, and cannot be themselves proved by experience, since all proof presupposes them. In this, therefore, which was the most important point of the controversy, the rationalists were in the right.

On the other hand, even that part of our knowledge which is *logically* independent of experience (in the sense that experience cannot prove it) is yet elicited and caused by experience. It is on occasion of particular experiences that we become aware of the general laws which their connexions exemplify. It would certainly be absurd to suppose that there are innate principles in the sense that babies are born with a knowledge of everything which men know and which cannot be deduced from what is experienced. For this reason, the word 'innate' would not now be employed to describe our knowledge of logical principles. The phrase '*a priori*' is less objectionable, and is more usual in modern writers. Thus, while admitting that all knowledge is elicited and caused by experience, we shall nevertheless hold that some knowledge is *a priori*, in the sense that the experience which makes us think of it does not suffice to prove it, but merely so directs our attention that we see its truth without requiring any proof from experience.

There is another point of great importance, in which the empiricists were in the right as against the rationalists. Nothing can be known to *exist* except by the help of experience. That is to say, if we wish to prove that something of which we have no direct experience exists, we must have among our premisses the existence of one or more things of which we have direct experience. Our belief that the Emperor of China exists, for example, rests upon testimony, and testimony consists, in the last analysis, of sense-data seen or heard in reading or being spoken to. Rationalists believed that, from general consideration as to what must be, they could deduce the existence of this or that in the actual world. In this belief they seem to have been mistaken. All the knowledge that we can acquire *a priori* concerning existence seems to be hypothetical: it tells us that if one thing exists, another must exist, or, more generally, that if one proposition is true, another must be true. This is exemplified by the principles we have already dealt with, such as '*if* this is true, and this implies that, then that is true', or '*if* this and that have been repeatedly found connected, they will probably be connected in the next instance in which one of them is found'. Thus the scope and power of *a priori* principles is strictly limited. All knowledge that something exists must be in part dependent on experience. When anything is known immediately, its existence is known by experience alone; when anything is proved to exist, without being known immediately, both experience and *a priori* principles must be required in the proof. Knowledge is called *empirical* when it rests wholly or partly upon experience. Thus all knowledge which asserts existence is empirical, and the only *a priori* knowledge concerning existence is hypothetical, giving connexions among things that exist or may exist, but not giving actual existence. *A priori* knowledge is not all of the logical kind we have been hitherto considering. Perhaps the most important example of non-logical *a priori* knowledge is knowledge as to ethical value. I am not speaking of judgements as to what is useful or as to what is virtuous, for such judgements do require empirical premisses; I am speaking of judgements as to the intrinsic desirability of things. If something is useful, it must be useful because it secures some end; the end must, if we have gone far enough, be valuable on its own account, and not merely because it is useful for some further end. Thus all judgements as to what is useful depend upon judgements as to what has value on its own account.

We judge, for example, that happiness is more desirable than misery, knowledge than ignorance, goodwill than hatred, and so on. Such judgements must, in part at least, be immediate and *a priori*. Like our previous *a priori* judgements, they may be elicited by experience, and indeed they must be; for it seems not possible to judge whether anything is intrinsically valuable unless we have experienced something of the same kind. But it is fairly obvious that they cannot be proved by experience; for the fact that a thing exists or does not exist cannot prove either that it is good that it should exist or that it is bad. The pursuit of this subject belongs to ethics, where the impossibility of deducing what ought to be from what is has to be established. In the present connexion, it is only important to realize that knowledge as to what is intrinsically of value is *a priori* in the same sense in which logic is *a priori*, namely in the sense that the truth of such knowledge can be neither proved nor disproved by experience.

All pure mathematics is *a priori*, like logic. This was strenuously denied by the empirical philosophers, who maintained that experience was as much the source of our knowledge of arithmetic as of our knowledge of geography. They maintained that by the repeated experience of seeing two things and two other things, and finding that altogether they made four things, we were led by induction to the conclusion that two things and two other things would *always* make four things altogether. If, however, this were the source of our knowledge that two and two are four, we should proceed differently, in persuading ourselves of its truth, from the way in which we do actually proceed. In fact, a certain number of instances are needed to make us think of two abstractly, rather than of two coins or two books or two people, or two of any other specified kind. But as soon as we are able to divest our thoughts of irrelevant particularity, we become able to see the general principle that two and two are four; any one instance is seen to be *typical*, and the examination of other instances becomes unnecessary.[1]

The same thing is exemplified in geometry. If we want to prove some property of *all* triangles, we draw some one triangle and reason about it; but we can avoid making use of any property which it does not share with all other triangles, and thus, from our particular case, we obtain a general result. We do not, in fact, feel our certainty that two and two are four increased by fresh instances, because, as soon as we have seen the truth of this proposition, our certainty becomes so great as to be incapable of growing greater. Moreover, we feel some quality of necessity about the proposition 'two and two are four', which is absent from even the best attested empirical generalizations. Such generalizations always remain mere facts: we feel that there might be a world in which they were false, though in the actual world they happen to be true. In any possible world, on the contrary, we feel that two and two would be four: this is not a mere fact, but a necessity to which everything actual and possible must conform. The case may be made clearer by considering a genuinely-empirical generalization, such as 'All men are mortal.' It is plain that we believe this proposition, in the first place, because there is no known instance of men living beyond a certain age, and in the second place because there seem to be physiological grounds for thinking that an organism such as a man's body must sooner or later wear out. Neglecting the second ground, and considering merely our experience of men's mortality, it is plain that we should not be content with one quite clearly understood instance of a man dying, whereas, in the case of 'two and two are four', one instance does suffice, when carefully considered, to persuade us that the same must happen in any other instance. Also we can be forced to admit, on reflection, that there may be some doubt, however slight, as to whether *all* men are mortal. This may be made plain by the attempt to imagine two different worlds, in one of which there are men who are not mortal, while in the other two and two make five. When Swift invites us to consider the race of Struldbugs who never die, we are able to acquiesce in imagination. But a world where two and two make five seems quite on a different level. We feel that such a world, if there were one, would upset the whole fabric of our knowledge and reduce us to utter doubt.

The fact is that, in simple mathematical judgements such as 'two and two are four', and also in many judgements of logic, we can know the general proposition without inferring it from instances, although some instance is usually necessary to make clear to us what the general proposition means. This is why there is real utility in the process of *deduction*, which goes from the general to the general, or from the general to the particular, as well as in the process of *induction*, which goes from the particular to the particular, or from the particular to the general. It is an old debate among philosophers whether deduction ever gives *new* knowledge. We can now see that in certain cases, at least, it does do so. If we already know that two and two always make four, and we know that Brown and Jones are two, and so are Robinson and Smith, we can deduce that Brown and Jones and Robinson and Smith are four. This is new knowledge, not contained in our premisses, because the general proposition, 'two and two are four', never told us there were such people as Brown and Jones and Robinson and Smith, and the particular premisses do not tell us that there were four of them, whereas the particular proposition deduced does tell us both these things.

But the newness of the knowledge is much less certain if we take the stock instance of deduction that is always given in books on logic, namely, 'All men are mortal; Socrates is a man, therefore Socrates is mortal.' In this case, what we really know beyond reasonable doubt is that certain men, A, B, C, were mortal, since, in fact, they have died. If Socrates is one of these men, it is foolish to go the roundabout way through 'all men are mortal' to arrive at the conclusion that *probably* Socrates is mortal. If Socrates is not one of the men on whom our induction is based, we shall still do better to argue straight from our A, B, C, to Socrates, than to go round by the general proposition, 'all men are mortal'. For the probability that Socrates is mortal is greater, on our data, than the probability that all men are mortal. (This is obvious, because if all men are mortal, so is Socrates; but if Socrates is mortal, it does not follow that all men are mortal.) Hence we shall reach the conclusion that Socrates is mortal with a greater approach to certainty if we make our argument purely inductive than if we go by way of 'all men are mortal' and then use deduction. This illustrates the difference between general propositions known *a priori* such as 'two and two are four', and empirical generalizations such as 'all men are mortal'. In regard to the former, deduction is the right mode of argument, whereas in regard to the latter, induction is always theoretically preferable, and warrants a greater confidence in the truth of our conclusion, because all empirical generalizations are more uncertain than the instances of them.

We have now seen that there are propositions known *a priori*, and that among them are the propositions of logic and pure mathematics, as well as the fundamental propositions of ethics. The question which must next occupy us is this: How is it possible that there should be such knowledge? And more particularly, how can there be knowledge of general propositions in cases where we have not examined all the instances, and indeed never can examine them all, because their number is infinite? These questions, which were first brought prominently forward by the German philosopher Kant (1724-1804), are very difficult, and historically very important.

John Stuart Mill (1806 – 1873) is probably best known for his ethical theory, Utilitarianism, which asks us to consider the consequences of our actions. But he also wrote widely on logic and scientific method, inventing various methods (called, appropriately enough, Mill's methods) for determining relations of cause and effect between observed phenomena. He was a radical empiricist, claiming that all of our knowledge is based on experience, and that none of it is a priori.

In this he differs from Russell, who wants to argue that some of our knowledge, for example logical and mathematical knowledge, is not based on experience: we know more about math than we have ever experienced first hand. While Russell does not mention him by name in Chapter VII, Mill is exactly the kind of philosopher he had in mind, and it is entirely possible that he had the following passage, from Mill's "A System of Logic," in mind.

There is an interesting biographical connection between Russell and Mill: Mill was Russell's godfather, although collaboration between the two wasimpossible as Mill died when Russell was only a year old.

J. S. Mill

from

A System of Logic, Chapter VI

§ 1. In the examination which formed the subject of the last chapter, into the nature of the evidence of those deductive sciences which are commonly represented to be systems of necessary truth, we have been led to the following conclusions. The results of those sciences are indeed necessary, in the sense of necessarily following from certain first principles, commonly called axioms and definitions; that is, of being certainly true if those axioms and definitions are so; for the word necessity, even in this acceptation of it, means no more than certainty. But their claim to the character of necessity in any sense beyond this, as implying an evidence independent of and superior to observation and experience, must depend on the previous establishment of such a claim in favor of the definitions and axioms themselves. With regard to axioms, we found that, considered as experimental truths, they rest on superabundant and obvious evidence. We inquired, whether, since this is the case, it be imperative to suppose any other evidence of those truths than experimental evidence, any other origin for our belief of them than an experimental origin. We decided, that the burden of proof lies with those who maintain the affirmative, and we examined, at considerable length, such arguments as they have produced. The examination having led to the rejection of those arguments, we have thought ourselves warranted in concluding that axioms are but a class, the most universal class, of inductions from experience; the simplest and easiest cases of generalization from the facts furnished to us by our senses or by our internal consciousness.

While the axioms of demonstrative sciences thus appeared to be experimental truths, the definitions, as they are incorrectly called, in those sciences, were found by us to be generalizations from experience which are not even, accurately speaking, truths; being propositions in which, while we assert of some kind of object, some property or properties which observation shows to belong to it, we at the same time deny that it possesses any other properties, though in truth other properties do in every individual instance accompany, and in almost all instances modify, the property thus exclusively predicated. The denial, therefore, is a mere fiction, or supposition, made for the purpose of excluding the consideration of those modifying circumstances, when their influence is of too trifling amount to be worth considering, or adjourning it, when important to a more convenient moment.

From these considerations it would appear that Deductive or Demonstrative Sciences are all, without exception, Inductive Sciences; that their evidence is that of experience; but that they are also, in virtue of the peculiar character of one indispensable portion of the general formulæ according to which their inductions are made, Hypothetical Sciences. Their conclusions are only true on certain suppositions, which are, or ought to be, approximations to the truth, but are seldom, if ever, exactly true; and to this hypothetical character is to be ascribed the peculiar certainty, which is supposed to be inherent in demonstration.

What we have now asserted, however, cannot be received as universally true of Deductive or Demonstrative Sciences, until verified by being applied to the most remarkable of all those sciences, that of Numbers; the theory of the Calculus; Arithmetic and Algebra. It is harder to believe of the doctrines of this science than of any other, either that they are not truths *a priori*, but experimental truths, or that their peculiar certainty is owing to their being not absolute but only conditional truths. This, therefore, is a case which merits examination apart; and the more so, because on this subject we have a double set of doctrines to contend with; that of the *a priori* philosophers on one side; and on the other, a theory the most opposite to theirs, which was at one time very generally received, and is still far from being altogether exploded, among metaphysicians.

§ 2. This theory attempts to solve the difficulty apparently inherent in the case, by representing the propositions of the science of numbers as merely verbal, and its processes as simple transformations of language, substitutions of one expression for another. The proposition, Two and one is equal to three, according to these writers, is not a truth, is not the assertion of a really existing fact, but a definition of the word three; a statement that mankind have agreed to use the name three as a sign exactly equivalent to two and one; to call by the former name whatever is called by the other more clumsy phrase. According to this doctrine, the longest process in algebra is but a succession of changes in terminology, by which equivalent expressions are substituted one for another; a series of translations of the same fact, from one into another language; though how, after such a series of translations, the fact itself comes out changed (as when we demonstrate a new geometrical theorem by algebra), they have not explained; and it is a difficulty which is fatal to their theory.

It must be acknowledged that there are peculiarities in the processes of arithmetic and algebra which render the theory in question very plausible, and have not unnaturally made those sciences the stronghold of Nominalism. The doctrine that we can discover facts, detect the hidden processes of nature, by an artful manipulation of language, is so contrary to common sense, that a person must have made some advances in philosophy to believe it: men fly to so paradoxical a belief to avoid, as they think, some even greater difficulty, which the vulgar do not see. What has led many to believe that reasoning is a mere verbal process, is, that no other theory seemed reconcilable with the nature of the Science of Numbers. For we do not carry any ideas along with us when we use the symbols of arithmetic or of algebra. In a geometrical demonstration we have a mental diagram, if not one on paper;

AB, AC, are present to our imagination as lines, intersecting other lines, forming an angle with one another, and the like; but not so *a* and *b.* These may represent lines or any other magnitudes, but those magnitudes are never thought of; nothing is realized in our imagination but *a* and *b.* The ideas which, on the particular occasion, they happen to represent, are banished from the mind during every intermediate part of the process, between the beginning, when the premises are translated from things into signs, and the end, when the conclusion is translated back from signs into things. Nothing, then, being in the reasoner's mind but the symbols, what can seem more inadmissible than to contend that the reasoning process has to do with any thing more? We seem to have come to one of Bacon's Prerogative Instances; an *experimentum crucis* on the nature of reasoning itself.

Nevertheless, it will appear on consideration, that this apparently so decisive instance is no instance at all; that there is in every step of an arithmetical or algebraical calculation a real induction, a real inference of facts from facts; and that what disguises the induction is simply its comprehensive nature, and the consequent extreme generality of the language. All numbers must be numbers of something: there are no such things as numbers in the abstract. *Ten* must mean ten bodies, or ten sounds, or ten beatings of the pulse. But though numbers must be numbers of something, they may be numbers of any thing. Propositions, therefore, concerning numbers, have the remarkable peculiarity that they are propositions concerning all things whatever; all objects, all existences of every kind, known to our experience. All things possess quantity; consist of parts which can be numbered; and in that character possess all the properties which are called properties of numbers. That half of four is two, must be true whatever the word four represents, whether four hours, four miles, or four pounds weight. We need only conceive a thing divided into four equal parts (and all things may be conceived as so divided), to be able to predicate of it every property of the number four, that is, every arithmetical proposition in which the number four stands on one side of the equation. Algebra extends the generalization still farther: every number represents that particular number of all things without distinction, but every algebraical symbol does more, it represents all numbers without distinction. As soon as we conceive a thing divided into equal parts, without knowing into what number of parts, we may call it *a* or *x*, and apply to it, without danger of error, every algebraical formula in the books. The proposition, $2\ (a + b) = 2\ a + 2\ b$, is a truth co-extensive with all nature. Since then algebraical truths are true of all things whatever, and not, like those of geometry, true of lines only or of angles only, it is no wonder that the symbols should not excite in our minds ideas of any things in particular. When we demonstrate the forty-seventh proposition of Euclid, it is not necessary that the words should raise in us an image of all right-angled triangles, but only of some one right-angled triangle: so in algebra we need not, under the symbol *a*, picture to ourselves all things whatever, but only some one thing; why not, then, the letter itself? The mere written characters, *a*, *b*, *x*, *y*, *z*, serve as well for representatives of Things in general, as any more complex and apparently more concrete conception. That we are conscious of them, however, in their character of things, and not of mere signs, is evident from the fact that our whole process of reasoning is carried on by predicating of them the properties of things. In resolving an algebraic equation, by what rules do we proceed? By applying at each step to *a*, *b*, and *x*, the proposition that equals added to equals make equals; that equals taken from equals leave equals; and other propositions founded on these two. These are not properties of language, or of signs as such, but of magnitudes, which is as much as to say, of all things. The inferences, therefore, which are successively drawn, are inferences concerning things, not symbols; though as any Things whatever will serve the turn, there is no necessity for keeping the idea of the Thing at all distinct, and consequently the process of thought may, in this case, be allowed without danger to do what all processes of thought, when they have been performed often, will do if permitted, namely, to become entirely mechanical. Hence the general language of algebra comes to be used familiarly without exciting ideas, as all other general language is prone to do from mere habit, though in no other case than this can it be done with complete safety. But when we look back to see from whence the probative force of the process is derived, we find that at every single step, unless we suppose ourselves to be thinking and talking of the things, and not the mere symbols, the evidence fails.

There is another circumstance, which, still more than that which we have now mentioned, gives plausibility to the notion that the propositions of arithmetic and algebra are merely verbal. That is, that when considered as propositions respecting Things, they all have the appearance of being identical propositions. The assertion, Two and one is equal to three, considered as an assertion respecting objects, as for instance, "Two pebbles and one pebble are equal to three pebbles," does not affirm equality between two collections of pebbles, but absolute identity. It affirms that if we put one pebble to two pebbles, those very pebbles are three. The objects, therefore, being the very same, and the mere assertion that "objects are themselves" being insignificant, it seems but natural to consider the proposition, Two and one is equal to three, as asserting mere identity of signification between the two names.

This, however, though it looks so plausible, will not bear examination. The expression "two pebbles and one pebble," and the expression "three pebbles," stand indeed for the same aggregation of objects, but they by no means stand for the same physical fact. They are names of the same objects, but of those objects in two different states: though they *de*note the same things, their *con*notation is different. Three pebbles in two separate parcels, and three pebbles in one parcel, do not make the same impression on our senses; and the assertion that the very same pebbles may by an alteration of place and arrangement be made to produce either the one set of sensations or the other, though a very familiar proposition, is not an identical one. It is a truth known to us by early and constant experience: an inductive truth; and such truths are the foundation of the science of Number. The fundamental truths of that science all rest on the evidence of sense; they are proved by showing to our eyes and our fingers that any given number of objects—ten balls, for example—may by separation and re-arrangement exhibit to our senses all the different sets of numbers the sums of which is equal to ten. All the improved methods of teaching arithmetic to children proceed on a knowledge of this fact. All who wish to carry the child's *mind* along with them in learning arithmetic; all who wish to teach numbers, and not mere ciphers—now teach it through the evidence of the senses, in the manner we have described.

We may, if we please, call the proposition, "Three is two and one," a definition of the number three, and assert that arithmetic, as it has been asserted that geometry, is a science founded on definitions. But they are definitions in the geometrical sense, not the logical; asserting not the meaning of a term only, but along with it an observed matter of fact. The proposition, "A circle is a figure bounded by a line which has all its points equally distant from a point within it," is called the definition of a circle; but the proposition from which so many consequences follow, and which is really a first principle in geometry, is, that figures answering to this description exist. And thus we may call "Three is two and one" a definition of three; but the calculations which depend on that proposition do not follow from the definition itself, but from an arithmetical theorem presupposed in it, namely, that collections of objects exist, which while they impress the senses thus, [figure 1], may be separated into two parts, thus, [figure 2]. This proposition being granted, we term all such parcels Threes, after which the enunciation of the above-mentioned physical fact will serve also for a definition of the word Three. The Science of Number is thus no exception to the conclusion we previously arrived at, that the processes even of deductive sciences are altogether inductive, and that their first principles are generalizations from experience. It remains to be examined whether this science resembles geometry in the further circumstance, that some of its inductions are not exactly true; and that the peculiar certainty ascribed to it, on account of which its propositions are called Necessary Truths, is fictitious and hypothetical, being true in no other sense than that those propositions legitimately follow from the hypothesis of the truth of premises which are avowedly mere approximations to truth.

Figure 1

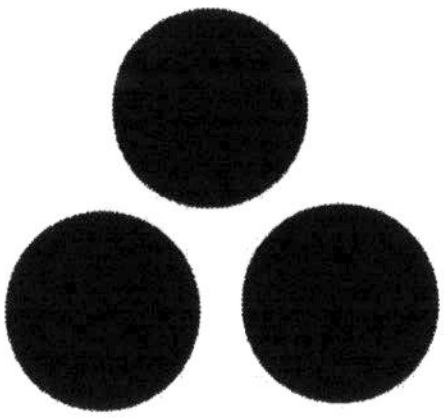

Figure 2

CHAPTER VIII.

HOW *A PRIORI* KNOWLEDGE IS POSSIBLE

Immanuel Kant is generally regarded as the greatest of the modern philosophers. Though he lived through the Seven Years War and the French Revolution, he never interrupted his teaching of philosophy at Konigsberg in East Prussia. His most distinctive contribution was the invention of what he called the 'critical' philosophy, which, assuming as a datum that there is knowledge of various kinds, inquired how such knowledge comes to be possible, and deduced, from the answer to this inquiry, many metaphysical results as to the nature of the world. Whether these results were valid may well be doubted. But Kant undoubtedly deserves credit for two things: first, for having perceived that we have *a priori* knowledge which is not purely 'analytic', i.e. such that the opposite would be self-contradictory, and secondly, for having made evident the philosophical importance of the theory of knowledge.

Before the time of Kant, it was generally held that whatever knowledge was *a priori* must be 'analytic'. What this word means will be best illustrated by examples. If I say, 'A bald man is a man', 'A plane figure is a figure', 'A bad poet is a poet', I make a purely analytic judgement: the subject spoken about is given as having at least two properties, of which one is singled out to be asserted of it. Such propositions as the above are trivial, and would never be enunciated in real life except by an orator preparing the way for a piece of sophistry. They are called 'analytic' because the predicate is obtained by merely analysing the subject. Before the time of Kant it was thought that all judgements of which we could be certain *a priori* were of this kind: that in all of them there was a predicate which was only part of the subject of which it was asserted. If this were so, we should be involved in a definite contradiction if we attempted to deny anything that could be known *a priori*. 'A bald man is not bald' would assert and deny baldness of the same man, and would therefore contradict itself. Thus according to the philosophers before Kant, the law of contradiction, which asserts that nothing can at the same time have and not have a certain property, sufficed to establish the truth of all *a priori* knowledge. Hume (1711-76), who preceded Kant, accepting the usual view as to what makes knowledge *a priori*, discovered that, in many cases which had previously been supposed analytic, and notably in the case of cause and effect, the connexion was really synthetic. Before Hume, rationalists at least had supposed that the effect could be logically deduced from the cause, if only we had sufficient knowledge. Hume argued- correctly, as would now be generally admitted--that this could not be done. Hence he inferred the far more doubtful proposition that nothing could be known *a priori* about the connexion of cause and effect. Kant, who had been educated in the rationalist tradition, was much perturbed by Hume's scepticism, and endeavoured to find an answer to it. He perceived that not only the connexion of cause and effect, but all the propositions of arithmetic and geometry, are 'synthetic', i.e. not analytic: in all these propositions, no analysis of the subject will reveal the predicate. His stock instance was the proposition 7 + 5 = 12. He pointed out, quite truly, that 7 and 5 have to be put together to give 12: the idea of 12 is not contained in them, nor even in the idea of adding them together. Thus he was led to the conclusion that all pure mathematics, though *a priori*, is synthetic; and this conclusion raised a new problem of which he endeavoured to find the solution.

The question which Kant put at the beginning of his philosophy, namely 'How is pure mathematics possible?' is an interesting and difficult one, to which every philosophy which is not purely sceptical must find some answer. The answer of the pure empiricists, that our mathematical knowledge is derived by induction from particular instances, we have already seen to be inadequate, for two reasons: first, that the validity of the inductive principle itself cannot be proved by induction; secondly, that the general propositions of mathematics, such as 'two and two always make four', can obviously be known with certainty by consideration of a single instance, and gain nothing by enumeration of other cases in which they have been found to be true. Thus our knowledge of the general propositions of mathematics (and the same applies to logic) must be accounted for otherwise than our (merely probable) knowledge of empirical generalizations such as 'all men are mortal'.

The problem arises through the fact that such knowledge is general, whereas all experience is particular. It seems strange that we should apparently be able to know some truths in advance about particular things of which we have as yet no experience; but it cannot easily be doubted that logic and arithmetic will apply to such things. We do not know who will be the inhabitants of London a hundred years hence; but we know that any two of them and any other two of them will make four of them. This apparent power of anticipating facts about things of which we have no experience is certainly surprising. Kant's solution of the problem, though not valid in my opinion, is interesting. It is, however, very difficult, and is differently understood by different philosophers. We can, therefore, only give the merest outline of it, and even that will be thought misleading by many exponents of Kant's system. What Kant maintained was that in all our experience there are two elements to be distinguished, the one due to the object (i.e. to what we have called the 'physical object'), the other due to our own nature. We saw, in discussing matter and sense-data, that the physical object is different from the associated sense-data, and that the sense-data are to be regarded as resulting from an interaction between the physical object and ourselves. So far, we are in agreement with Kant. But what is distinctive of Kant is the way in which he apportions the shares of ourselves and the physical object respectively. He considers that the crude material given in sensation--the colour, hardness, etc.--is due to the object, and that what we supply is the arrangement in space and time, and all the relations between sense-data which result from comparison or from considering one as the cause of the other or in any other way. His chief reason in favour of this view is that we seem to have *a priori* knowledge as to space and time and causality and comparison, but not as to the actual crude material of sensation. We can be sure, he says, that anything we shall ever experience must show the characteristics affirmed of it in our *a priori* knowledge, because these characteristics are due to our own nature, and therefore nothing can ever come into our experience without acquiring these characteristics.

The physical object, which he calls the 'thing in itself'[2], he regards as essentially unknowable; what can be known is the object as we have it in experience, which he calls the 'phenomenon'. The phenomenon, being a joint product of us and the thing in itself, is sure to have those characteristics which are due to us, and is therefore sure to conform to our *a priori* knowledge. Hence this knowledge, though true of all actual and possible experience, must not be supposed to apply outside experience. Thus in spite of the existence of *a priori* knowledge, we cannot know anything about the thing in itself or about what is not an actual or possible object of experience. In this way he tries to reconcile and harmonize the contentions of the rationalists with the arguments of the empiricists.

Apart from minor grounds on which Kant's philosophy may be criticized, there is one main objection which seems fatal to any attempt to deal with the problem of *a priori* knowledge by his method. The thing to be accounted for is our certainty that the facts must always conform to logic and arithmetic. To say that logic and arithmetic are contributed by us does not account for this. Our nature is as much a fact of the existing world as anything, and there can be no certainty that it will remain constant. It might happen, if Kant is right, that to-morrow our nature would so change as to make two and two become five. This possibility seems never to have occurred to him, yet it is one which utterly destroys the certainty and universality which he is anxious to vindicate for arithmetical propositions. It is true that this possibility, formally, is inconsistent with the Kantian view that time itself is a form imposed by the subject upon phenomena, so that our real Self is not in time and has no to-morrow. But he will still have to suppose that the time-order of phenomena is determined by characteristics of what is behind phenomena, and this suffices for the substance of our argument. Reflection, moreover, seems to make it clear that, if there is any truth in our arithmetical beliefs, they must apply to things equally whether we think of them or not. Two physical objects and two other physical objects must make four physical objects, even if physical objects cannot be experienced. To assert this is certainly within the scope of what we mean when we state that two and two are four. Its truth is just as indubitable as the truth of the assertion that two phenomena and two other phenomena make four phenomena. Thus Kant's solution unduly limits the scope of *a priori* propositions, in addition to failing in the attempt at explaining their certainty.

Apart from the special doctrines advocated by Kant, it is very common among philosophers to regard what is *a priori* as in some sense mental, as concerned rather with the way we must think than with any fact of the outer world. We noted in the preceding chapter the three principles commonly called 'laws of thought'. The view which led to their being so named is a natural one, but there are strong reasons for thinking that it is erroneous. Let us take as an illustration the law of contradiction. This is commonly stated in the form 'Nothing can both be and not be', which is intended to express the fact that nothing can at once have and not have a given quality. Thus, for example, if a tree is a beech it cannot also be not a beech; if my table is rectangular it cannot also be not rectangular, and so on.

Now what makes it natural to call this principle a law of *thought* is that it is by thought rather than by outward observation that we persuade ourselves of its necessary truth. When we have seen that a tree is a beech, we do not need to look again in order to ascertain whether it is also not a beech; thought alone makes us know that this is impossible. But the conclusion that the law of contradiction is a law of *thought* is nevertheless erroneous. What we believe, when we believe the law of contradiction, is not that the mind is so made that it must believe the law of contradiction. *This* belief is a subsequent result of psychological reflection, which presupposes the belief in the law of contradiction. The belief in the law of contradiction is a belief about things, not only about thoughts. It is not, e.g., the belief that if we *think* a certain tree is a beech, we cannot at the same time *think* that it is not a beech; it is the belief that if the tree *is* a beech, it cannot at the same time *be* not a beech. Thus the law of contradiction is about things, and not merely about thoughts; and although belief in the law of contradiction is a thought, the law of contradiction itself is not a thought, but a fact concerning the things in the world. If this, which we believe when we believe the law of contradiction, were not true of the things in the world, the fact that we were compelled to *think* it true would not save the law of contradiction from being false; and this shows that the law is not a law of *thought*.

A similar argument applies to any other *a priori* judgement. When we judge that two and two are four, we are not making a judgement about our thoughts, but about all actual or possible couples. The fact that our minds are so constituted as to believe that two and two are four, though it is true, is emphatically not what we assert when we assert that two and two are four. And no fact about the constitution of our minds could make it *true* that two and two are four. Thus our *a priori* knowledge, if it is not erroneous, is not merely knowledge about the constitution of our minds, but is applicable to whatever the world may contain, both what is mental and what is non-mental. The fact seems to be that all our *a priori* knowledge is concerned with entities which do not, properly speaking, *exist*, either in the mental or in the physical world. These entities are such as can be named by parts of speech which are not substantives; they are such entities as qualities and relations. Suppose, for instance, that I am in my room. I exist, and my room exists; but does 'in' exist? Yet obviously the word 'in' has a meaning; it denotes a relation which holds between me and my room. This relation is something, although we cannot say that it exists *in the same sense* in which I and my room exist. The relation 'in' is something which we can think about and understand, for, if we could not understand it, we could not understand the sentence 'I am in my room'. Many philosophers, following Kant, have maintained that relations are the work of the mind, that things in themselves have no relations, but that the mind brings them together in one act of thought and thus produces the relations which it judges them to have.

This view, however, seems open to objections similar to those which we urged before against Kant. It seems plain that it is not thought which produces the truth of the proposition 'I am in my room'. It may be true that an earwig is in my room, even if neither I nor the earwig nor any one else is aware of this truth; for this truth concerns only the earwig and the room, and does not depend upon anything else. Thus relations, as we shall see more fully in the next chapter, must be placed in a world which is neither mental nor physical. This world is of great importance to philosophy, and in particular to the problems of *a priori* knowledge. In the next chapter we shall proceed to develop its nature and its bearing upon the questions with which we have been dealing.

Immanuel Kant (1724 – 1804) is the foremost representative of German Idealism, and a major influence on 19th and even 20th century philosophy and beyond. He wrote on a number of philosophical topics, including ethics, aesthetics and epistemology.

In epistemology, he was primarily concerned to respond to the challenge presented by Hume concerning Induction. Kant tried to prove that while the content of our beliefs were based on experience, the form of that belief, in particular the Principle of Induction, was based on something sturdier, something that would enable us to know with certainty that the future will resemble the past. His treatment of the problem would influence even those philosophers who rejected his conclusions.

Immanuel Kant

from

The Critique Of Pure Reason, Introduction

1. *Of The Difference Between Pure And Empirical Knowledge*

That all our knowledge begins with experience there can be no doubt. For how is it possible that the faculty of cognition should be awakened into exercise otherwise than by means of objects which affect our senses, and partly of themselves produce representations, partly rouse our powers of understanding into activity, to compare to connect, or to separate these, and so to convert the raw material of our sensuous impressions into a knowledge of objects, which is called experience? In respect of time, therefore, no knowledge of ours is antecedent to experience, but begins with it.

But, though all our knowledge begins with experience, it by no means follows that all arises out of experience. For, on the contrary, it is quite possible that our empirical knowledge is a compound of that which we receive through impressions, and that which the faculty of cognition supplies from itself (sensuous impressions giving merely the occasion), an addition which we cannot distinguish from the original element given by sense, till long practice has made us attentive to, and skillful in separating it. It is, therefore, a question which requires close investigation, and not to be answered at first sight, whether there exists a knowledge altogether independent of experience, and even of all sensuous impressions? Knowledge of this kind is called a priori, in contradistinction to empirical knowledge, which has its sources a posteriori, that is, in experience.

But the expression, "a priori," is not as yet definite enough adequately to indicate the whole meaning of the question above started. For, in speaking of knowledge which has its sources in experience, we are wont to say, that this or that may be known a priori, because we do not derive this knowledge immediately from experience, but from a general rule, which, however, we have itself borrowed from experience. Thus, if a man undermined his house, we say, "he might know a priori that it would have fallen;" that is, he needed not to have waited for the experience that it did actually fall. But still, a priori, he could not know even this much. For, that bodies are heavy, and, consequently, that they fall when their supports are taken away, must have been known to him previously, by means of experience.

By the term "knowledge a priori," therefore, we shall in the sequel understand, not such as is independent of this or that kind of experience, but such as is absolutely so of all experience. Opposed to this is empirical knowledge, or that which is possible only a posteriori, that is, through experience. Knowledge a priori is either pure or impure. Pure knowledge a priori is that with which no empirical element is mixed up. For example, the proposition, "Every change has a cause," is a proposition a priori, but impure, because change is a conception which can only be derived from experience.

II. The Human Intellect, even in an Unphilosophical State, is in Possession of Certain Cognitions "a priori".

The question now is as to a criterion, by which we may securely distinguish a pure from an empirical cognition. Experience no doubt teaches us that this or that object is constituted in such and such a manner, but not that it could not possibly exist otherwise. Now, in the first place, if we have a proposition which contains the idea of necessity in its very conception, it is a if, moreover, it is not derived from any other proposition, unless from one equally involving the idea of necessity, it is absolutely priori. Secondly, an empirical judgement never exhibits strict and absolute, but only assumed and comparative universality (by induction); therefore, the most we can say is—so far as we have hitherto observed, there is no exception to this or that rule. If, on the other hand, a judgement carries with it strict and absolute universality, that is, admits of no possible exception, it is not derived from experience, but is valid absolutely a priori.

Empirical universality is, therefore, only an arbitrary extension of validity, from that which may be predicated of a proposition valid in most cases, to that which is asserted of a proposition which holds good in all; as, for example, in the affirmation, "All bodies are heavy." When, on the contrary, strict universality characterizes a judgement, it necessarily indicates another peculiar source of knowledge, namely, a faculty of cognition a priori. Necessity and strict universality, therefore, are infallible tests for distinguishing pure from empirical knowledge, and are inseparably connected with each other. But as in the use of these criteria the empirical limitation is sometimes more easily detected than the contingency of the judgement, or the unlimited universality which we attach to a judgement is often a more convincing proof than its necessity, it may be advisable to use the criteria separately, each being by itself infallible.

Now, that in the sphere of human cognition we have judgements which are necessary, and in the strictest sense universal, consequently pure a priori, it will be an easy matter to show. If we desire an example from the sciences, we need only take any proposition in mathematics. If we cast our eyes upon the commonest operations of the understanding, the proposition, "Every change must have a cause," will amply serve our purpose. In the latter case, indeed, the conception of a cause so plainly involves the conception of a necessity of connection with an effect, and of a strict universality of the law, that the very notion of a cause would entirely disappear, were we to derive it, like Hume, from a frequent association of what happens with that which precedes; and the habit thence originating of connecting representations—the necessity inherent in the judgement being therefore merely subjective. Besides, without seeking for such examples of principles existing a priori in cognition, we might easily show that such principles are the indispensable basis of the possibility of experience itself, and consequently prove their existence a priori. For whence could our experience itself acquire certainty, if all the rules on which it depends were themselves empirical, and consequently fortuitous? No one, therefore, can admit the validity of the use of such rules as first principles. But, for the present, we may content ourselves with having established the fact, that we do possess and exercise a faculty of pure a priori cognition; and, secondly, with having pointed out the proper tests of such cognition, namely, universality and necessity.

Not only in judgements, however, but even in conceptions, is an a priori origin manifest. For example, if we take away by degrees from our conceptions of a body all that can be referred to mere sensuous experience—colour, hardness or softness, weight, even impenetrability—the body will then vanish; but the space which it occupied still remains, and this it is utterly impossible to annihilate in thought. Again, if we take away, in like manner, from our empirical conception of any object, corporeal or incorporeal, all properties which mere experience has taught us to connect with it, still we cannot think away those through which we cogitate it as substance, or adhering to substance, although our conception of substance is more determined than that of an object. Compelled, therefore, by that necessity with which the conception of substance forces itself upon us, we must confess that it has its seat in our faculty of cognition a priori.

III. Philosophy stands in need of a Science which shall Determine the Possibility, Principles, and Extent of Human Knowledge "a priori"

Of far more importance than all that has been above said, is the consideration that certain of our cognitions rise completely above the sphere of all possible experience, and by means of conceptions, to which there exists in the whole extent of experience no corresponding object, seem to extend the range of our judgements beyond its bounds. And just in this transcendental or supersensible sphere, where experience affords us neither instruction nor guidance, lie the investigations of reason, which, on account of their importance, we consider far preferable to, and as having a far more elevated aim than, all that the understanding can achieve within the sphere of sensuous phenomena. So high a value do we set upon these investigations, that even at the risk of error, we persist in following them out, and permit neither doubt nor disregard nor indifference to restrain us from the pursuit. These unavoidable problems of mere pure reason are God, freedom (of will), and immortality. The science which, with all its preliminaries, has for its especial object the solution of these problems is named metaphysics—a science which is at the very outset dogmatical, that is, it confidently takes upon itself the execution of this task without any previous investigation of the ability or inability of reason for such an undertaking.

Now the safe ground of experience being thus abandoned, it seems nevertheless natural that we should hesitate to erect a building with the cognitions we possess, without knowing whence they come, and on the strength of principles, the origin of which is undiscovered. Instead of thus trying to build without a foundation, it is rather to be expected that we should long ago have put the question, how the understanding can arrive at these a priori cognitions, and what is the extent, validity, and worth which they may possess? We say, "This is natural enough," meaning by the word natural, that which is consistent with a just and reasonable way of thinking; but if we understand by the term, that which usually happens, nothing indeed could be more natural and more comprehensible than that this investigation should be left long unattempted. For one part of our pure knowledge, the science of mathematics, has been long firmly established, and thus leads us to form flattering expectations with regard to others, though these may be of quite a different nature. Besides, when we get beyond the bounds of experience, we are of course safe from opposition in that quarter; and the charm of widening the range of our knowledge is so great that, unless we are brought to a standstill by some evident contradiction, we hurry on undoubtingly in our course. This, however, may be avoided, if we are sufficiently cautious in the construction of our fictions, which are not the less fictions on that account.

Mathematical science affords us a brilliant example, how far, independently of all experience, we may carry our a priori knowledge. It is true that the mathematician occupies himself with objects and cognitions only in so far as they can be represented by means of intuition. But this circumstance is easily overlooked, because the said intuition can itself be given a priori, and therefore is hardly to be distinguished from a mere pure conception. Deceived by such a proof of the power of reason, we can perceive no limits to the extension of our knowledge. The light dove cleaving in free flight the thin air, whose resistance it feels, might imagine that her movements would be far more free and rapid in airless space. Just in the same way did Plato, abandoning the world of sense because of the narrow limits it sets to the understanding, venture upon the wings of ideas beyond it, into the void space of pure intellect. He did not reflect that he made no real progress by all his efforts; for he met with no resistance which might serve him for a support, as it were, whereon to rest, and on which he might apply his powers, in order to let the intellect acquire momentum for its progress. It is, indeed, the common fate of human reason in speculation, to finish the imposing edifice of thought as rapidly as possible, and then for the first time to begin to examine whether the foundation is a solid one or no. Arrived at this point, all sorts of excuses are sought after, in order to console us for its want of stability, or rather, indeed, to enable Us to dispense altogether with so late and dangerous an investigation. But what frees us during the process of building from all apprehension or suspicion, and flatters us into the belief of its solidity, is this. A great part, perhaps the greatest part, of the business of our reason consists in the analysation of the conceptions which we already possess of objects. By this means we gain a multitude of cognitions, which although really nothing more than elucidations or explanations of that which (though in a confused manner) was already thought in our conceptions, are, at least in respect of their form, prized as new introspections; whilst, so far as regards their matter or content, we have really made no addition to our conceptions, but only disinvolved them. But as this process does furnish a real priori knowledge, which has a sure progress and useful results, reason, deceived by this, slips in, without being itself aware of it, assertions of a quite different kind; in which, to given conceptions it adds others, a priori indeed, but entirely foreign to them, without our knowing how it arrives at these, and, indeed, without such a question ever suggesting itself. I shall therefore at once proceed to examine the difference between these two modes of knowledge.

IV. Of the Difference Between Analytical and Synthetical Judgements.

In all judgements wherein the relation of a subject to the predicate is cogitated (I mention affirmative judgements only here; the application to negative will be very easy), this relation is possible in two different ways. Either the predicate B belongs to the subject A, as somewhat which is contained (though covertly) in the conception A; or the predicate B lies completely out of the conception A, although it stands in connection with it. In the first instance, I term the judgement analytical, in the second, synthetical. Analytical judgements (affirmative) are therefore those in which the connection of the predicate with the subject is cogitated through identity; those in which this connection is cogitated without identity, are called synthetical judgements. The former may be called explicative, the latter augmentative judgements; because the former add in the predicate nothing to the conception of the subject, but only analyse it into its constituent conceptions, which were thought already in the subject, although in a confused manner; the latter add to our conceptions of the subject a predicate which was not contained in it, and which no analysis could ever have discovered therein. For example, when I say, "All bodies are extended," this is an analytical judgement. For I need not go beyond the conception of body in order to find extension connected with it, but merely analyse the conception, that is, become conscious of the manifold properties which I think in that conception, in order to discover this predicate in it: it is therefore an analytical judgement. On the other hand, when I say, "All bodies are heavy," the predicate is something totally different from that which I think in the mere conception of a body. By the addition of such a predicate, therefore, it becomes a synthetical judgement.

Judgements of experience, as such, are always synthetical. For it would be absurd to think of grounding an analytical judgement on experience, because in forming such a judgement I need not go out of the sphere of my conceptions, and therefore recourse to the testimony of experience is quite unnecessary. That "bodies are extended" is not an empirical judgement, but a proposition which stands firm a priori. For before addressing myself to experience, I already have in my conception all the requisite conditions for the judgement, and I have only to extract the predicate from the conception, according to the principle of contradiction, and thereby at the same time become conscious of the necessity of the judgement, a necessity which I could never learn from experience. On the other hand, though at first I do not at all include the predicate of weight in my conception of body in general, that conception still indicates an object of experience, a part of the totality of experience, to which I can still add other parts; and this I do when I recognize by observation that bodies are heavy. I can cognize beforehand by analysis the conception of body through the characteristics of extension, impenetrability, shape, etc., all which are cogitated in this conception. But now I extend my knowledge, and looking back on experience from which I had derived this conception of body, I find weight at all times connected with the above characteristics, and therefore I synthetically add to my conceptions this as a predicate, and say, "All bodies are heavy." Thus it is experience upon which rests the possibility of the synthesis of the predicate of weight with the conception of body, because both conceptions, although the one is not contained in the other, still belong to one another (only contingently, however), as parts of a whole, namely, of experience, which is itself a synthesis of intuitions.

But to synthetical judgements a priori, such aid is entirely wanting. If I go out of and beyond the conception A, in order to recognize another B as connected with it, what foundation have I to rest on, whereby to render the synthesis possible? I have here no longer the advantage of looking out in the sphere of experience for what I want. Let us take, for example, the proposition, "Everything that happens has a cause." In the conception of "something that happens," I indeed think an existence which a certain time antecedes, and from this I can derive analytical judgements. But the conception of a cause lies quite out of the above conception, and indicates something entirely different from "that which happens," and is consequently not contained in that conception. How then am I able to assert concerning the general conception—"that which happens"—something entirely different from that conception, and to recognize the conception of cause although not contained in it, yet as belonging to it, and even necessarily? what is here the unknown = X, upon which the understanding rests when it believes it has found, out of the conception A a foreign predicate B, which it nevertheless considers to be connected with it? It cannot be experience, because the principle adduced annexes the two representations, cause and effect, to the representation existence, not only with universality, which experience cannot give, but also with the expression of necessity, therefore completely a priori and from pure conceptions. Upon such synthetical, that is augmentative propositions, depends the whole aim of our speculative knowledge a priori; for although analytical judgements are indeed highly important and necessary, they are so, only to arrive at that clearness of conceptions which is requisite for a sure and extended synthesis, and this alone is a real acquisition.

In all Theoretical Sciences of Reason, Synthetical Judgements "a priori" are contained as Principles.

1. Mathematical judgements are always synthetical. Hitherto this fact, though incontestably true and very important in its consequences, seems to have escaped the analysts of the human mind, nay, to be in complete opposition to all their conjectures. For as it was found that mathematical conclusions all proceed according to the principle of contradiction (which the nature of every apodeictic certainty requires), people became persuaded that the fundamental principles of the science also were recognized and admitted in the same way. But the notion is fallacious; for although a synthetical proposition can certainly be discerned by means of the principle of contradiction, this is possible only when another synthetical proposition precedes, from which the latter is deduced, but never of itself.

Before all, be it observed, that proper mathematical propositions are always judgements a priori, and not empirical, because they carry along with them the conception of necessity, which cannot be given by experience. If this be demurred to, it matters not; I will then limit my assertion to pure mathematics, the very conception of which implies that it consists of knowledge altogether non-empirical and a priori.

We might, indeed at first suppose that the proposition 7 + 5 = 12 is a merely analytical proposition, following (according to the principle of contradiction) from the conception of a sum of seven and five. But if we regard it more narrowly, we find that our conception of the sum of seven and five contains nothing more than the uniting of both sums into one, whereby it cannot at all be cogitated what this single number is which embraces both. The conception of twelve is by no means obtained by merely cogitating the union of seven and five; and we may analyse our conception of such a possible sum as long as we will, still we shall never discover in it the notion of twelve. We must go beyond these conceptions, and have recourse to an intuition which corresponds to one of the two—our five fingers, for example, or like Segner in his Arithmetic five points, and so by degrees, add the units contained in the five given in the intuition, to the conception of seven. For I first take the number 7, and, for the conception of 5 calling in the aid of the fingers of my hand as objects of intuition, I add the units, which I before took together to make up the number 5, gradually now by means of the material image my hand, to the number 7, and by this process, I at length see the number 12 arise. That 7 should be added to 5, I have certainly cogitated in my conception of a sum = 7 + 5, but not that this sum was equal to 12. Arithmetical propositions are therefore always synthetical, of which we may become more clearly convinced by trying large numbers. For it will thus become quite evident that, turn and twist our conceptions as we may, it is impossible, without having recourse to intuition, to arrive at the sum total or product by means of the mere analysis of our conceptions. Just as little is any principle of pure geometry analytical. "A straight line between two points is the shortest," is a synthetical proposition. For my conception of straight contains no notion of quantity, but is merely qualitative. The conception of the shortest is therefore fore wholly an addition, and by no analysis can it be extracted from our conception of a straight line. Intuition must therefore here lend its aid, by means of which, and thus only, our synthesis is possible.

Some few principles preposited by geometricians are, indeed, really analytical, and depend on the principle of contradiction. They serve, however, like identical propositions, as links in the chain of method, not as principles—for example, a = a, the whole is equal to itself, or (a+b) > a, the whole is greater than its part. And yet even these principles themselves, though they derive their validity from pure conceptions, are only admitted in mathematics because they can be presented in intuition. What causes us here commonly to believe that the predicate of such apodeictic judgements is already contained in our conception, and that the judgement is therefore analytical, is merely the equivocal nature of the expression. We must join in thought a certain predicate to a given conception, and this necessity cleaves already to the conception. But the question is, not what we must join in thought to the given conception, but what we really think therein, though only obscurely, and then it becomes manifest that the predicate pertains to these conceptions, necessarily indeed, yet not as thought in the conception itself, but by virtue of an intuition, which must be added to the conception.

2. The science of natural philosophy (physics) contains in itself synthetical judgements a priori, as principles. I shall adduce two propositions. For instance, the proposition, "In all changes of the material world, the quantity of matter remains unchanged"; or, that, "In all communication of motion, action and reaction must always be equal." In both of these, not only is the necessity, and therefore their origin a priori clear, but also that they are synthetical propositions. For in the conception of matter, I do not cogitate its permanency, but merely its presence in space, which it fills. I therefore really go out of and beyond the conception of matter, in order to think on to it something a priori, which I did not think in it. The proposition is therefore not analytical, but synthetical, and nevertheless conceived a priori; and so it is with regard to the other propositions of the pure part of natural philosophy.

3. As to metaphysics, even if we look upon it merely as an attempted science, yet, from the nature of human reason, an indispensable one, we find that it must contain synthetical propositions a priori. It is not merely the duty of metaphysics to dissect, and thereby analytically to illustrate the conceptions which we form a priori of things; but we seek to widen the range of our a priori knowledge. For this purpose, we must avail ourselves of such principles as add something to the original conception—something not identical with, nor contained in it, and by means of synthetical judgements a priori, leave far behind us the limits of experience; for example, in the proposition, "the world must have a beginning," and such like. Thus metaphysics, according to the proper aim of the science, consists merely of synthetical propositions a priori.

CHAPTER IX.

THE WORLD OF UNIVERSALS

At the end of the preceding chapter we saw that such entities as relations appear to have a being which is in some way different from that of physical objects, and also different from that of minds and from that of sense-data. In the present chapter we have to consider what is the nature of this kind of being, and also what objects there are that have this kind of being. We will begin with the latter question.

The problem with which we are now concerned is a very old one, since it was brought into philosophy by Plato. Plato's 'theory of ideas' is an attempt to solve this very problem, and in my opinion it is one of the most successful attempts hitherto made. The theory to be advocated in what follows is largely Plato's, with merely such modifications as time has shown to be necessary.

The way the problem arose for Plato was more or less as follows. Let us consider, say, such a notion as *justice*. If we ask ourselves what justice is, it is natural to proceed by considering this, that, and the other just act, with a view to discovering what they have in common. They must all, in some sense, partake of a common nature, which will be found in whatever is just and in nothing else. This common nature, in virtue of which they are all just, will be justice itself, the pure essence the admixture of which with facts of ordinary life produces the multiplicity of just acts. Similarly with any other word which may be applicable to common facts, such as 'whiteness' for example. The word will be applicable to a number of particular things because they all participate in a common nature or essence. This pure essence is what Plato calls an 'idea' or 'form'. (It must not be supposed that 'ideas', in his sense, exist in minds, though they may be apprehended by minds.)

The 'idea' *justice* is not identical with anything that is just: it is something other than particular things, which particular things partake of. Not being particular, it cannot itself exist in the world of sense. Moreover it is not fleeting or changeable like the things of sense: it is eternally itself, immutable and indestructible. Thus Plato is led to a supra-sensible world, more real than the common world of sense, the unchangeable world of ideas, which alone gives to the world of sense whatever pale reflection of reality may belong to it. The truly real world, for Plato, is the world of ideas; for whatever we may attempt to say about things in the world of sense, we can only succeed in saying that they participate in such and such ideas, which, therefore, constitute all their character. Hence it is easy to pass on into a mysticism. We may hope, in a mystic illumination, to see the ideas as we see objects of sense; and we may imagine that the ideas exist in heaven. These mystical developments are very natural, but the basis of the theory is in logic, and it is as based in logic that we have to consider it.

The word 'idea' has acquired, in the course of time, many associations which are quite misleading when applied to Plato's 'ideas'. We shall therefore use the word 'universal' instead of the word 'idea', to describe what Plato meant. The essence of the sort of entity that Plato meant is that it is opposed to the particular things that are given in sensation. We speak of whatever is given in sensation, or is of the same nature as things given in sensation, as a *particular*; by opposition to this, a *universal* will be anything which may be shared by many particulars, and has those characteristics which, as we saw, distinguish justice and whiteness from just acts and white things.

When we examine common words, we find that, broadly speaking, proper names stand for particulars, while other substantives, adjectives, prepositions, and verbs stand for universals. Pronouns stand for particulars, but are ambiguous: it is only by the context or the circumstances that we know what particulars they stand for. The word 'now' stands for a particular, namely the present moment; but like pronouns, it stands for an ambiguous particular, because the present is always changing.

It will be seen that no sentence can be made up without at least one word which denotes a universal. The nearest approach would be some such statement as 'I like this'. But even here the word 'like' denotes a universal, for I may like other things, and other people may like things. Thus all truths involve universals, and all knowledge of truths involves acquaintance with universals.

Seeing that nearly all the words to be found in the dictionary stand for universals, it is strange that hardly anybody except students of philosophy ever realizes that there are such entities as universals. We do not naturally dwell upon those words in a sentence which do not stand for particulars; and if we are forced to dwell upon a word which stands for a universal, we naturally think of it as standing for some one of the particulars that come under the universal. When, for example, we hear the sentence, 'Charles I's head was cut off', we may naturally enough think of Charles I, of Charles I's head, and of the operation of cutting off *his* head, which are all particulars; but we do not naturally dwell upon what is meant by the word 'head' or the word 'cut', which is a universal: We feel such words to be incomplete and insubstantial; they seem to demand a context before anything can be done with them. Hence we succeed in avoiding all notice of universals as such, until the study of philosophy forces them upon our attention. Even among philosophers, we may say, broadly, that only those universals which are named by adjectives or substantives have been much or often recognized, while those named by verbs and prepositions have been usually overlooked. This omission has had a very great effect upon philosophy; it is hardly too much to say that most metaphysics, since Spinoza, has been largely determined by it. The way this has occurred is, in outline, as follows: Speaking generally, adjectives and common nouns express qualities or properties of single things, whereas prepositions and verbs tend to express relations between two or more things. Thus the neglect of prepositions and verbs led to the belief that every proposition can be regarded as attributing a property to a single thing, rather than as expressing a relation between two or more things. Hence it was supposed that, ultimately, there can be no such entities as relations between things. Hence either there can be only one thing in the universe, or, if there are many things, they cannot possibly interact in any way, since any interaction would be a relation, and relations are impossible.

The first of these views, advocated by Spinoza and held in our own day by Bradley and many other philosophers, is called *monism*; the second, advocated by Leibniz but not very common nowadays, is called *monadism*, because each of the isolated things is called a *monad*. Both these opposing philosophies, interesting as they are, result, in my opinion, from an undue attention to one sort of universals, namely the sort represented by adjectives and substantives rather than by verbs and prepositions.

As a matter of fact, if any one were anxious to deny altogether that there are such things as universals, we should find that we cannot strictly prove that there are such entities as *qualities*, i.e. the universals represented by adjectives and substantives, whereas we can prove that there must be *relations*, i.e. the sort of universals generally represented by verbs and prepositions. Let us take in illustration the universal *whiteness*. If we believe that there is such a universal, we shall say that things are white because they have the quality of whiteness. This view, however, was strenuously denied by Berkeley and Hume, who have been followed in this by later empiricists. The form which their denial took was to deny that there are such things as 'abstract ideas '. When we want to think of whiteness, they said, we form an image of some particular white thing, and reason concerning this particular, taking care not to deduce anything concerning it which we cannot see to be equally true of any other white thing. As an account of our actual mental processes, this is no doubt largely true. In geometry, for example, when we wish to prove something about all triangles, we draw a particular triangle and reason about it, taking care not to use any characteristic which it does not share with other triangles. The beginner, in order to avoid error, often finds it useful to draw several triangles, as unlike each other as possible, in order to make sure that his reasoning is equally applicable to all of them. But a difficulty emerges as soon as we ask ourselves how we know that a thing is white or a triangle. If we wish to avoid the universals *whiteness* and *triangularity*, we shall choose some particular patch of white or some particular triangle, and say that anything is white or a triangle if it has the right sort of resemblance to our chosen particular. But then the resemblance required will have to be a universal. Since there are many white things, the resemblance must hold between many pairs of particular white things; and this is the characteristic of a universal. It will be useless to say that there is a different resemblance for each pair, for then we shall have to say that these resemblances resemble each other, and thus at last we shall be forced to admit resemblance as a universal. The relation of resemblance, therefore, must be a true universal. And having been forced to admit this universal, we find that it is no longer worth while to invent difficult and unplausible theories to avoid the admission of such universals as whiteness and triangularity. Berkeley and Hume failed to perceive this refutation of their rejection of 'abstract ideas', because, like their adversaries, they only thought of *qualities*, and altogether ignored *relations* as universals. We have therefore here another respect in which the rationalists appear to have been in the right as against the empiricists, although, owing to the neglect or denial of relations, the deductions made by rationalists were, if anything, more apt to be mistaken than those made by empiricists.

Having now seen that there must be such entities as universals, the next point to be proved is that their being is not merely mental. By this is meant that whatever being belongs to them is independent of their being thought of or in any way apprehended by minds. We have already touched on this subject at the end of the preceding chapter, but we must now consider more fully what sort of being it is that belongs to universals.

Consider such a proposition as 'Edinburgh is north of London'. Here we have a relation between two places, and it seems plain that the relation subsists independently of our knowledge of it. When we come to know that Edinburgh is north of London, we come to know something which has to do only with Edinburgh and London: we do not cause the truth of the proposition by coming to know it, on the contrary we merely apprehend a fact which was there before we knew it. The part of the earth's surface where Edinburgh stands would be north of the part where London stands, even if there were no human being to know about north and south, and even if there were no minds at all in the universe. This is, of course, denied by many philosophers, either for Berkeley's reasons or for Kant's. But we have already considered these reasons, and decided that they are inadequate. We may therefore now assume it to be true that nothing mental is presupposed in the fact that Edinburgh is north of London. But this fact involves the relation 'north of', which is a universal; and it would be impossible for the whole fact to involve nothing mental if the relation 'north of', which is a constituent part of the fact, did involve anything mental. Hence we must admit that the relation, like the terms it relates, is not dependent upon thought, but belongs to the independent world which thought apprehends but does not create.

This conclusion, however, is met by the difficulty that the relation 'north of' does not seem to *exist* in the same sense in which Edinburgh and London exist. If we ask 'Where and when does this relation exist?' the answer must be 'Nowhere and nowhen'. There is no place or time where we can find the relation 'north of'. It does not exist in Edinburgh any more than in London, for it relates the two and is neutral as between them. Nor can we say that it exists at any particular time. Now everything that can be apprehended by the senses or by introspection exists at some particular time. Hence the relation 'north of' is radically different from such things. It is neither in space nor in time, neither material nor mental; yet it is something. It is largely the very peculiar kind of being that belongs to universals which has led many people to suppose that they are really mental. We can think *of* a universal, and our thinking then exists in a perfectly ordinary sense, like any other mental act. Suppose, for example, that we are thinking of whiteness. Then *in one sense* it may be said that whiteness is 'in our mind'. We have here the same ambiguity as we noted in discussing Berkeley in Chapter IV. In the strict sense, it is not whiteness that is in our mind, but the act of thinking of whiteness. The connected ambiguity in the word 'idea', which we noted at the same time, also causes confusion here. In one sense of this word, namely the sense in which it denotes the *object* of an act of thought, whiteness is an 'idea'. Hence, if the ambiguity is not guarded against, we may come to think that whiteness is an 'idea' in the other sense, i.e. an act of thought; and thus we come to think that whiteness is mental. But in so thinking, we rob it of its essential quality of universality. One man's act of thought is necessarily a different thing from another man's; one man's act of thought at one time is necessarily a different thing from the same man's act of thought at another time. Hence, if whiteness were the thought as opposed to its object, no two different men could think of it, and no one man could think of it twice. That which many different thoughts of whiteness have in common is their *object*, and this object is different from all of them. Thus universals are not thoughts, though when known they are the objects of thoughts.

We shall find it convenient only to speak of things *existing* when they are in time, that is to say, when we can point to some time at which they exist (not excluding the possibility of their existing at all times). Thus thoughts and feelings, minds and physical objects exist. But universals do not exist in this sense; we shall say that they *subsist* or *have being*, where 'being' is opposed to 'existence' as being timeless. The world of universals, therefore, may also be described as the world of being. The world of being is unchangeable, rigid, exact, delightful to the mathematician, the logician, the builder of metaphysical systems, and all who love perfection more than life. The world of existence is fleeting, vague, without sharp boundaries, without any clear plan or arrangement, but it contains all thoughts and feelings, all the data of sense, and all physical objects, everything that can do either good or harm, everything that makes any difference to the value of life and the world. According to our temperaments, we shall prefer the contemplation of the one or of the other. The one we do not prefer will probably seem to us a pale shadow of the one we prefer, and hardly worthy to be regarded as in any sense real. But the truth is that both have the same claim on our impartial attention, both are real, and both are important to the metaphysician. Indeed no sooner have we distinguished the two worlds than it becomes necessary to consider their relations.

But first of all we must examine our knowledge of universals. This consideration will occupy us in the following chapter, where we shall find that it solves the problem of *a priori* knowledge, from which we were first led to consider universals.

Plato (ca. 424 BC– ca. 348 BC) hardly needs an introduction. If Descartes was the father of modern philosophy, Plato was the father of Western philosophy. Hardly a thinker since his time has been uninfluenced by his work, for better or worse. Given that Plato wrote dialogues, that is, dramatic accounts of philosophical discussions, it can be difficult to say exactly what Plato himself believed. Just because a character in a dialogue holds a given position does not mean that Plato himself endorsed that view. However there is a certain consensus about what Plato believed, and a philosophy by the name of Platonism has been extracted from his dialogues and argued over for centuries.

Roughly speaking, Platonism is the theory that certain knowledge is possible because the mind does not rely on the senses, but has access to a realm of perfect Ideas or Forms. The Forms provide an eternal and unchanging object for our thoughts, and without such eternal and unchanging objects, knowledge would be impossible.

Russell is a Platonist in this regard, although, as we shall see, he might disagree with Plato as to the exact nature of these Forms.

Plato

from

THE PHAEDO

PERSONS OF THE DIALOGUE:

Phaedo, who is the narrator of the dialogue to Echecrates of Phlius. Socrates, Apollodorus, Simmias, Cebes, Crito and an Attendant of the Prison.

SCENE: The Prison of Socrates.

PLACE OF THE NARRATION: Phlius.

And what is the nature of this knowledge or recollection? I mean to ask, Whether a person who, having seen or heard or in any way perceived anything, knows not only that, but has a conception of something else which is the subject, not of the same but of some other kind of knowledge, may not be fairly said to recollect that of which he has the conception?

What do you mean?

I mean what I may illustrate by the following instance:—The knowledge of a lyre is not the same as the knowledge of a man?

True.

And yet what is the feeling of lovers when they recognize a lyre, or a garment, or anything else which the beloved has been in the habit of using? Do not they, from knowing the lyre, form in the mind's eye an image of the youth to whom the lyre belongs? And this is recollection. In like manner any one who sees Simmias may remember Cebes; and there are endless examples of the same thing.

Endless, indeed, replied Simmias.

And recollection is most commonly a process of recovering that which has been already forgotten through time and inattention.

Very true, he said.

Well; and may you not also from seeing the picture of a horse or a lyre remember a man? and from the picture of Simmias, you may be led to remember Cebes?

True.

Or you may also be led to the recollection of Simmias himself?

Quite so.

And in all these cases, the recollection may be derived from things either like or unlike?

It may be.

And when the recollection is derived from like things, then another consideration is sure to arise, which is—whether the likeness in any degree falls short or not of that which is recollected?

Very true, he said.

And shall we proceed a step further, and affirm that there is such a thing as equality, not of one piece of wood or stone with another, but that, over and above this, there is absolute equality? Shall we say so?

Say so, yes, replied Simmias, and swear to it, with all the confidence in life.

And do we know the nature of this absolute essence?

To be sure, he said.

And whence did we obtain our knowledge? Did we not see equalities of material things, such as pieces of wood and stones, and gather from them the idea of an equality which is different from them? For you will acknowledge that there is a difference. Or look at the matter in another way:—Do not the same pieces of wood or stone appear at one time equal, and at another time unequal?

That is certain.

But are real equals ever unequal? or is the idea of equality the same as of inequality?

Impossible, Socrates.

Then these (so-called) equals are not the same with the idea of equality?

I should say, clearly not, Socrates.

And yet from these equals, although differing from the idea of equality, you conceived and attained that idea?

Very true, he said.

Which might be like, or might be unlike them?

Yes.

But that makes no difference; whenever from seeing one thing you conceived another, whether like or unlike, there must surely have been an act of recollection?

Very true.

But what would you say of equal portions of wood and stone, or other material equals? and what is the impression produced by them? Are they equals in the same sense in which absolute equality is equal? or do they fall short of this perfect equality in a measure?

Yes, he said, in a very great measure too.

And must we not allow, that when I or any one, looking at any object, observes that the thing which he sees aims at being some other thing, but falls short of, and cannot be, that other thing, but is inferior, he who makes this observation must have had a previous knowledge of that to which the other, although similar, was inferior?

Certainly.

And has not this been our own case in the matter of equals and of absolute equality?

Precisely.

Then we must have known equality previously to the time when we first saw the material equals, and reflected that all these apparent equals strive to attain absolute equality, but fall short of it?

Very true.

And we recognize also that this absolute equality has only been known, and can only be known, through the medium of sight or touch, or of some other of the senses, which are all alike in this respect?

Yes, Socrates, as far as the argument is concerned, one of them is the same as the other.

From the senses then is derived the knowledge that all sensible things aim at an absolute equality of which they fall short?

Yes.

Then before we began to see or hear or perceive in any way, we must have had a knowledge of absolute equality, or we could not have referred to that standard the equals which are derived from the senses?—for to that they all aspire, and of that they fall short.

No other inference can be drawn from the previous statements.

And did we not see and hear and have the use of our other senses as soon as we were born?

Certainly.

Then we must have acquired the knowledge of equality at some previous time?

Yes.

That is to say, before we were born, I suppose?

True.

And if we acquired this knowledge before we were born, and were born having the use of it, then we also knew before we were born and at the instant of birth not only the equal or the greater or the less, but all other ideas; for we are not speaking only of equality, but of beauty, goodness, justice, holiness, and of all which we stamp with the name of essence in the dialectical process, both when we ask and when we answer questions. Of all this we may certainly affirm that we acquired the knowledge before birth?

We may.

But if, after having acquired, we have not forgotten what in each case we acquired, then we must always have come into life having knowledge, and shall always continue to know as long as life lasts —for knowing is the acquiring and retaining knowledge and not forgetting. Is not forgetting, Simmias, just the losing of knowledge?

Quite true, Socrates.

But if the knowledge which we acquired before birth was lost by us at birth, and if afterwards by the use of the senses we recovered what we previously knew, will not the process which we call learning be a recovering of the knowledge which is natural to us, and may not this be rightly termed recollection?

Very true.

So much is clear—that when we perceive something, either by the help of sight, or hearing, or some other sense, from that perception we are able to obtain a notion of some other thing like or unlike which is associated with it but has been forgotten. Whence, as I was saying, one of two alternatives follows:—either we had this knowledge at birth, and continued to know through life; or, after birth, those who are said to learn only remember, and learning is simply recollection.

Yes, that is quite true, Socrates.

And which alternative, Simmias, do you prefer? Had we the knowledge at our birth, or did we recollect the things which we knew previously to our birth?

I cannot decide at the moment.

At any rate you can decide whether he who has knowledge will or will not be able to render an account of his knowledge? What do you say?

Certainly, he will.

But do you think that every man is able to give an account of these very matters about which we are speaking?

Would that they could, Socrates, but I rather fear that to-morrow, at this time, there will no longer be any one alive who is able to give an account of them such as ought to be given.

Then you are not of opinion, Simmias, that all men know these things?

Certainly not.

They are in process of recollecting that which they learned before?

Certainly.

But when did our souls acquire this knowledge?—not since we were born as men?

Certainly not.

And therefore, previously?

Yes.

Then, Simmias, our souls must also have existed without bodies before they were in the form of man, and must have had intelligence.

Unless indeed you suppose, Socrates, that these notions are given us at the very moment of birth; for this is the only time which remains.

Yes, my friend, but if so, when do we lose them? for they are not in us when we are born—that is admitted. Do we lose them at the moment of receiving them, or if not at what other time?

No, Socrates, I perceive that I was unconsciously talking nonsense.

Then may we not say, Simmias, that if, as we are always repeating, there is an absolute beauty, and goodness, and an absolute essence of all things; and if to this, which is now discovered to have existed in our former state, we refer all our sensations, and with this compare them, finding these ideas to be pre-existent and our inborn possession—then our souls must have had a prior existence, but if not, there would be no force in the argument? There is the same proof that these ideas must have existed before we were born, as that our souls existed before we were born; and if not the ideas, then not the souls.

Yes, Socrates; I am convinced that there is precisely the same necessity for the one as for the other; and the argument retreats successfully to the position that the existence of the soul before birth cannot be separated from the existence of the essence of which you speak. For there is nothing which to my mind is so patent as that beauty, goodness, and the other notions of which you were just now speaking, have a most real and absolute existence; and I am satisfied with the proof.

Well, but is Cebes equally satisfied? for I must convince him too.

I think, said Simmias, that Cebes is satisfied: although he is the most incredulous of mortals, yet I believe that he is sufficiently convinced of the existence of the soul before birth. But that after death the soul will continue to exist is not yet proven even to my own satisfaction. I cannot get rid of the feeling of the many to which Cebes was referring—the feeling that when the man dies the soul will be dispersed, and that this may be the extinction of her. For admitting that she may have been born elsewhere, and framed out of other elements, and was in existence before entering the human body, why after having entered in and gone out again may she not herself be destroyed and come to an end?

Very true, Simmias, said Cebes; about half of what was required has been proven; to wit, that our souls existed before we were born:—that the soul will exist after death as well as before birth is the other half of which the proof is still wanting, and has to be supplied; when that is given the demonstration will be complete.

But that proof, Simmias and Cebes, has been already given, said Socrates, if you put the two arguments together—I mean this and the former one, in which we admitted that everything living is born of the dead. For if the soul exists before birth, and in coming to life and being born can be born only from death and dying, must she not after death continue to exist, since she has to be born again?—Surely the proof which you desire has been already furnished. Still I suspect that you and Simmias would be glad to probe the argument further. Like children, you are haunted with a fear that when the soul leaves the body, the wind may really blow her away and scatter her; especially if a man should happen to die in a great storm and not when the sky is calm.

Cebes answered with a smile: Then, Socrates, you must argue us out of our fears—and yet, strictly speaking, they are not our fears, but there is a child within us to whom death is a sort of hobgoblin; him too we must persuade not to be afraid when he is alone in the dark.

Socrates said: Let the voice of the charmer be applied daily until you have charmed away the fear.

And where shall we find a good charmer of our fears, Socrates, when you are gone?

Hellas, he replied, is a large place, Cebes, and has many good men, and there are barbarous races not a few: seek for him among them all, far and wide, sparing neither pains nor money; for there is no better way of spending your money. And you must seek among yourselves too; for you will not find others better able to make the search.

The search, replied Cebes, shall certainly be made. And now, if you please, let us return to the point of the argument at which we digressed.

By all means, replied Socrates; what else should I please?

Very good.

Must we not, said Socrates, ask ourselves what that is which, as we imagine, is liable to be scattered, and about which we fear? and what again is that about which we have no fear? And then we may proceed further to enquire whether that which suffers dispersion is or is not of the nature of soul—our hopes and fears as to our own souls will turn upon the answers to these questions.

Very true, he said.

Now the compound or composite may be supposed to be naturally capable, as of being compounded, so also of being dissolved; but that which is uncompounded, and that only, must be, if anything is, indissoluble.

Yes; I should imagine so, said Cebes.

And the uncompounded may be assumed to be the same and unchanging, whereas the compound is always changing and never the same.

I agree, he said.

Then now let us return to the previous discussion. Is that idea or essence, which in the dialectical process we define as essence or true existence—whether essence of equality, beauty, or anything else—are these essences, I say, liable at times to some degree of change? or are they each of them always what they are, having the same simple self-existent and unchanging forms, not admitting of variation at all, or in any way, or at any time?

They must be always the same, Socrates, replied Cebes.

And what would you say of the many beautiful—whether men or horses or garments or any other things which are named by the same names and may be called equal or beautiful,—are they all unchanging and the same always, or quite the reverse? May they not rather be described as almost always changing and hardly ever the same, either with themselves or with one another?

The latter, replied Cebes; they are always in a state of change.

And these you can touch and see and perceive with the senses, but the unchanging things you can only perceive with the mind—they are invisible and are not seen?

That is very true, he said.

Well, then, added Socrates, let us suppose that there are two sorts of existences—one seen, the other unseen.

Let us suppose them.

The seen is the changing, and the unseen is the unchanging?

That may be also supposed.

And, further, is not one part of us body, another part soul?

To be sure.

And to which class is the body more alike and akin?

Clearly to the seen—no one can doubt that.

And is the soul seen or not seen?

Not by man, Socrates.

And what we mean by 'seen' and 'not seen' is that which is or is not visible to the eye of man?

Yes, to the eye of man.

And is the soul seen or not seen?

Not seen.

Unseen then?

Yes.

Then the soul is more like to the unseen, and the body to the seen?

That follows necessarily, Socrates.

And were we not saying long ago that the soul when using the body as an instrument of perception, that is to say, when using the sense of sight or hearing or some other sense (for the meaning of perceiving through the body is perceiving through the senses)—were we not saying that the soul too is then dragged by the body into the region of the changeable, and wanders and is confused; the world spins round her, and she is like a drunkard, when she touches change?

Very true.

But when returning into herself she reflects, then she passes into the other world, the region of purity, and eternity, and immortality, and unchangeableness, which are her kindred, and with them she ever lives, when she is by herself and is not let or hindered; then she ceases from her erring ways, and being in communion with the unchanging is unchanging. And this state of the soul is called wisdom?

That is well and truly said, Socrates, he replied.

CHAPTER X.

ON OUR KNOWLEDGE OF UNIVERSALS

In regard to one man's knowledge at a given time, universals, like particulars, may be divided into those known by acquaintance, those known only by description, and those not known either by acquaintance or by description.

Let us consider first the knowledge of universals by acquaintance. It is obvious, to begin with, that we are acquainted with such universals as white, red, black, sweet, sour, loud, hard, etc., i.e. with qualities which are exemplified in sense-data. When we see a white patch, we are acquainted, in the first instance, with the particular patch; but by seeing many white patches, we easily learn to abstract the whiteness which they all have in common, and in learning to do this we are learning to be acquainted with whiteness. A similar process will make us acquainted with any other universal of the same sort. Universals of this sort may be called 'sensible qualities'. They can be apprehended with less effort of abstraction than any others, and they seem less removed from particulars than other universals are.

We come next to relations. The easiest relations to apprehend are those which hold between the different parts of a single complex sense-datum. For example, I can see at a glance the whole of the page on which I am writing; thus the whole page is included in one sense-datum. But I perceive that some parts of the page are to the left of other parts, and some parts are above other parts. The process of abstraction in this case seems to proceed somewhat as follows: I see successively a number of sense-data in which one part is to the left of another; I perceive, as in the case of different white patches, that all these sense-data have something in common, and by abstraction I find that what they have in common is a certain relation between their parts, namely the relation which I call 'being to the left of'. In this way I become acquainted with the universal relation.

In like manner I become aware of the relation of before and after in time. Suppose I hear a chime of bells: when the last bell of the chime sounds, I can retain the whole chime before my mind, and I can perceive that the earlier bells came before the later ones. Also in memory I perceive that what I am remembering came before the present time. From either of these sources I can abstract the universal relation of before and after, just as I abstracted the universal relation 'being to the left of'. Thus time-relations, like space-relations, are among those with which we are acquainted.

Another relation with which we become acquainted in much the same way is resemblance. If I see simultaneously two shades of green, I can see that they resemble each other; if I also see a shade of red: at the same time, I can see that the two greens have more resemblance to each other than either has to the red. In this way I become acquainted with the universal *resemblance* or *similarity*. Between universals, as between particulars, there are relations of which we may be immediately aware. We have just seen that we can perceive that the resemblance between two shades of green is greater than the resemblance between a shade of red and a shade of green. Here we are dealing with a relation, namely 'greater than', between two relations. Our knowledge of such relations, though it requires more power of abstraction than is required for perceiving the qualities of sense-data, appears to be equally immediate, and (at least in some cases) equally indubitable. Thus there is immediate knowledge concerning universals as well as concerning sense-data.

Returning now to the problem of *a priori* knowledge, which we left unsolved when we began the consideration of universals, we find ourselves in a position to deal with it in a much more satisfactory manner than was possible before. Let us revert to the proposition 'two and two are four'. It is fairly obvious, in view of what has been said, that this proposition states a relation between the universal 'two' and the universal 'four'. This suggests a proposition which we shall now endeavour to establish: namely, *All a priori knowledge deals exclusively with the relations of universals.* This proposition is of great importance, and goes a long way towards solving our previous difficulties concerning *a priori* knowledge.

The only case in which it might seem, at first sight, as if our proposition were untrue, is the case in which an *a priori* proposition states that *all* of one class of particulars belong to some other class, or (what comes to the same thing) that *all* particulars having some one property also have some other. In this case it might seem as though we were dealing with the particulars that have the property rather than with the property. The proposition 'two and two are four' is really a case in point, for this may be stated in the form 'any two and any other two are four', or 'any collection formed of two twos is a collection of four'. If we can show that such statements as this really deal only with universals, our proposition may be regarded as proved.

One way of discovering what a proposition deals with is to ask ourselves what words we must understand --in other words, what objects we must be acquainted with-- in order to see what the proposition means. As soon as we see what the proposition means, even if we do not yet know whether it is true or false, it is evident that we must have acquaintance with whatever is really dealt with by the proposition. By applying this test, it appears that many propositions which might seem to be concerned with particulars are really concerned only with universals. In the special case of 'two and two are four', even when we interpret it as meaning 'any collection formed of two twos is a collection of four', it is plain that we can understand the proposition, i.e. we can see what it is that it asserts, as soon as we know what is meant by 'collection' and 'two' and 'four'. It is quite unnecessary to know all the couples in the world: if it were necessary, obviously we could never understand the proposition, since the couples are infinitely numerous and therefore cannot all be known to us. Thus although our general statement *implies* statements about particular couples, *as soon as we know that there are such particular couples*, yet it does not itself assert or imply that there are such particular couples, and thus fails to make any statement whatever about any actual particular couple. The statement made is about 'couple', the universal, and not about this or that couple. Thus the statement 'two and two are four' deals exclusively with universals, and therefore may be known by anybody who is acquainted with the universals concerned and can perceive the relation between them which the statement asserts. It must be taken as a fact, discovered by reflecting upon our knowledge, that we have the power of sometimes perceiving such relations between universals, and therefore of sometimes knowing general *a priori* propositions such as those of arithmetic and logic. The thing that seemed mysterious, when we formerly considered such knowledge, was that it seemed to anticipate and control experience. This, however, we can now see to have been an error. *No* fact concerning anything capable of being experienced can be known independently of experience. We know *a priori* that two things and two other things together make four things, but we do *not* know *a priori* that if Brown and Jones are two, and Robinson and Smith are two, then Brown and Jones and Robinson and Smith are four. The reason is that this proposition cannot be understood at all unless we know that there are such people as Brown and Jones and Robinson and Smith, and this we can only know by experience. Hence, although our general proposition is *a priori*, all its applications to actual particulars involve experience and therefore contain an empirical element. In this way what seemed mysterious in our *a priori* knowledge is seen to have been based upon an error.

It will serve to make the point clearer if we contrast our genuine *a priori* judgement with an empirical generalization, such as 'all men are mortals'. Here as before, we can *understand* what the proposition means as soon as we understand the universals involved, namely *man* and *mortal.* It is obviously unnecessary to have an individual acquaintance with the whole human race in order to understand what our proposition means. Thus the difference between an *a priori* general proposition and an empirical generalization does not come in the *meaning* of the proposition; it comes in the nature of the *evidence* for it. In the empirical case, the evidence consists in the particular instances. We believe that all men are mortal because we know that there are innumerable instances of men dying, and no instances of their living beyond a certain age. We do not believe it because we see a connexion between the universal *man* and the universal *mortal*. It is true that if physiology can prove, assuming the general laws that govern living bodies, that no living organism can last for ever, that gives a connexion between *man* and *mortality* which would enable us to assert our proposition without appealing to the special evidence of *men* dying. But that only means that our generalization has been subsumed under a wider generalization, for which the evidence is still of the same kind, though more extensive. The progress of science is constantly producing such subsumptions, and therefore giving a constantly wider inductive basis for scientific generalizations. But although this gives a greater *degree* of certainty, it does not give a different *kind*: the ultimate ground remains inductive, i.e. derived from instances, and not an *a priori* connexion of universals such as we have in logic and arithmetic. Two opposite points are to be observed concerning *a priori* general propositions. The first is that, if many particular instances are known, our general proposition may be arrived at in the first instance by induction, and the connexion of universals may be only subsequently perceived. For example, it is known that if we draw perpendiculars to the sides of a triangle from the opposite angles, all three perpendiculars meet in a point. It would be quite possible to be first led to this proposition by actually drawing perpendiculars in many cases, and finding that they always met in a point; this experience might lead us to look for the general proof and find it. Such cases are common in the experience of every mathematician.

The other point is more interesting, and of more philosophical importance. It is, that we may sometimes know a general proposition in cases where we do not know a single instance of it.

Take such a case as the following: We know that any two numbers can be multiplied together, and will give a third called their *product.* We know that all pairs of integers the product of which is less than 100 have been actually multiplied together, and the value of the product recorded in the multiplication table. But we also know that the number of integers is infinite, and that only a finite number of pairs of integers ever have been or ever will be thought of by human beings. Hence it follows that there are pairs of integers which never have been and never will be thought of by human beings, and that all of them deal with integers the product of which is over 100. Hence we arrive at the proposition: 'All products of two integers, which never have been and never will be thought of by any human being, are over 100.' Here is a general proposition of which the truth is undeniable, and yet, from the very nature of the case, we can never give an instance; because any two numbers we may think of are excluded by the terms of the proposition. This possibility, of knowledge of general propositions of which no instance can be given, is often denied, because it is not perceived that the knowledge of such propositions only requires a knowledge of the relations of universals, and does not require any knowledge of instances of the universals in question. Yet the knowledge of such general propositions is quite vital to a great deal of what is generally admitted to be known. For example, we saw, in our early chapters, that knowledge of physical objects, as opposed to sense-data, is only obtained by an inference, and that they are not things with which we are acquainted. Hence we can never know any proposition of the form 'this is a physical object', where 'this' is something immediately known. It follows that all our knowledge concerning physical objects is such that no actual instance can be given. We can give instances of the associated sense-data, but we cannot give instances of the actual physical objects. Hence our knowledge as to physical objects depends throughout upon this possibility of general knowledge where no instance can be given. And the same applies to our knowledge of other people's minds, or of any other class of things of which no instance is known to us by acquaintance. We may now take a survey of the sources of our knowledge, as they have appeared in the course of our analysis. We have first to distinguish knowledge of things and knowledge of truths. In each there are two kinds, one immediate and one derivative. Our immediate knowledge of things, which we called *acquaintance*, consists of two sorts, according as the things known are particulars or universals. Among particulars, we have acquaintance with sense-data and (probably) with ourselves. Among universals, there seems to be no principle by which we can decide which can be known by acquaintance, but it is clear that among those that can be so known are sensible qualities, relations of space and time, similarity, and certain abstract logical universals. Our derivative knowledge of things, which we call knowledge by *description*, always involves both acquaintance with something and knowledge of truths. Our immediate knowledge of *truths* may be called *intuitive* knowledge, and the truths so known may be called *self-evident* truths. Among such truths are included those which merely state what is given in sense, and also certain abstract logical and arithmetical principles, and (though with less certainty) some ethical propositions. Our *derivative* knowledge of truths consists of everything that we can deduce from self-evident truths by the use of self-evident principles of deduction. If the above account is correct, all our knowledge of truths depends upon our intuitive knowledge. It therefore becomes important to consider the nature and scope of intuitive knowledge, in much the same way as, at an earlier stage, we considered the nature and scope of knowledge by acquaintance. But knowledge of truths raises a further problem, which does not arise in regard to knowledge of things, namely the problem of *error*. Some of our beliefs turn out to be erroneous, and therefore it becomes necessary to consider how, if at all, we can distinguish knowledge from error. This problem does not arise with regard to knowledge by acquaintance, for, whatever may be the object of acquaintance, even in dreams and hallucinations, there is no error involved so long as we do not go beyond the immediate object: error can only arise when we regard the immediate object, i.e. the sense-datum, as the mark of some physical object. Thus the problems connected with knowledge of truths are more difficult than those connected with knowledge of things. As the first of the problems connected with knowledge of truths, let us examine the nature and scope of our intuitive judgements.

Ralph Waldo Emerson (1803 – 1882) was a leading intellectual and literary figure in 19th century America. He was a poet as well as a philosopher, as is perhaps obvious from this selection, from his essay "Nominalist and Realist." The style is very different than Russell's, choosing flowery language and metaphor over more sober argumentation. This is entirely appropriate, since going back to Plato, it has often been claimed that the world of the Ideas is not easily described in the everyday language.

Emerson focusses in this essay on the difference between the Ideal of "manhood" (or in the less sexist manner of today, "personhood") and the particular men (and women) that we encounter on a daily basis. The particulars are perceptible, but they suggest an imperceptible Form that gives them their meaning. Emerson seems to have ethical or even spiritual considerations in mind, whereas Russell is dealing with more mundane problems of math and logic. The theory of Forms has historically had a role to play in both of these kinds of discussions.

Ralph Waldo Emerson

from

Nominalist and Realist

I cannot often enough say that a man is only a relative and representative nature. Each is a hint of the truth, but far enough from being that truth which yet he quite newly and inevitably suggests to us. If I seek it in him I shall not find it. Could any man conduct into me the pure stream of that which he pretends to be! Long afterwards I find that quality elsewhere which he promised me. The genius of the Platonists is intoxicating to the student, yet how few particulars of it can I detach from all their books. The man momentarily stands for the thought, but will not bear examination; and a society of men will cursorily represent well enough a certain quality and culture, for example, chivalry or beauty of manners; but separate them and there is no gentleman and no lady in the group. The least hint sets us on the pursuit of a character which no man realizes. We have such exorbitant eyes that on seeing the smallest arc we complete the curve, and when the curtain is lifted from the diagram which it seemed to veil, we are vexed to find that no more was drawn than just that fragment of an arc which we first beheld. We are greatly too liberal in our construction of each other's faculty and promise. Exactly what the parties have already done they shall do again; but that which we inferred from their nature and inception, they will not do. That is in nature, but not in them. That happens in the world, which we often witness in a public debate. Each of the speakers expresses himself imperfectly; no one of them hears much that another says, such is the preoccupation of mind of each; and the audience, who have only to hear and not to speak, judge very wisely and superiorly how wrongheaded and unskilful is each of the debaters to his own affair. Great men or men of great gifts you shall easily find, but symmetrical men never. When I meet a pure intellectual force or a generosity of affection, I believe here then is man; and am presently mortified by the discovery that this individual is no more available to his own or to the general ends than his companions; because the power which drew my respect is not supported by the total symphony of his talents. All persons exist to society by some shining trait of beauty or utility which they have. We borrow the proportions of the man from that one fine feature, and finish the portrait symmetrically; which is false, for the rest of his body is small or deformed. I observe a person who makes a good public appearance, and conclude thence the perfection of his private character, on which this is based; but he has no private character. He is a graceful cloak or lay-figure for holidays. All our poets, heroes, and saints, fail utterly in some one or in many parts to satisfy our idea, fail to draw our spontaneous interest, and so leave us without any hope of realization but in our own future. Our exaggeration of all fine characters arises from the fact that we identify each in turn with the soul. But there are no such men as we fable; no Jesus, nor Pericles, nor Caesar, nor Angelo, nor Washington, such as we have made. We consecrate a great deal of nonsense because it was allowed by great men. There is none without his foible. I verily believe if an angel should come to chant the chorus of the moral law, he would eat too much gingerbread, or take liberties with private letters, or do some precious atrocity. It is bad enough that our geniuses cannot do anything useful, but it is worse that no man is fit for society who has fine traits. He is admired at a distance, but he cannot come near without appearing a cripple. The men of fine parts protect themselves by solitude, or by courtesy, or by satire, or by an acid worldly manner, each concealing as he best can his incapacity for useful association, but they want either love or self-reliance.

Our native love of reality joins with this experience to teach us a little reserve, and to dissuade a too sudden surrender to the brilliant qualities of persons. Young people admire talents or particular excellences; as we grow older we value total powers and effects, as the impression, the quality, the spirit of men and things. The genius is all. The man,—it is his system: we do not try a solitary word or act, but his habit. The acts which you praise, I praise not, since they are departures from his faith, and are mere compliances. The magnetism which arranges tribes and races in one polarity is alone to be respected; the men are steel-filings. Yet we unjustly select a particle, and say, 'O steel-filing number one! what heart-drawings I feel to thee! what prodigious virtues are these of thine! how constitutional to thee, and incommunicable.' Whilst we speak the loadstone is withdrawn; down falls our filing in a heap with the rest, and we continue our mummery to the wretched shaving. Let us go for universals; for the magnetism, not for the needles. Human life and its persons are poor empirical pretensions. A personal influence is an ignis fatuus. If they say it is great, it is great; if they say it is small, it is small; you see it, and you see it not, by turns; it borrows all its size from the momentary estimation of the speakers: the Will-of-the-wisp vanishes if you go too near, vanishes if you go too far, and only blazes at one angle. Who can tell if Washington be a great man or no? Who can tell if Franklin be? Yes, or any but the twelve, or six, or three great gods of fame? And they too loom and fade before the eternal.

We are amphibious creatures, weaponed for two elements, having two sets of faculties, the particular and the catholic. We adjust our instrument for general observation, and sweep the heavens as easily as we pick out a single figure in the terrestrial landscape. We are practically skillful in detecting elements for which we have no place in our theory, and no name. Thus we are very sensible of an atmospheric influence in men and in bodies of men, not accounted for in an arithmetical addition of all their measurable properties. There is a genius of a nation, which is not to be found in the numerical citizens, but which characterizes the society. England, strong, punctual, practical, well-spoken England I should not find if I should go to the island to seek it. In the parliament, in the play-house, at dinner-tables, I might see a great number of rich, ignorant, book-read, conventional, proud men, —many old women,—and not anywhere the Englishman who made the good speeches, combined the accurate engines, and did the bold and nervous deeds. It is even worse in America, where, from the intellectual quickness of the race, the genius of the country is more splendid in its promise and more slight in its performance. Webster cannot do the work of Webster. We conceive distinctly enough the French, the Spanish, the German genius, and it is not the less real that perhaps we should not meet in either of those nations a single individual who corresponded with the type. We infer the spirit of the nation in great measure from the language, which is a sort of monument to which each forcible individual in a course of many hundred years has contributed a stone. And, universally, a good example of this social force is the veracity of language, which cannot be debauched. In any controversy concerning morals, an appeal may be made with safety to the sentiments which the language of the people expresses. Proverbs, words, and grammar-inflections convey the public sense with more purity and precision than the wisest individual.

In the famous dispute with the Nominalists, the Realists had a good deal of reason. General ideas are essences. They are our gods: they round and ennoble the most partial and sordid way of living. Our proclivity to details cannot quite degrade our life and divest it of poetry. The day-laborer is reckoned as standing at the foot of the social scale, yet he is saturated with the laws of the world. His measures are the hours; morning and night, solstice and equinox, geometry, astronomy and all the lovely accidents of nature play through his mind. Money, which represents the prose of life, and which is hardly spoken of in parlors without an apology, is, in its effects and laws, as beautiful as roses. Property keeps the accounts of the world, and is always moral. The property will be found where the labor, the wisdom, and the virtue have been in nations, in classes, and (the whole life-time considered, with the compensations) in the individual also. How wise the world appears, when the laws and usages of nations are largely detailed, and the completeness of the municipal system is considered! Nothing is left out. If you go into the markets and the custom-houses, the insurers' and notaries' offices, the offices of sealers of weights and measures, of inspection of provisions,—it will appear as if one man had made it all. Wherever you go, a wit like your own has been before you, and has realized its thought.

The Eleusinian mysteries, the Egyptian architecture, the Indian astronomy, the Greek sculpture, show that there always were seeing and knowing men in the planet. The world is full of masonic ties, of guilds, of secret and public legions of honor; that of scholars, for example; and that of gentlemen, fraternizing with the upper class of every country and every culture.

I am very much struck in literature by the appearance that one person wrote all the books; as if the editor of a journal planted his body of reporters in different parts of the field of action, and relieved some by others from time to time; but there is such equality and identity both of judgment and point of view in the narrative that it is plainly the work of one all-seeing, all-hearing gentleman. I looked into Pope's Odyssey yesterday: it is as correct and elegant after our canon of to-day as if it were newly written. The modernness of all good books seems to give me an existence as wide as man. What is well done I feel as if I did; what is ill done I reck not of. Shakespeare's passages of passion (for example, in Lear and Hamlet) are in the very dialect of the present year. I am faithful again to the whole over the members in my use of books. I find the most pleasure in reading a book in a manner least flattering to the author. I read Proclus, and sometimes Plato, as I might read a dictionary, for a mechanical help to the fancy and the imagination. I read for the lustres, as if one should use a fine picture in a chromatic experiment, for its rich colors. 'Tis not Proclus, but a piece of nature and fate that I explore. It is a greater joy to see the author's author, than himself. A higher pleasure of the same kind I found lately at a concert, where I went to hear Handel's Messiah. As the master overpowered the littleness and incapableness of the performers and made them conductors of his electricity, so it was easy to observe what efforts nature was making, through so many hoarse, wooden, and imperfect persons, to produce beautiful voices, fluid and soul-guided men and women. The genius of nature was paramount at the oratorio.

This preference of the genius to the parts is the secret of that deification of art, which is found in all superior minds. Art, in the artist, is proportion, or a habitual respect to the whole by an eye loving beauty in details. And the wonder and charm of it is the sanity in insanity which it denotes. Proportion is almost impossible to human beings. There is no one who does not exaggerate. In conversation, men are encumbered with personality, and talk too much. In modern sculpture, picture, and poetry, the beauty is miscellaneous; the artist works here and there and at all points, adding and adding, instead of unfolding the unit of his thought. Beautiful details we must have, or no artist; but they must be means and never other. The eye must not lose sight for a moment of the purpose. Lively boys write to their ear and eye, and the cool reader finds nothing but sweet jingles in it. When they grow older, they respect the argument.

We obey the same intellectual integrity when we study in exceptions the law of the world. Anomalous facts, as the never quite obsolete rumors of magic and demonology, and the new allegations of phrenologists and neurologists, are of ideal use. They are good indications. Homoeopathy is insignificant as an art of healing, but of great value as criticism on the hygeia or medical practice of the time. So with Mesmerism, Swedenborgism, Fourierism, and the Millennial Church; they are poor pretensions enough, but good criticism on the science, philosophy, and preaching of the day. For these abnormal insights of the adepts ought to be normal, and things of course.

All things show us that on every side we are very near to the best. It seems not worth while to execute with too much pains some one intellectual, or aesthetical, or civil feat, when presently the dream will scatter, and we shall burst into universal power. The reason of idleness and of crime is the deferring of our hopes. Whilst we are waiting we beguile the time with jokes, with sleep, with eating, and with crimes.

Thus we settle it in our cool libraries, that all the agents with which we deal are subalterns, which we can well afford to let pass, and life will be simpler when we live at the centre and flout the surfaces. I wish to speak with all respect of persons, but sometimes I must pinch myself to keep awake and preserve the due decorum. They melt so fast into each other that they are like grass and trees, and it needs an effort to treat them as individuals. Though the uninspired man certainly finds persons a conveniency in household matters, the divine man does not respect them; he sees them as a rack of clouds, or a fleet of ripples which the wind drives over the surface of the water. But this is flat rebellion. Nature will not be Buddhist: she resents generalizing, and insults the philosopher in every moment with a million of fresh particulars. It is all idle talking: as much as a man is a whole, so is he also a part; and it were partial not to see it. What you say in your pompous distribution only distributes you into your class and section. You have not got rid of parts by denying them, but are the more partial. You are one thing, but Nature is one thing and the other thing, in the same moment. She will not remain orbed in a thought, but rushes into persons; and when each person, inflamed to a fury of personality, would conquer all things to his poor crotchet, she raises up against him another person, and by many persons incarnates again a sort of whole. She will have all. Nick Bottom cannot play all the parts, work it how he may; there will be somebody else, and the world will be round. Everything must have its flower or effort at the beautiful, coarser or finer according to its stuff. They relieve and recommend each other, and the sanity of society is a balance of a thousand insanities. She punishes abstractionists, and will only forgive an induction which is rare and casual. We like to come to a height of land and see the landscape, just as we value a general remark in conversation. But it is not the intention of Nature that we should live by general views. We fetch fire and water, run about all day among the shops and markets, and get our clothes and shoes made and mended, and are the victims of these details; and once in a fortnight we arrive perhaps at a rational moment. If we were not thus infatuated, if we saw the real from hour to hour, we should not be here to write and to read, but should have been burned or frozen long ago. She would never get anything done, if she suffered admirable Crichtons and universal geniuses. She loves better a wheelwright who dreams all night of wheels, and a groom who is part of his horse; for she is full of work, and these are her hands. As the frugal farmer takes care that his cattle shall eat down the rowen, and swine shall eat the waste of his house, and poultry shall pick the crumbs,—so our economical mother dispatches a new genius and habit of mind into every district and condition of existence, plants an eye wherever a new ray of light can fall, and gathering up into some man every property in the universe, establishes thousandfold occult mutual attractions among her offspring, that all this wash and waste of power may be imparted and exchanged.

Great dangers undoubtedly accrue from this incarnation and distribution of the godhead, and hence Nature has her maligners, as if she were Circe; and Alphonso of Castille fancied he could have given useful advice. But she does not go unprovided; she has hellebore at the bottom of the cup. Solitude would ripen a plentiful crop of despots. The recluse thinks of men as having his manner, or as not having his manner; and as having degrees of it, more and less. But when he comes into a public assembly he sees that men have very different manners from his own, and in their way admirable. In his childhood and youth he has had many checks and censures, and thinks modestly enough of his own endowment. When afterwards he comes to unfold it in propitious circumstance, it seems the only talent; he is delighted with his success, and accounts himself already the fellow of the great. But he goes into a mob, into a banking house, into a mechanic's shop, into a mill, into a laboratory, into a ship, into a camp, and in each new place he is no better than an idiot; other talents take place, and rule the hour. The rotation which whirls every leaf and pebble to the meridian, reaches to every gift of man, and we all take turns at the top.

For Nature, who abhors mannerism, has set her heart on breaking up all styles and tricks, and it is so much easier to do what one has done before than to do a new thing, that there is a perpetual tendency to a set mode. In every conversation, even the highest, there is a certain trick, which may be soon learned by an acute person and then that particular style continued indefinitely. Each man too is a tyrant in tendency, because he would impose his idea on others; and their trick is their natural defence. Jesus would absorb the race; but Tom Paine or the coarsest blasphemer helps humanity by resisting this exuberance of power. Hence the immense benefit of party in politics, as it reveals faults of character in a chief, which the intellectual force of the persons, with ordinary opportunity and not hurled into aphelion by hatred, could not have seen. Since we are all so stupid, what benefit that there should be two stupidities! It is like that brute advantage so essential to astronomy, of having the diameter of the earth's orbit for a base of its triangles. Democracy is morose, and runs to anarchy, but in the State and in the schools it is indispensable to resist the consolidation of all men into a few men. If John was perfect, why are you and I alive? As long as any man exists, there is some need of him; let him fight for his own. A new poet has appeared; a new character approached us; why should we refuse to eat bread until we have found his regiment and section in our old army-files? Why not a new man? Here is a new enterprise of Brook Farm, of Skeneateles, of Northampton: why so impatient to baptize them Essenes, or Port-Royalists, or Shakers, or by any known and effete name? Let it be a new way of living. Why have only two or three ways of life, and not thousands? Every man is wanted, and no man is wanted much. We came this time for condiments, not for corn. We want the great genius only for joy; for one star more in our constellation, for one tree more in our grove. But he thinks we wish to belong to him, as he wishes to occupy us. He greatly mistakes us. I think I have done well if I have acquired a new word from a good author; and my business with him is to find my own, though it were only to melt him down into an epithet or an image for daily use:—

"Into paint will I grind thee, my bride!"

To embroil the confusion, and make it impossible to arrive at any general statement,—when we have insisted on the imperfection of individuals, our affections and our experience urge that every individual is entitled to honor, and a very generous treatment is sure to be repaid. A recluse sees only two or three persons, and allows them all their room; they spread themselves at large. The statesman looks at many, and compares the few habitually with others, and these look less. Yet are they not entitled to this generosity of reception? and is not munificence the means of insight? For though gamesters say that the cards beat all the players, though they were never so skillful, yet in the contest we are now considering, the players are also the game, and share the power of the cards. If you criticise a fine genius, the odds are that you are out of your reckoning, and instead of the poet, are censuring your own caricature of him. For there is somewhat spheral and infinite in every man, especially in every genius, which, if you can come very near him, sports with all your limitations. For rightly every man is a channel through which heaven floweth, and whilst I fancied I was criticising him, I was censuring or rather terminating my own soul. After taxing Goethe as a courtier, artificial, unbelieving, worldly,—I took up this book of Helena, and found him an Indian of the wilderness, a piece of pure nature like an apple or an oak, large as morning or night, and virtuous as a brier-rose.

But care is taken that the whole tune shall be played. If we were not kept among surfaces, every thing would be large and universal; now the excluded attributes burst in on us with the more brightness that they have been excluded. "Your turn now, my turn next," is the rule of the game. The universality being hindered in its primary form, comes in the secondary form of all sides; the points come in succession to the meridian, and by the speed of rotation a new whole is formed. Nature keeps herself whole and her representation complete in the experience of each mind. She suffers no seat to be vacant in her college. It is the secret of the world that all things subsist and do not die but only retire a little from sight and afterwards return again. Whatever does not concern us is concealed from us. As soon as a person is no longer related to our present well-being, he is concealed, or dies, as we say. Really, all things and persons are related to us, but according to our nature they act on us not at once but in succession, and we are made aware of their presence one at a time. All persons, all things which we have known, are here present, and many more than we see; the world is full. As the ancient said, the world is a plenum or solid; and if we saw all things that really surround us we should be imprisoned and unable to move. For though nothing is impassable to the soul, but all things are pervious to it and like highways, yet this is only whilst the soul does not see them. As soon as the soul sees any object, it stops before that object. Therefore, the divine Providence which keeps the universe open in every direction to the soul, conceals all the furniture and all the persons that do not concern a particular soul, from the senses of that individual. Through solidest eternal things the man finds his road as if they did not subsist, and does not once suspect their being. As soon as he needs a new object, suddenly he beholds it, and no longer attempts to pass through it, but takes another way. When he has exhausted for the time the nourishment to be drawn from any one person or thing, that object is withdrawn from his observation, and though still in his immediate neighborhood, he does not suspect its presence. Nothing is dead: men feign themselves dead, and endure mock funerals and mournful obituaries, and there they stand looking out of the window, sound and well, in some new and strange disguise. Jesus is not dead; he is very well alive: nor John, nor Paul, nor Mahomet, nor Aristotle; at times we believe we have seen them all, and could easily tell the names under which they go.

If we cannot make voluntary and conscious steps in the admirable science of universals, let us see the parts wisely, and infer the genius of nature from the best particulars with a becoming charity. What is best in each kind is an index of what should be the average of that thing. Love shows me the opulence of nature, by disclosing to me in my friend a hidden wealth, and I infer an equal depth of good in every other direction. It is commonly said by farmers that a good pear or apple costs no more time or pains to rear than a poor one; so I would have no work of art, no speech, or action, or thought, or friend, but the best.

The end and the means, the gamester and the game,—life is made up of the intermixture and reaction of these two amicable powers, whose marriage appears beforehand monstrous, as each denies and tends to abolish the other. We must reconcile the contradictions as we can, but their discord and their concord introduce wild absurdities into our thinking and speech. No sentence will hold the whole truth, and the only way in which we can be just, is by giving ourselves the lie; Speech is better than silence; silence is better than speech;—All things are in contact; every atom has a sphere of repulsion;—Things are, and are not, at the same time;—and the like. All the universe over, there is but one thing, this old Two-Face, creator-creature, mind-matter, right-wrong, of which any proposition may be affirmed or denied. Very fitly therefore I assert that every man is a partialist, that nature secures him as an instrument by self-conceit, preventing the tendencies to religion and science; and now further assert, that, each man's genius being nearly and affectionately explored, he is justified in his individuality, as his nature is found to be immense; and now I add that every man is a universalist also, and, as our earth, whilst it spins on its own axis, spins all the time around the sun through the celestial spaces, so the least of its rational children, the most dedicated to his private affair, works out, though as it were under a disguise, the universal problem. We fancy men are individuals; so are pumpkins; but every pumpkin in the field goes through every point of pumpkin history. The rabid democrat, as soon as he is senator and rich man, has ripened beyond possibility of sincere radicalism, and unless he can resist the sun, he must be conservative the remainder of his days. Lord Eldon said in his old age that "if he were to begin life again, he would be damned but he would begin as agitator."

We hide this universality if we can, but it appears at all points. We are as ungrateful as children. There is nothing we cherish and strive to draw to us but in some hour we turn and rend it. We keep a running fire of sarcasm at ignorance and the life of the senses; then goes by, perchance, a fair girl, a piece of life, gay and happy, and making the commonest offices beautiful by the energy and heart with which she does them; and seeing this we admire and love her and them, and say, 'Lo! a genuine creature of the fair earth, not dissipated or too early ripened by books, philosophy, religion, society, or care!' insinuating a treachery and contempt for all we had so long loved and wrought in ourselves and others.

If we could have any security against moods! If the profoundest prophet could be holden to his words, and the hearer who is ready to sell all and join the crusade could have any certificate that tomorrow his prophet shall not unsay his testimony! But the Truth sits veiled there on the Bench, and never interposes an adamantine syllable; and the most sincere and revolutionary doctrine, put as if the ark of God were carried forward some furlongs, and planted there for the succor of the world, shall in a few weeks be coldly set aside by the same speaker, as morbid; "I thought I was right, but I was not,"—and the same immeasurable credulity demanded for new audacities. If we were not of all opinions! if we did not in any moment shift the platform on which we stand, and look and speak from another! if there could be any regulation, any 'one-hour-rule,' that a man should never leave his point of view without sound of trumpet. I am always insincere, as always knowing there are other moods.

How sincere and confidential we can be, saying all that lies in the mind, and yet go away feeling that all is yet unsaid, from the incapacity of the parties to know each other, although they use the same words! My companion assumes to know my mood and habit of thought, and we go on from explanation to explanation until all is said which words can, and we leave matters just as they were at first, because of that vicious assumption. Is it that every man believes every other to be an incurable partialist, and himself a universalist? I talked yesterday with a pair of philosophers; I endeavored to show my good men that I love everything by turns and nothing long; that I loved the centre, but doted on the superficies; that I loved man, if men seemed to me mice and rats; that I revered saints, but woke up glad that the old pagan world stood its ground and died hard; that I was glad of men of every gift and nobility, but would not live in their arms.

Could they but once understand that I loved to know that they existed, and heartily wished them God-speed, yet, out of my poverty of life and thought, had no word or welcome for them when they came to see me, and could well consent to their living in Oregon, for any claim I felt on them,—it would be a great satisfaction.

CHAPTER XI.

ON INTUITIVE KNOWLEDGE

There is a common impression that everything that we believe ought to be capable of proof, or at least of being shown to be highly probable. It is felt by many that a belief for which no reason can be given is an unreasonable belief. In the main, this view is just. Almost all our common beliefs are either inferred, or capable of being inferred, from other beliefs which may be regarded as giving the reason for them. As a rule, the reason has been forgotten, or has even never been consciously present to our minds. Few of us ever ask ourselves, for example, what reason there is to suppose the food we are just going to eat will not turn out to be poison. Yet we feel, when challenged, that a perfectly good reason could be found, even if we are not ready with it at the moment. And in this belief we are usually justified.

But let us imagine some insistent Socrates, who, whatever reason we give him, continues to demand a reason for the reason. We must sooner or later, and probably before very long, be driven to a point where we cannot find any further reason, and where it becomes almost certain that no further reason is even theoretically discoverable. Starting with the common beliefs of daily life, we can be driven back from point to point, until we come to some general principle, or some instance of a general principle, which seems luminously evident, and is not itself capable of being deduced from anything more evident. In most questions of daily life, such as whether our food is likely to be nourishing and not poisonous, we shall be driven back to the inductive principle, which we discussed in Chapter VI. But beyond that, there seems to be no further regress. The principle itself is constantly used in our reasoning, sometimes consciously, sometimes unconsciously; but there is no reasoning which, starting from some simpler self-evident principle, leads us to the principle of induction as its conclusion. And the same holds for other logical principles. Their truth is evident to us, and we employ them in constructing demonstrations; but they themselves, or at least some of them, are incapable of demonstration.

Self-evidence, however, is not confined to those among general principles which are incapable of proof. When a certain number of logical principles have been admitted, the rest can be deduced from them; but the propositions deduced are often just as self-evident as those that were assumed without proof. All arithmetic, moreover, can be deduced from the general principles of logic, yet the simple propositions of arithmetic, such as 'two and two are four', are just as self-evident as the principles of logic.

It would seem, also, though this is more disputable, that there are some self-evident ethical principles, such as 'we ought to pursue what is good'. It should be observed that, in all cases of general principles, particular instances, dealing with familiar things, are more evident than the general principle. For example, the law of contradiction states that nothing can both have a certain property and not have it. This is evident as soon as it is understood, but it is not so evident as that a particular rose which we see cannot be both red and not red. (It is of course possible that parts of the rose may be red and parts not red, or that the rose may be of a shade of pink which we hardly know whether to call red or not; but in the former case it is plain that the rose as a whole is not red, while in the latter case the answer is theoretically definite as soon as we have decided on a precise definition of 'red'.) It is usually through particular instances that we come to be able to see the general principle. Only those who are practised in dealing with abstractions can readily grasp a general principle without the help of instances.

In addition to general principles, the other kind of self-evident truths are those immediately derived from sensation. We will call such truths 'truths of perception', and the judgements expressing them we will call 'judgements of perception'. But here a certain amount of care is required in getting at the precise nature of the truths that are self-evident. The actual sense-data are neither true nor false. A particular patch of colour which I see, for example, simply exists: it is not the sort of thing that is true or false. It is true that there is such a patch, true that it has a certain shape and degree of brightness, true that it is surrounded by certain other colours. But the patch itself, like everything else in the world of sense, is of a radically different kind from the things that are true or false, and therefore cannot properly be said to be _*true*_. Thus whatever self-evident truths may be obtained from our senses must be different from the sense-data from which they are obtained. It would seem that there are two kinds of self-evident truths of perception, though perhaps in the last analysis the two kinds may coalesce. First, there is the kind which simply asserts the _*existence*_ of the sense-datum, without in any way analysing it. We see a patch of red, and we judge 'there is such-and-such a patch of red', or more strictly 'there is that'; this is one kind of intuitive judgement of perception. The other kind arises when the object of sense is complex, and we subject it to some degree of analysis. If, for instance, we see a _*round*_ patch of red, we may judge 'that patch of red is round'. This is again a judgement of perception, but it differs from our previous kind. In our present kind we have a single sense-datum which has both colour and shape: the colour is red and the shape is round. Our judgement analyses the datum into colour and shape, and then recombines them by stating that the red colour is round in shape. Another example of this kind of judgement is 'this is to the right of that', where 'this' and 'that' are seen simultaneously. In this kind of judgement the sense-datum contains constituents which have some relation to each other, and the judgement asserts that these constituents have this relation.

Another class of intuitive judgements, analogous to those of sense and yet quite distinct from them, are judgements of _*memory*_. There is some danger of confusion as to the nature of memory, owing to the fact that memory of an object is apt to be accompanied by an image of the object, and yet the image cannot be what constitutes memory. This is easily seen by merely noticing that the image is in the present, whereas what is remembered is known to be in the past. Moreover, we are certainly able to some extent to compare our image with the object remembered, so that we often know, within somewhat wide limits, how far our image is accurate; but this would be impossible, unless the object, as opposed to the image, were in some way before the mind. Thus the essence of memory is not constituted by the image, but by having immediately before the mind an object which is recognized as past. But for the fact of memory in this sense, we should not know that there ever was a past at all, nor should we be able to understand the word 'past', any more than a man born blind can understand the word 'light'. Thus there must be intuitive judgements of memory, and it is upon them, ultimately, that all our knowledge of the past depends.

The case of memory, however, raises a difficulty, for it is notoriously fallacious, and thus throws doubt on the trustworthiness of intuitive judgements in general. This difficulty is no light one. But let us first narrow its scope as far as possible. Broadly speaking, memory is trustworthy in proportion to the vividness of the experience and to its nearness in time. If the house next door was struck by lightning half a minute ago, my memory of what I saw and heard will be so reliable that it would be preposterous to doubt whether there had been a flash at all. And the same applies to less vivid experiences, so long as they are recent. I am absolutely certain that half a minute ago I was sitting in the same chair in which I am sitting now. Going backward over the day, I find things of which I am quite certain, other things of which I am almost certain, other things of which I can become certain by thought and by calling up attendant circumstances, and some things of which I am by no means certain. I am quite certain that I ate my breakfast this morning, but if I were as indifferent to my breakfast as a philosopher should be, I should be doubtful. As to the conversation at breakfast, I can recall some of it easily, some with an effort, some only with a large element of doubt, and some not at all. Thus there is a continual gradation in the degree of self-evidence of what I remember, and a corresponding gradation in the trustworthiness of my memory. Thus the first answer to the difficulty of fallacious memory is to say that memory has degrees of self-evidence, and that these correspond to the degrees of its trustworthiness, reaching a limit of perfect self-evidence and perfect trustworthiness in our memory of events which are recent and vivid.

It would seem, however, that there are cases of very firm belief in a memory which is wholly false. It is probable that, in these cases, what is really remembered, in the sense of being immediately before the mind, is something other than what is falsely believed in, though something generally associated with it. George IV is said to have at last believed that he was at the battle of Waterloo, because he had so often said that he was. In this case, what was immediately remembered was his repeated assertion; the belief in what he was asserting (if it existed) would be produced by association with the remembered assertion, and would therefore not be a genuine case of memory. It would seem that cases of fallacious memory can probably all be dealt with in this way, i.e. they can be shown to be not cases of memory in the strict sense at all.

One important point about self-evidence is made clear by the case of memory, and that is, that self-evidence has degrees: it is not a quality which is simply present or absent, but a quality which may be more or less present, in gradations ranging from absolute certainty down to an almost imperceptible faintness. Truths of perception and some of the principles of logic have the very highest degree of self-evidence; truths of immediate memory have an almost equally high degree. The inductive principle has less self-evidence than some of the other principles of logic, such as 'what follows from a true premiss must be true'. Memories have a diminishing self-evidence as they become remoter and fainter; the truths of logic and mathematics have (broadly speaking) less self-evidence as they become more complicated. Judgements of intrinsic ethical or aesthetic value are apt to have some self-evidence, but not much.

Degrees of self-evidence are important in the theory of knowledge, since, if propositions may (as seems likely) have some degree of self-evidence without being true, it will not be necessary to abandon all connexion between self-evidence and truth, but merely to say that, where there is a conflict, the more self-evident proposition is to be retained and the less self-evident rejected.

It seems, however, highly probable that two different notions are combined in 'self-evidence' as above explained; that one of them, which corresponds to the highest degree of self-evidence, is really an infallible guarantee of truth, while the other, which corresponds to all the other degrees, does not give an infallible guarantee, but only a greater or less presumption. This, however, is only a suggestion, which we cannot as yet develop further. After we have dealt with the nature of truth, we shall return to the subject of self-evidence, in connexion with the distinction between knowledge and error.

Josiah Royce (1855 – 1916) was an American idealist, who wrote and taught on a number of topics inside and outside of philosophy. He is philosophy is not widely read today, but he had a definite influence on the philosophers of his time, especially in the area of logic. He was influenced by the Pragmatists C.S. Peirce and William James, but had a distinctive philosophy of his own.

In particular he wrote on the possibility of religious knowledge, and in doing so elaborated on the notion of "intuition," a term that is often used but seldom well defined. "Intuitive knowledge" was supposed, going back to Descartes, to be immediate and certain, but philosophers have differed as to what an "intuition" is. Here Royce we see Royce defining the term, as part of a broader attempt to define "reason." So "intuition" and "reason" are two different things, and both differ from "common sense."

It is worth noting that "intuition" or "immediate knowledge," which is so crucial to so many philosophical systems, has no standard, uncontroversial definition.

Josiah Royce

from

THE SOURCES OF RELIGIOUS INSIGHT

I

"What does one mean by the Reason?" As I attempt to answer this question, with an especial effort to show the relations of reason and religion, I shall be aided by reminding you at the outset that, at the present time, there is a widespread tendency to discredit the reason as a source of any notable insight into life or into the universe. And this tendency depends upon so defining the business of the reason as sharply to oppose, on the one hand, intuition and reason, and, on the other hand, reason and common-sense experience. That is, some of our recent teachers tell us that the only sort of insight which can be of any use in religion must be won by intuitions and cannot be obtained by what these teachers call the abstract reason. By intuition, at least in the religious field, such men mean some sort of direct feeling of the nature of things, some experience such as the mystics have reported, or such as many religious people, whether technical mystics or not, call illumination through faith. Intuitions of this sort, they say, are our only guides in the religious field. As opposed to such direct apprehension, the use of reason would mean the effort to be guided by formulas, by explicitly stated abstract principles, by processes of inference, by calculations, or by logical demonstrations. James is prominent amongst those who thus oppose the abstract reason to the revelations of intuition; and, especially in his later works, he is never weary of emphasising the inarticulate character of all our deepest sources of religious insight. When we get true religious insight, so he teaches, we simply feel convinced that these things are so. If we try to give reasons for our beliefs, James holds that the reasons are inapt afterthoughts, the outcome of sophistication, or are at best useful only in putting our convictions into convenient order for purposes of record or of teaching. James's favourite statement of the contrast here in question identifies the partisans of reason with the defenders of what he calls "barren intellectualism." He maintains that religion is hindered rather than helped by such people. You attain conviction by processes of which the "barren intellect" can give no adequate account. Conviction, in religious matters, emanates, according to James, from those mysterious depths of the subconscious about which I said something in the last lecture. And convictions thus resulting feel overwhelming to the persons who have them. Such convictions are what many denote by the word "intuitions." The effort to define abstract principles, as grounds for holding your convictions to be true, constitutes the only effort of the reason in religious matters which James recognises. According to James, such reasoning processes are inevitably bad. And as a fact, so he insists, nobody seriously believes in God because some theologian or philosopher pretends to have demonstrated his existence. On the contrary, he says, belief in God is intuitive or is nothing of value. And reason is employed in such matters merely because of a frequent overfondness for abstract conceptions, or at best because formulas are useful for the teachers of religious traditions.

Another form of contrast, and one upon which James also often insists, while many other recent writers, whose interests are not those of James, emphasise the same matter, depends upon opposing reason to experience in general, including under the latter term not only the intuitions of the devout, but whatever goes by the name experience in ordinary speech. We see and hear and touch, and by such means get experience. But we make hypotheses and deduce their consequences; we assume premises and demonstrate conclusions; and, according to such writers, what we then do constitutes the typical work of our reason. The characteristic of the reason is that it attempts either to elucidate the meaning of an assertion, or to prove some proposition to be true, without appealing to experience to verify the proposition in question. And such work of the reason, as these writers tell us, is of very limited use, in comparison to the use of our direct experience as a guide. What is found to be true through empirical tests is rightly tested. What is supposed to be proved true by abstract reasoning is thus at best made dependent for its explicit warrant upon the presupposed truth of the premises used in the reasoning process. Or, as is sometimes said, the reason can discover nothing essentially new. It turns its premises over and over, and gets out of them only what has already been put into them. Experience, on the other hand, is full of countless novelties; for what you can find through observation and experiment depends not upon previous assumptions, but upon the skill and the good fortune of the inquirer, and upon the wealth of life and of the real world.

In brief, for those who look at reason in this way, to use your reason is simply to draw necessary inferences from assumed premises. And no premises, as such writers insist, can warrant any inference except the inference of a conclusion which is already hidden away, so to speak, in the premises themselves. Thus reasoning, as they tell us, is a process which, in the conclusion inferred, merely lets out of the bag the cat which was concealed in that bag, namely, in the premises. Reason, therefore, is indeed (so such writers assert) barren wherever novelty is sought. It is useful only for purposes of formulation, and in certain parts of the abstract sciences, where deduction has a technical place, as a means for preparing the way for experimental tests. In life, experience is the guide to true novelty. And therefore, if religious insight can be attained at all, it must be due not to the reason, but to some sort of religious experience.

Such objections to the use of reason in the religious field depend, as you see, upon identifying the reasoning process with the combination of two well-known mental processes; first, the process of forming and using abstract conceptions; secondly, the process of analysing assertions, or combinations of assertions, to make more explicit what is already contained in their meaning. Our next question may well be this: Is such an account of the work of reason just to the actual usage that common-sense is accustomed to make of this familiar name?

II

To this question I must at once answer that we all of us daily use the word reason as the name for a process, or a set of processes, which certainly cannot be reduced to the mere power to form and to use abstract ideas, and to analyse the already predetermined meaning of statements. When we speak of an ill-tempered or of a prejudiced man as "unreasonable," we do not merely mean that he is unable to form or to define abstract ideas, or that he cannot analyse the meaning of his own statements. For sometimes such a man is contentiously thoughtful, and fond of using too many one-sided abstractions, and eager to argue altogether too vehemently. No, when we call him unreasonable, we mean that he takes a narrow view of his life, or of his duties, or of the interests of his fellow-men. We mean, in brief, that he lacks vision for the true relations and for the total values of things. When we try to correct this sort of unreasonableness, we do not say to the petulant or to the one-sided man: "Go to the dictionary, and learn how to define your abstract terms." Sometimes contentiously prejudiced men are altogether too fond of the dictionary. Nor do we merely urge him to form the habit of analysis. No, we may indeed say to him: "Be reasonable"; but we mean: "Take a wider outlook; see things not one at a time, but many at once; be broad; consider more than one side; bring your ideas together; in a word, get insight." For precisely what I defined in my opening lecture as insight is what we have in mind when, in such cases, we counsel a man to be reasonable. So, in such uses of the word reason, reason is not opposed to intuition, as the power to form abstract ideas is supposed by James to be opposed to the power to see things by direct vision. No, reason, in such cases, means simply broader intuition, the sort of seeing that grasps many views in one, that surveys life as it were from above, that sees, as the wanderer views the larger landscape from a mountain top.

When, not long since, in a famous decision, the Supreme Court of the United States called attention to what it called "The rule of reason," and declared its intention to judge the workings of well-known modern business methods by that rule, the court certainly did not mean by "the rule of reason" the requirement that acts said to be "in restraint of trade" must be judged merely through a process of forming abstract ideas or of analysing the signification of assertions. No, the court was explicitly opposing certain methods of estimate which it regarded as falsely abstract; and it proposed to substitute for these false abstractions a mode of judging the workings of certain trade combinations which was to involve taking as wide and concrete and practical a view as possible of their total effects. Everybody who read the court's words understood that, in this case, it was precisely the merely abstract conception of something technically defined as a "restraint of trade" which the court wished, not to make sovereign, but to subordinate to the wider intuition of a fair-minded observer of the whole result, of a given sort of corporate combination. The "rule of reason" was intended to bring the whole question out of the realm of barren abstractions and of mere analysis, and nearer to the realm where the trained observation of the fair minded man would decide the case--nearer, in fact, to the realm of intuition. Only, the decisive intuition must be something broad, and far-seeing, and synthetic, and fair.

Now I submit that this meaning of the word reason is perfectly familiar to all of you. Reason, from this point of view, is the power to see widely and steadily and connectedly. Its true opponent is not intuition, but whatever makes us narrow in outlook, and consequently the prey of our own caprices. The unreasonable person is the person who can see but one thing at a time, when he ought to see two or many things together; who can grasp but one idea, when a synthesis of ideas is required. The reasonable man is capable of synopsis, of viewing both or many sides of a question, of comparing various motives, of taking interest in a totality rather than in a scattered multiplicity.

You may, of course, admit that this use of the word reason is familiar; and still you may say that James's contention is nevertheless sound. For, as you may declare, the real issue is not regarding the meanings that chance to be linked with the word reason, but regarding the relative impotence of that process which James chose to call by this name. As a fact, so you may assert, there exists the familiar process of forming abstract conceptions; and there also exists the process of drawing conclusions through an analysis of what is already contained in the meaning of the assumed premises. Whether or no one calls these two processes, in their usual combination, by the name reasoning, James is right in saying that abstractions, and that such sorts of purely analytic abstract reasoning as he has in mind, are incapable of giving us religious insight. And both James and the others who oppose reason to concrete experience are right in asserting that you get no novel insight whatever through mere abstractions, or through mere analysis, but are dependent for your advances in knowledge upon experience. Therefore, as you may continue, the issue which James and other empiricists raise must not be evaded by any appeal to vaguer uses of the word reason, whether common-sense or the Supreme Court chances to authorise such special forms of expression.

I fully agree to the importance of this comment and of the issue as thus stated. I am ready to consider the issue. But I also insist upon estimating the whole use of reason in its proper context. James, in common with countless other partisans of intuition in religious matters, is fond of insisting that all our nobler intuitions and all our deeper faiths are, in their foundations, inwardly compelling, but inarticulate, and that we degrade them rather than help them when we define their meaning in abstract terms or employ processes of explicit demonstration in their defence. James, in common with many empiricists, also opposes experience in general to all processes of reasoning, and asserts that the latter never teach us anything novel. The issue, fairly viewed, is therefore not a perfectly simple one. It involves the question whether the two modes of getting knowledge between which we are asked to choose are the only modes actually in use. Intuition, and experience in general, are by James and by others sharply contrasted with certain processes of abstraction and of analysis. It is then pointed out that since these latter processes, taken by themselves, never give us any essentially novel insights, you must on the whole cease to use your powers of abstraction and of analysis, except for the mere purpose of record or of teaching, or of some other such technical end--computation, analysis of hypotheses, and the like. You must, at least in religious matters, depend upon the uprushes from your subconscious self or upon whatever else is persuasively inarticulate. In the ultimate decisions of life, inarticulate intuition, mere faith, and that alone, can save you. Hereupon the perfectly fair question arises whether the alternatives are thus exhaustively stated. Must one choose between inarticulate faith and barren abstractions? Must one face the alternative: Either intuition without reasoning, or else relatively fruitless analysis without intuition? Perhaps there is a third possibility. Perhaps one may use one's process of abstraction {90} as a sort of preparation for certain articulate and noble intuitions that cannot be approached, by our human sort of consciousness, through any other way. Perhaps analysis is not the whole process which determines demonstrations. Perhaps synthesis--the viewing of many facts or principles or relations in some sort of unity and wholeness--perhaps a synoptic survey of various articulate truths, can lead us to novel insights. In that case inarticulate intuitions and barren abstractions are not the only instruments between which we must choose. For in that case there will be another sort of aid, a more explicit sort of intuition, a more considerate view of our life and its meaning, which we may adopt, and which may lead us to novel results. And these results may be not only articulate but saving.

Or, to state the issue more generally: In seeking for any sort of novel truth, have we only the choice between the experience of the data of sense or of feeling on the one hand and the analysis of abstract ideas and assertions upon the other? May there not be another source of knowledge? May not this source consist in the synthetic view of many facts in their unity--in the grasping of a complex of relations in their total significance? And may not just this be a source of insight which is employed in many of the processes ordinarily known as reasoning processes? May not the formation of abstract ideas, when wisely used, be merely a means of helping us toward an easier view of larger unities of fact than our present sort of human consciousness could grasp except for this auxiliary device? May not analysis be merely an aspect, a part of our live thinking? May not all genuine demonstration involve synthesis as well as analysis, the making of new constructions as well as the dissection of old assertions? If so, then the issue as presented by James and his allies is not rightly stated, because an essential part of its context is neglected. Abstract conceptions are, in fact, in the live and serious work of thought, a mere preparation for intuitions and experiences that lie on higher levels than those which, apart from abstract conceptions, we men can reach. Reasoning processes are fruitful because they involve sorts of experience, forms of intuition, that you cannot reach without them. In brief, reason and experience are not opposed. There is an opposition between inarticulate intuition and articulate insight. There is also an opposition between relatively blind experience of any sort and relatively rational experience. And, in view of such oppositions, it will be perfectly fair to define reason as the power to get articulate insight--insight into wholes rather than fragments. It will also be fair to define the reasoning process as the process of getting connected experience on a large scale.

Whoever views the matter thus will indeed not be forced to be a one-sided partisan of the reasoning process as thus defined. He will, first, fully admit that the formation of abstract ideas is but a means to an end, and that this end is the enlargement of the range of our view of the connections of our experience. He will secondly admit that, as soon as the process of forming abstract ideas is pursued as an end in itself, pedantry and formalism result, whether the topic be one of religion, or of science, or of the world's daily work. He will further agree with James, and with the empiricists generally, that merely analytic reasoning, if such were, in its isolation, a possible thing, would be indeed "barren intellectualism." And finally, if he is wise, he will go still further. He will not despise instinct, and feeling, and the movings of faith, and the inarticulate intuitions. For he will know that all these things are human, are indispensable, and are the basis upon which the genuine work of the reason, the wider view of life, must be carried toward its fulfillment. For whoever is to comprehend the unities of life must first live. Whoever is to be best able to survey the landscape from the mountain top must first have wandered in its paths and its byways, and must have grown familiar with its valleys and its recesses. Whoever is to get the mature insight must first have become a little child.

But whoever, remembering the New Testament word about becoming as a little child, one-sidedly defends the inarticulate intuitions, as the only source of religious insight, should remember also the word of St. Paul: "When I was a child, I spake as a child, I thought as a child, I understood as a child; but when I became a man I put away childish things."

It is the business of reason not to make naught of the indispensable intuitions of the childlike and of the faithful, but to work toward the insight such that, if we possessed it, we should "know even as we are known." That which is weak in this world may indeed confound many who are called wise; but there is no objection to its becoming also truly wise itself. For then it would all the better know why it had been able to confound false wisdom.

CHAPTER XII.

TRUTH AND FALSEHOOD

Our knowledge of truths, unlike our knowledge of things, has an opposite, namely *error*. So far as things are concerned, we may know them or not know them, but there is no positive state of mind which can be described as erroneous knowledge of things, so long, at any rate, as we confine ourselves to knowledge by acquaintance. Whatever we are acquainted with must be something; we may draw wrong inferences from our acquaintance, but the acquaintance itself cannot be deceptive. Thus there is no dualism as regards acquaintance. But as regards knowledge of truths, there is a dualism. We may believe what is false as well as what is true. We know that on very many subjects different people hold different and incompatible opinions: hence some beliefs must be erroneous. Since erroneous beliefs are often held just as strongly as true beliefs, it becomes a difficult question how they are to be distinguished from true beliefs. How are we to know, in a given case, that our belief is not erroneous? This is a question of the very greatest difficulty, to which no completely satisfactory answer is possible. There is, however, a preliminary question which is rather less difficult, and that is: What do we *mean* by truth and falsehood? It is this preliminary question which is to be considered in this chapter. In this chapter we are not asking how we can know whether a belief is true or false: we are asking what is meant by the question whether a belief is true or false. It is to be hoped that a clear answer to this question may help us to obtain an answer to the question what beliefs are true, but for the present we ask only 'What is truth?' and 'What is falsehood?' not 'What beliefs are true?' and 'What beliefs are false?' It is very important to keep these different questions entirely separate, since any confusion between them is sure to produce an answer which is not really applicable to either.

There are three points to observe in the attempt to discover the nature of truth, three requisites which any theory must fulfill.

(1) Our theory of truth must be such as to admit of its opposite, falsehood. A good many philosophers have failed adequately to satisfy this condition: they have constructed theories according to which all our thinking ought to have been true, and have then had the greatest difficulty in finding a place for falsehood. In this respect our theory of belief must differ from our theory of acquaintance, since in the case of acquaintance it was not necessary to take account of any opposite.

(2) It seems fairly evident that if there were no beliefs there could be no falsehood, and no truth either, in the sense in which truth is correlative to falsehood. If we imagine a world of mere matter, there would be no room for falsehood in such a world, and although it would contain what may be called 'facts', it would not contain any truths, in the sense in which truths are things of the same kind as falsehoods. In fact, truth and falsehood are properties of beliefs and statements: hence a world of mere matter, since it would contain no beliefs or statements, would also contain no truth or falsehood.

(3) But, as against what we have just said, it is to be observed that the truth or falsehood of a belief always depends upon something which lies outside the belief itself. If I believe that Charles I died on the scaffold, I believe truly, not because of any intrinsic quality of my belief, which could be discovered by merely examining the belief, but because of an historical event which happened two and a half centuries ago. If I believe that Charles I died in his bed, I believe falsely: no degree of vividness in my belief, or of care in arriving at it, prevents it from being false, again because of what happened long ago, and not because of any intrinsic property of my belief. Hence, although truth and falsehood are properties of beliefs, they are properties dependent upon the relations of the beliefs to other things, not upon any internal quality of the beliefs.

The third of the above requisites leads us to adopt the view--which has on the whole been commonest among philosophers--that truth consists in some form of correspondence between belief and fact. It is, however, by no means an easy matter to discover a form of correspondence to which there are no irrefutable objections. By this partly--and partly by the feeling that, if truth consists in a correspondence of thought with something outside thought, thought can never know when truth has been attained--many philosophers have been led to try to find some definition of truth which shall not consist in relation to something wholly outside belief. The most important attempt at a definition of this sort is the theory that truth consists in *coherence*. It is said that the mark of falsehood is failure to cohere in the body of our beliefs, and that it is the essence of a truth to form part of the completely rounded system which is The Truth.

There is, however, a great difficulty in this view, or rather two great difficulties. The first is that there is no reason to suppose that only *one* coherent body of beliefs is possible. It may be that, with sufficient imagination, a novelist might invent a past for the world that would perfectly fit on to what we know, and yet be quite different from the real past. In more scientific matters, it is certain that there are often two or more hypotheses which account for all the known facts on some subject, and although, in such cases, men of science endeavour to find facts which will rule out all the hypotheses except one, there is no reason why they should always succeed.

In philosophy, again, it seems not uncommon for two rival hypotheses to be both able to account for all the facts. Thus, for example, it is possible that life is one long dream, and that the outer world has only that degree of reality that the objects of dreams have; but although such a view does not seem inconsistent with known facts, there is no reason to prefer it to the common-sense view, according to which other people and things do really exist. Thus coherence as the definition of truth fails because there is no proof that there can be only one coherent system. The other objection to this definition of truth is that it assumes the meaning of 'coherence' known, whereas, in fact, 'coherence' presupposes the truth of the laws of logic. Two propositions are coherent when both may be true, and are incoherent when one at least must be false. Now in order to know whether two propositions can both be true, we must know such truths as the law of contradiction. For example, the two propositions, 'this tree is a beech' and 'this tree is not a beech', are not coherent, because of the law of contradiction. But if the law of contradiction itself were subjected to the test of coherence, we should find that, if we choose to suppose it false, nothing will any longer be incoherent with anything else. Thus the laws of logic supply the skeleton or framework within which the test of coherence applies, and they themselves cannot be established by this test.

For the above two reasons, coherence cannot be accepted as giving the *meaning* of truth, though it is often a most important *test* of truth after a certain amount of truth has become known.

Hence we are driven back to *correspondence with fact* as constituting the nature of truth. It remains to define precisely what we mean by 'fact', and what is the nature of the correspondence which must subsist between belief and fact, in order that belief may be true.

In accordance with our three requisites, we have to seek a theory of truth which (1) allows truth to have an opposite, namely falsehood, (2) makes truth a property of beliefs, but (3) makes it a property wholly dependent upon the relation of the beliefs to outside things.

The necessity of allowing for falsehood makes it impossible to regard belief as a relation of the mind to a single object, which could be said to be what is believed. If belief were so regarded, we should find that, like acquaintance, it would not admit of the opposition of truth and falsehood, but would have to be always true. This may be made clear by examples. Othello believes falsely that Desdemona loves Cassio. We cannot say that this belief consists in a relation to a single object, 'Desdemona's love for Cassio', for if there were such an object, the belief would be true. There is in fact no such object, and therefore Othello cannot have any relation to such an object. Hence his belief cannot possibly consist in a relation to this object.

It might be said that his belief is a relation to a different object, namely 'that Desdemona loves Cassio'; but it is almost as difficult to suppose that there is such an object as this, when Desdemona does not love Cassio, as it was to suppose that there is 'Desdemona's love for Cassio'. Hence it will be better to seek for a theory of belief which does not make it consist in a relation of the mind to a single object.

It is common to think of relations as though they always held between two terms, but in fact this is not always the case. Some relations demand three terms, some four, and so on. Take, for instance, the relation 'between'. So long as only two terms come in, the relation 'between' is impossible: three terms are the smallest number that render it possible. York is between London and Edinburgh; but if London and Edinburgh were the only places in the world, there could be nothing which was between one place and another. Similarly *jealousy* requires three people: there can be no such relation that does not involve three at least. Such a proposition as 'A wishes B to promote C's marriage with D' involves a relation of four terms; that is to say, A and B and C and D all come in, and the relation involved cannot be expressed otherwise than in a form involving all four. Instances might be multiplied indefinitely, but enough has been said to show that there are relations which require more than two terms before they can occur. The relation involved in *judging* or *believing* must, if falsehood is to be duly allowed for, be taken to be a relation between several terms, not between two. When Othello believes that Desdemona loves Cassio, he must not have before his mind a single object, 'Desdemona's love for Cassio', or 'that Desdemona loves Cassio ', for that would require that there should be objective falsehoods, which subsist independently of any minds; and this, though not logically refutable, is a theory to be avoided if possible. Thus it is easier to account for falsehood if we take judgement to be a relation in which the mind and the various objects concerned all occur severally; that is to say, Desdemona and loving and Cassio must all be terms in the relation which subsists when Othello believes that Desdemona loves Cassio. This relation, therefore, is a relation of four terms, since Othello also is one of the terms of the relation. When we say that it is a relation of four terms, we do not mean that Othello has a certain relation to Desdemona, and has the same relation to loving and also to Cassio. This may be true of some other relation than believing; but believing, plainly, is not a relation which Othello has to *each* of the three terms concerned, but to *all* of them together: there is only one example of the relation of believing involved, but this one example knits together four terms. Thus the actual occurrence, at the moment when Othello is entertaining his belief, is that the relation called 'believing' is knitting together into one complex whole the four terms Othello, Desdemona, loving, and Cassio. What is called belief or judgement is nothing but this relation of believing or judging, which relates a mind to several things other than itself. An *act* of belief or of judgement is the occurrence between certain terms at some particular time, of the relation of believing or judging.

We are now in a position to understand what it is that distinguishes a true judgement from a false one. For this purpose we will adopt certain definitions. In every act of judgement there is a mind which judges, and there are terms concerning which it judges. We will call the mind the *subject* in the judgement, and the remaining terms the *objects*. Thus, when Othello judges that Desdemona loves Cassio, Othello is the subject, while the objects are Desdemona and loving and Cassio. The subject and the objects together are called the *constituents* of the judgement. It will be observed that the relation of judging has what is called a 'sense' or 'direction'. We may say, metaphorically, that it puts its objects in a certain *order*, which we may indicate by means of the order of the words in the sentence. (In an inflected language, the same thing will be indicated by inflections, e.g. by the difference between nominative and accusative.) Othello's judgement that Cassio loves Desdemona differs from his judgement that Desdemona loves Cassio, in spite of the fact that it consists of the same constituents, because the relation of judging places the constituents in a different order in the two cases. Similarly, if Cassio judges that Desdemona loves Othello, the constituents of the judgement are still the same, but their order is different. This property of having a 'sense' or 'direction' is one which the relation of judging shares with all other relations. The 'sense' of relations is the ultimate source of order and series and a host of mathematical concepts; but we need not concern ourselves further with this aspect. We spoke of the relation called 'judging' or 'believing' as knitting together into one complex whole the subject and the objects. In this respect, judging is exactly like every other relation. Whenever a relation holds between two or more terms, it unites the terms into a complex whole. If Othello loves Desdemona, there is such a complex whole as 'Othello's love for Desdemona'. The terms united by the relation may be themselves complex, or may be simple, but the whole which results from their being united must be complex. Wherever there is a relation which relates certain terms, there is a complex object formed of the union of those terms; and conversely, wherever there is a complex object, there is a relation which relates its constituents. When an act of believing occurs, there is a complex, in which 'believing' is the uniting relation, and subject and objects are arranged in a certain order by the 'sense' of the relation of believing. Among the objects, as we saw in considering 'Othello believes that Desdemona loves Cassio', one must be a relation--in this instance, the relation 'loving'. But this relation, as it occurs in the act of believing, is not the relation which creates the unity of the complex whole consisting of the subject and the objects. The relation 'loving', as it occurs in the act of believing, is one of the objects--it is a brick in the structure, not the cement. The cement is the relation 'believing'. When the belief is *true*, there is another complex unity, in which the relation which was one of the objects of the belief relates the other objects. Thus, e.g., if Othello believes *truly* that Desdemona loves Cassio, then there is a complex unity, 'Desdemona's love for Cassio', which is composed exclusively of the *objects* of the belief, in the same order as they had in the belief, with the relation which was one of the objects occurring now as the cement that binds together the other objects of the belief. On the other hand, when a belief is *false*, there is no such complex unity composed only of the objects of the belief. If Othello believes *falsely* that Desdemona loves Cassio, then there is no such complex unity as 'Desdemona's love for Cassio'.

Thus a belief is *true* when it *corresponds* to a certain associated complex, and *false* when it does not. Assuming, for the sake of definiteness, that the objects of the belief are two terms and a relation, the terms being put in a certain order by the 'sense' of the believing, then if the two terms in that order are united by the relation into a complex, the belief is true; if not, it is false. This constitutes the definition of truth and falsehood that we were in search of. Judging or believing is a certain complex unity of which a mind is a constituent; if the remaining constituents, taken in the order which they have in the belief, form a complex unity, then the belief is true; if not, it is false.

Thus although truth and falsehood are properties of beliefs, yet they are in a sense extrinsic properties, for the condition of the truth of a belief is something not involving beliefs, or (in general) any mind at all, but only the *objects* of the belief. A mind, which believes, believes truly when there is a *corresponding* complex not involving the mind, but only its objects. This correspondence ensures truth, and its absence entails falsehood. Hence we account simultaneously for the two facts that beliefs (a) depend on minds for their *existence*, (b) do not depend on minds for their *truth*. We may restate our theory as follows: If we take such a belief as 'Othello believes that Desdemona loves Cassio', we will call Desdemona and Cassio the *object-terms*, and loving the *object-relation*. If there is a complex unity 'Desdemona's love for Cassio', consisting of the object-terms related by the object-relation in the same order as they have in the belief, then this complex unity is called the *fact corresponding to the belief*. Thus a belief is true when there is a corresponding fact, and is false when there is no corresponding fact. It will be seen that minds do not *create* truth or falsehood. They create beliefs, but when once the beliefs are created, the mind cannot make them true or false, except in the special case where they concern future things which are within the power of the person believing, such as catching trains. What makes a belief true is a *fact*, and this fact does not (except in exceptional cases) in any way involve the mind of the person who has the belief.

Having now decided what we *mean* by truth and falsehood, we have next to consider what ways there are of knowing whether this or that belief is true or false. This consideration will occupy the next chapter.

William James *(1842 - -1910) came from a prominent family. His father was a well known intellectual, and his brother Henry is an important American novelist, several of whose books have been turned into movies. William James is best known for his defense of Pragmatism, which is considered to be a distinctively American school of thought.*

Pragmatism is a theory of truth, one that equates the truth of a belief with it's usefulness. This stands in stark contrast to what has been called the Coherence theory of truth, which is associated with Idealism, and also to what is called the Correspondence theory of truth, whereby a proposition is said to be true if it corresponds with "the facts." whatever they may be. Russell (and Wittgenstein, in the supplement to Chapter V of this volume) represents the Correspondence theory. Russell defends it against the Coherence theory; this selection, from James' book Pragmatism, lays out the case against Correspondence.

William James

from

Pragmatism, Lecture VI

Pragmatism's Conception of Truth

When Clerk Maxwell was a child it is written that he had a mania for having everything explained to him, and that when people put him off with vague verbal accounts of any phenomenon he would interrupt them impatiently by saying, "Yes; but I want you to tell me the PARTICULAR GO of it!" Had his question been about truth, only a pragmatist could have told him the particular go of it. I believe that our contemporary pragmatists, especially Messrs. Schiller and Dewey, have given the only tenable account of this subject. It is a very ticklish subject, sending subtle rootlets into all kinds of crannies, and hard to treat in the sketchy way that alone befits a public lecture. But the Schiller-Dewey view of truth has been so ferociously attacked by rationalistic philosophers, and so abominably misunderstood, that here, if anywhere, is the point where a clear and simple statement should be made.

I fully expect to see the pragmatist view of truth run through the classic stages of a theory's career. First, you know, a new theory is attacked as absurd; then it is admitted to be true, but obvious and insignificant; finally it is seen to be so important that its adversaries claim that they themselves discovered it. Our doctrine of truth is at present in the first of these three stages, with symptoms of the second stage having begun in certain quarters. I wish that this lecture might help it beyond the first stage in the eyes of many of you.

Truth, as any dictionary will tell you, is a property of certain of our ideas. It means their 'agreement,' as falsity means their disagreement, with 'reality.' Pragmatists and intellectualists both accept this definition as a matter of course. They begin to quarrel only after the question is raised as to what may precisely be meant by the term 'agreement,' and what by the term 'reality,' when reality is taken as something for our ideas to agree with.

In answering these questions the pragmatists are more analytic and painstaking, the intellectualists more offhand and irreflective. The popular notion is that a true idea must copy its reality. Like other popular views, this one follows the analogy of the most usual experience. Our true ideas of sensible things do indeed copy them. Shut your eyes and think of yonder clock on the wall, and you get just such a true picture or copy of its dial. But your idea of its 'works' (unless you are a clock-maker) is much less of a copy, yet it passes muster, for it in no way clashes with the reality. Even tho it should shrink to the mere word 'works,' that word still serves you truly; and when you speak of the 'time-keeping function' of the clock, or of its spring's 'elasticity,' it is hard to see exactly what your ideas can copy.

You perceive that there is a problem here. Where our ideas cannot copy definitely their object, what does agreement with that object mean? Some idealists seem to say that they are true whenever they are what God means that we ought to think about that object. Others hold the copy-view all through, and speak as if our ideas possessed truth just in proportion as they approach to being copies of the Absolute's eternal way of thinking.

These views, you see, invite pragmatistic discussion. But the great assumption of the intellectualists is that truth means essentially an inert static relation. When you've got your true idea of anything, there's an end of the matter. You're in possession; you KNOW; you have fulfilled your thinking destiny. You are where you ought to be mentally; you have obeyed your categorical imperative; and nothing more need follow on that climax of your rational destiny. Epistemologically you are in stable equilibrium.

Pragmatism, on the other hand, asks its usual question. "Grant an idea or belief to be true," it says, "what concrete difference will its being true make in anyone's actual life? How will the truth be realized? What experiences will be different from those which would obtain if the belief were false? What, in short, is the truth's cash-value in experiential terms?"

The moment pragmatism asks this question, it sees the answer: TRUE IDEAS ARE THOSE THAT WE CAN ASSIMILATE, VALIDATE, CORROBORATE AND VERIFY. FALSE IDEAS ARE THOSE THAT WE CANNOT. That is the practical difference it makes to us to have true ideas; that, therefore, is the meaning of truth, for it is all that truth is known-as.

This thesis is what I have to defend. The truth of an idea is not a stagnant property inherent in it. Truth HAPPENS to an idea. It BECOMES true, is MADE true by events. Its verity is in fact an event, a process: the process namely of its verifying itself, its veri-FICATION. Its validity is the process of its valid-ATION.

But what do the words verification and validation themselves pragmatically mean? They again signify certain practical consequences of the verified and validated idea. It is hard to find any one phrase that characterizes these consequences better than the ordinary agreement-formula—just such consequences being what we have in mind whenever we say that our ideas 'agree' with reality. They lead us, namely, through the acts and other ideas which they instigate, into or up to, or towards, other parts of experience with which we feel all the while-such feeling being among our potentialities—that the original ideas remain in agreement. The connexions and transitions come to us from point to point as being progressive, harmonious, satisfactory. This function of agreeable leading is what we mean by an idea's verification. Such an account is vague and it sounds at first quite trivial, but it has results which it will take the rest of my hour to explain.

Let me begin by reminding you of the fact that the possession of true thoughts means everywhere the possession of invaluable instruments of action; and that our duty to gain truth, so far from being a blank command from out of the blue, or a 'stunt' self-imposed by our intellect, can account for itself by excellent practical reasons.

The importance to human life of having true beliefs about matters of fact is a thing too notorious. We live in a world of realities that can be infinitely useful or infinitely harmful. Ideas that tell us which of them to expect count as the true ideas in all this primary sphere of verification, and the pursuit of such ideas is a primary human duty. The possession of truth, so far from being here an end in itself, is only a preliminary means towards other vital satisfactions. If I am lost in the woods and starved, and find what looks like a cow-path, it is of the utmost importance that I should think of a human habitation at the end of it, for if I do so and follow it, I save myself. The true thought is useful here because the house which is its object is useful. The practical value of true ideas is thus primarily derived from the practical importance of their objects to us. Their objects are, indeed, not important at all times. I may on another occasion have no use for the house; and then my idea of it, however verifiable, will be practically irrelevant, and had better remain latent. Yet since almost any object may some day become temporarily important, the advantage of having a general stock of extra truths, of ideas that shall be true of merely possible situations, is obvious. We store such extra truths away in our memories, and with the overflow we fill our books of reference. Whenever such an extra truth becomes practically relevant to one of our emergencies, it passes from cold-storage to do work in the world, and our belief in it grows active. You can say of it then either that 'it is useful because it is true' or that 'it is true because it is useful.' Both these phrases mean exactly the same thing, namely that here is an idea that gets fulfilled and can be verified. True is the name for whatever idea starts the verification-process, useful is the name for its completed function in experience. True ideas would never have been singled out as such, would never have acquired a class-name, least of all a name suggesting value, unless they had been useful from the outset in this way.

From this simple cue pragmatism gets her general notion of truth as something essentially bound up with the way in which one moment in our experience may lead us towards other moments which it will be worth while to have been led to. Primarily, and on the common-sense level, the truth of a state of mind means this function of A LEADING THAT IS WORTH WHILE. When a moment in our experience, of any kind whatever, inspires us with a thought that is true, that means that sooner or later we dip by that thought's guidance into the particulars of experience again and make advantageous connexion with them. This is a vague enough statement, but I beg you to retain it, for it is essential.

Our experience meanwhile is all shot through with regularities. One bit of it can warn us to get ready for another bit, can 'intend' or be 'significant of' that remoter object. The object's advent is the significance's verification. Truth, in these cases, meaning nothing but eventual verification, is manifestly incompatible with waywardness on our part. Woe to him whose beliefs play fast and loose with the order which realities follow in his experience: they will lead him nowhere or else make false connexions.

By 'realities' or 'objects' here, we mean either things of common sense, sensibly present, or else common-sense relations, such as dates, places, distances, kinds, activities. Following our mental image of a house along the cow-path, we actually come to see the house; we get the image's full verification. SUCH SIMPLY AND FULLY VERIFIED LEADINGS ARE CERTAINLY THE ORIGINALS AND PROTOTYPES OF THE TRUTH-PROCESS. Experience offers indeed other forms of truth-process, but they are all conceivable as being primary verifications arrested, multiplied or substituted one for another.

Take, for instance, yonder object on the wall. You and I consider it to be a 'clock,' altho no one of us has seen the hidden works that make it one. We let our notion pass for true without attempting to verify. If truths mean verification-process essentially, ought we then to call such unverified truths as this abortive? No, for they form the overwhelmingly large number of the truths we live by. Indirect as well as direct verifications pass muster. Where circumstantial evidence is sufficient, we can go without eye-witnessing. Just as we here assume Japan to exist without ever having been there, because it WORKS to do so, everything we know conspiring with the belief, and nothing interfering, so we assume that thing to be a clock. We USE it as a clock, regulating the length of our lecture by it. The verification of the assumption here means its leading to no frustration or contradiction. VerifiABILITY of wheels and weights and pendulum is as good as verification. For one truth-process completed there are a million in our lives that function in this state of nascency. They turn us TOWARDS direct verification; lead us into the SURROUNDINGS of the objects they envisage; and then, if everything runs on harmoniously, we are so sure that verification is possible that we omit it, and are usually justified by all that happens.

Truth lives, in fact, for the most part on a credit system. Our thoughts and beliefs 'pass,' so long as nothing challenges them, just as bank-notes pass so long as nobody refuses them. But this all points to direct face-to-face verifications somewhere, without which the fabric of truth collapses like a financial system with no cash- basis whatever. You accept my verification of one thing, I yours of another. We trade on each other's truth. But beliefs verified concretely by SOMEBODY are the posts of the whole superstructure.

Another great reason—beside economy of time—for waiving complete verification in the usual business of life is that all things exist in kinds and not singly. Our world is found once for all to have that peculiarity. So that when we have once directly verified our ideas about one specimen of a kind, we consider ourselves free to apply them to other specimens without verification. A mind that habitually discerns the kind of thing before it, and acts by the law of the kind immediately, without pausing to verify, will be a 'true' mind in ninety-nine out of a hundred emergencies, proved so by its conduct fitting everything it meets, and getting no refutation.

INDIRECTLY OR ONLY POTENTIALLY VERIFYING PROCESSES MAY THUS BE TRUE AS WELL AS FULL VERIFICATION-PROCESSES. They work as true processes would work, give us the same advantages, and claim our recognition for the same reasons. All this on the common-sense level of, matters of fact, which we are alone considering.

CHAPTER XIII.

KNOWLEDGE, ERROR, AND PROBABLE OPINION

The question as to what we mean by truth and falsehood, which we considered in the preceding chapter, is of much less interest than the question as to how we can know what is true and what is false. This question will occupy us in the present chapter. There can be no doubt that *some* of our beliefs are erroneous; thus we are led to inquire what certainty we can ever have that such and such a belief is not erroneous. In other words, can we ever *know* anything at all, or do we merely sometimes by good luck believe what is true? Before we can attack this question, we must, however, first decide what we mean by 'knowing', and this question is not so easy as might be supposed.

At first sight we might imagine that knowledge could be defined as 'true belief'. When what we believe is true, it might be supposed that we had achieved a knowledge of what we believe. But this would not accord with the way in which the word is commonly used. To take a very trivial instance: If a man believes that the late Prime Minister's last name began with a B, he believes what is true, since the late Prime Minister was Sir Henry Campbell Bannerman. But if he believes that Mr. Balfour was the late Prime Minister, he will still believe that the late Prime Minister's last name began with a B, yet this belief, though true, would not be thought to constitute knowledge. If a newspaper, by an intelligent anticipation, announces the result of a battle before any telegram giving the result has been received, it may by good fortune announce what afterwards turns out to be the right result, and it may produce belief in some of its less experienced readers. But in spite of the truth of their belief, they cannot be said to have knowledge. Thus it is clear that a true belief is not knowledge when it is deduced from a false belief. In like manner, a true belief cannot be called knowledge when it is deduced by a fallacious process of reasoning, even if the premisses from which it is deduced are true. If I know that all Greeks are men and that Socrates was a man, and I infer that Socrates was a Greek, I cannot be said to *know* that Socrates was a Greek, because, although my premisses and my conclusion are true, the conclusion does not follow from the premisses.

But are we to say that nothing is knowledge except what is validly deduced from true premisses? Obviously we cannot say this. Such a definition is at once too wide and too narrow. In the first place, it is too wide, because it is not enough that our premisses should be *true*, they must also be *known*. The man who believes that Mr. Balfour was the late Prime Minister may proceed to draw valid deductions from the true premiss that the late Prime Minister's name began with a B, but he cannot be said to *know* the conclusions reached by these deductions. Thus we shall have to amend our definition by saying that knowledge is what is validly deduced from *known* premisses. This, however, is a circular definition: it assumes that we already know what is meant by 'known premisses'. It can, therefore, at best define one sort of knowledge, the sort we call derivative, as opposed to intuitive knowledge. We may say: '*Derivative* knowledge is what is validly deduced from premisses known intuitively'. In this statement there is no formal defect, but it leaves the definition of *intuitive* knowledge still to seek.

Leaving on one side, for the moment, the question of intuitive knowledge, let us consider the above suggested definition of derivative knowledge. The chief objection to it is that it unduly limits knowledge. It constantly happens that people entertain a true belief, which has grown up in them because of some piece of intuitive knowledge from which it is capable of being validly inferred, but from which it has not, as a matter of fact, been inferred by any logical process.

Take, for example, the beliefs produced by reading. If the newspapers announce the death of the King, we are fairly well justified in believing that the King is dead, since this is the sort of announcement which would not be made if it were false. And we are quite amply justified in believing that the newspaper asserts that the King is dead. But here the intuitive knowledge upon which our belief is based is knowledge of the existence of sense-data derived from looking at the print which gives the news. This knowledge scarcely rises into consciousness, except in a person who cannot read easily. A child may be aware of the shapes of the letters, and pass gradually and painfully to a realization of their meaning. But anybody accustomed to reading passes at once to what the letters mean, and is not aware, except on reflection, that he has derived this knowledge from the sense-data called seeing the printed letters. Thus although a valid inference from the-letters to their meaning is possible, and *could* be performed by the reader, it is not in fact performed, since he does not in fact perform any operation which can be called logical inference. Yet it would be absurd to say that the reader does not *know* that the newspaper announces the King's death. We must, therefore, admit as derivative knowledge whatever is the result of intuitive knowledge even if by mere association, provided there *is* a valid logical connexion, and the person in question could become aware of this connexion by reflection. There are in fact many ways, besides logical inference, by which we pass from one belief to another: the passage from the print to its meaning illustrates these ways. These ways may be called 'psychological inference'. We shall, then, admit such psychological inference as a means of obtaining derivative knowledge, provided there is a discoverable logical inference which runs parallel to the psychological inference. This renders our definition of derivative knowledge less precise than we could wish, since the word 'discoverable' is vague: it does not tell us how much reflection may be needed in order to make the discovery. But in fact 'knowledge' is not a precise conception: it merges into 'probable opinion', as we shall see more fully in the course of the present chapter. A very precise definition, therefore, should not be sought, since any such definition must be more or less misleading.

The chief difficulty in regard to knowledge, however, does not arise over derivative knowledge, but over intuitive knowledge. So long as we are dealing with derivative knowledge, we have the test of intuitive knowledge to fall back upon. But in regard to intuitive beliefs, it is by no means easy to discover any criterion by which to distinguish some as true and others as erroneous. In this question it is scarcely possible to reach any very precise result: all our knowledge of truths is infected with some degree of doubt, and a theory which ignored this fact would be plainly wrong. Something may be done, however, to mitigate the difficulties of the question.

Our theory of truth, to begin with, supplies the possibility of distinguishing certain truths as *self-evident* in a sense which ensures infallibility. When a belief is true, we said, there is a corresponding fact, in which the several objects of the belief form a single complex. The belief is said to constitute *knowledge* of this fact, provided it fulfills those further somewhat vague conditions which we have been considering in the present chapter. But in regard to any fact, besides the knowledge constituted by belief, we may also have the kind of knowledge constituted by *perception* (taking this word in its widest possible sense). For example, if you know the hour of the sunset, you can at that hour know the fact that the sun is setting: this is knowledge of the fact by way of knowledge of *truths*; but you can also, if the weather is fine, look to the west and actually see the setting sun: you then know the same fact by the way of knowledge of *things*.

Thus in regard to any complex fact, there are, theoretically, two ways in which it may be known: (1) by means of a judgement, in which its several parts are judged to be related as they are in fact related; (2) by means of *acquaintance* with the complex fact itself, which may (in a large sense) be called perception, though it is by no means confined to objects of the senses. Now it will be observed that the second way of knowing a complex fact, the way of acquaintance, is only possible when there really is such a fact, while the first way, like all judgement, is liable to error. The second way gives us the complex whole, and is therefore only possible when its parts do actually have that relation which makes them combine to form such a complex. The first way, on the contrary, gives us the parts and the relation severally, and demands only the reality of the parts and the relation: the relation may not relate those parts in that way, and yet the judgement may occur. It will be remembered that at the end of Chapter XI we suggested that there might be two kinds of self-evidence, one giving an absolute guarantee of truth, the other only a partial guarantee. These two kinds can now be distinguished.

We may say that a truth is self-evident, in the first and most absolute sense, when we have acquaintance with the fact which corresponds to the truth. When Othello believes that Desdemona loves Cassio, the corresponding fact, if his belief were true, would be 'Desdemona's love for Cassio'. This would be a fact with which no one could have acquaintance except Desdemona; hence in the sense of self-evidence that we are considering, the truth that Desdemona loves Cassio (if it were a truth) could only be self-evident to Desdemona. All mental facts, and all facts concerning sense-data, have this same privacy: there is only one person to whom they can be self-evident in our present sense, since there is only one person who can be acquainted with the mental things or the sense-data concerned. Thus no fact about any particular existing thing can be self-evident to more than one person. On the other hand, facts about universals do not have this privacy. Many minds may be acquainted with the same universals; hence a relation between universals may be known by acquaintance to many different people. In all cases where we know by acquaintance a complex fact consisting of certain terms in a certain relation, we say that the truth that these terms are so related has the first or absolute kind of self-evidence, and in these cases the judgement that the terms are so related *must* be true. Thus this sort of self-evidence is an absolute guarantee of truth.

But although this sort of self-evidence is an absolute guarantee of truth, it does not enable us to be *absolutely* certain, in the case of any given judgement, that the judgement in question is true. Suppose we first perceive the sun shining, which is a complex fact, and thence proceed to make the judgement 'the sun is shining'. In passing from the perception to the judgement, it is necessary to analyse the given complex fact: we have to separate out 'the sun' and 'shining' as constituents of the fact. In this process it is possible to commit an error; hence even where a *fact* has the first or absolute kind of self-evidence, a judgement believed to correspond to the fact is not absolutely infallible, because it may not really correspond to the fact. But if it does correspond (in the sense explained in the preceding chapter), then it *must* be true.

The second sort of self-evidence will be that which belongs to judgements in the first instance, and is not derived from direct perception of a fact as a single complex whole. This second kind of self-evidence will have degrees, from the very highest degree down to a bare inclination in favour of the belief. Take, for example, the case of a horse trotting away from us along a hard road. At first our certainty that we hear the hoofs is complete; gradually, if we listen intently, there comes a moment when we think perhaps it was imagination or the blind upstairs or our own heartbeats; at last we become doubtful whether there was any noise at all; then we *think* we no longer hear anything, and at last we *know* we no longer hear anything. In this process, there is a continual gradation of self-evidence, from the highest degree to the least, not in the sense-data themselves, but in the judgements based on them. Or again: Suppose we are comparing two shades of colour, one blue and one green. We can be quite sure they are different shades of colour; but if the green colour is gradually altered to be more and more like the blue, becoming first a blue-green, then a greeny-blue, then blue, there will come a moment when we are doubtful whether we can see any difference, and then a moment when we know that we cannot see any difference. The same thing happens in tuning a musical instrument, or in any other case where there is a continuous gradation. Thus self-evidence of this sort is a matter of degree; and it seems plain that the higher degrees are more to be trusted than the lower degrees.

In derivative knowledge our ultimate premisses must have some degree of self-evidence, and so must their connexion with the conclusions deduced from them. Take for example a piece of reasoning in geometry. It is not enough that the axioms from which we start should be self-evident: it is necessary also that, at each step in the reasoning, the connexion of premiss and conclusion should be self-evident. In difficult reasoning, this connexion has often only a very small degree of self-evidence; hence errors of reasoning are not improbable where the difficulty is great.

From what has been said it is evident that, both as regards intuitive knowledge and as regards derivative knowledge, if we assume that intuitive knowledge is trustworthy in proportion to the degree of its self-evidence, there will be a gradation in trustworthiness, from the existence of noteworthy sense-data and the simpler truths of logic and arithmetic, which may be taken as quite certain, down to judgements which seem only just more probable than their opposites. What we firmly believe, if it is true, is called *knowledge*, provided it is either intuitive or inferred (logically or psychologically) from intuitive knowledge from which it follows logically. What we firmly believe, if it is not true, is called *error*. What we firmly believe, if it is neither knowledge nor error, and also what we believe hesitatingly, because it is, or is derived from, something which has not the highest degree of self-evidence, may be called *probable opinion*. Thus the greater part of what would commonly pass as knowledge is more or less probable opinion.

In regard to probable opinion, we can derive great assistance from *coherence*, which we rejected as the *definition* of truth, but may often use as a *criterion*. A body of individually probable opinions, if they are mutually coherent, become more probable than any one of them would be individually. It is in this way that many scientific hypotheses acquire their probability. They fit into a coherent system of probable opinions, and thus become more probable than they would be in isolation. The same thing applies to general philosophical hypotheses. Often in a single case such hypotheses may seem highly doubtful, while yet, when we consider the order and coherence which they introduce into a mass of probable opinion, they become pretty nearly certain. This applies, in particular, to such matters as the distinction between dreams and waking life. If our dreams, night after night, were as coherent one with another as our days, we should hardly know whether to believe the dreams or the waking life. As it is, the test of coherence condemns the dreams and confirms the waking life. But this test, though it increases probability where it is successful, never gives absolute certainty, unless there is certainty already at some point in the coherent system. Thus the mere organization of probable opinion will never, by itself, transform it into indubitable knowledge.

John Locke (1632 - - 1704) is one of the earliest of the British Empiricists, a tradition that includes Berkeley and Hume as well. He wrote political philosophy as well as epistemology, and is often cited by defenders of property rights.

He disagrees with Descartes substantively, in that he denies that we can have any knowledge that isn't based on experience. He also differs from Descartes temperamentally, in that he is less concerned with proving that we can have certain knowledge, and more concerned with discovering what degree of knowledge we do in fact have, and becoming comfortable with whatever limitations to human knowledge there might be.

He differs from Russell in one important respect: where Russell says that "the greater part of what would commonly pass as knowledge is more or less probable opinion," Locke seems to think that all of what we call knowledge is merely probable opinion, and that this is a perfectly satisfactory state of affairs.

John Locke

From

An ESSAY CONCERNING HUMAN UNDERSTANDING, INTRODUCTION.

1. An Inquiry into the Understanding pleasant and useful.

Since it is the UNDERSTANDING that sets man above the rest of sensible beings, and gives him all the advantage and dominion which he has over them; it is certainly a subject, even for its nobleness, worth our labour to inquire into. The understanding, like the eye, whilst it makes us see and perceive all other things, takes no notice of itself; and it requires and art and pains to set it at a distance and make it its own object. But whatever be the difficulties that lie in the way of this inquiry; whatever it be that keeps us so much in the dark to ourselves; sure I am that all the light we can let in upon our minds, all the acquaintance we can make with our own understandings, will not only be very pleasant, but bring us great advantage, in directing our thoughts in the search of other things.

2. Design.

This, therefore, being my purpose—to inquire into the original, certainty, and extent of HUMAN KNOWLEDGE, together with the grounds and degrees of BELIEF, OPINION, and ASSENT; —I shall not at present meddle with the physical consideration of the mind; or trouble myself to examine wherein its essence consists; or by what motions of our spirits or alterations of our bodies we come to have any SENSATION by our organs, or any IDEAS in our understandings; and whether those ideas do in their formation, any or all of them, depend on matter or not.

These are speculations which, however curious and entertaining, I shall decline, as lying out of my way in the design I am now upon. It shall suffice to my present purpose, to consider the discerning faculties of a man, as they are employed about the objects which they have to do with. And I shall imagine I have not wholly misemployed myself in the thoughts I shall have on this occasion, if, in this historical, plain method, I can give any account of the ways whereby our understandings come to attain those notions of things we have; and can set down any measures of the certainty of our knowledge; or the grounds of those persuasions which are to be found amongst men, so various, different, and wholly contradictory; and yet asserted somewhere or other with such assurance and confidence, that he that shall take a view of the opinions of mankind, observe their opposition, and at the same time consider the fondness and devotion wherewith they are embraced, the resolution and eagerness wherewith they are maintained, may perhaps have reason to suspect, that either there is no such thing as truth at all, or that mankind hath no sufficient means to attain a certain knowledge of it.

3. Method.

It is therefore worth while to search out the bounds between opinion and knowledge; and examine by what measures, in things whereof we have no certain knowledge, we ought to regulate our assent and moderate our persuasion. In order whereunto I shall pursue this following method:— First, I shall inquire into the original of those ideas, notions, or whatever else you please to call them, which a man observes, and is conscious to himself he has in his mind; and the ways whereby the understanding comes to be furnished with them.

Secondly, I shall endeavour to show what knowledge the understanding hath by those ideas; and the certainty, evidence, and extent of it.

Thirdly, I shall make some inquiry into the nature and grounds of FAITH or OPINION: whereby I mean that assent which we give to any proposition as true, of whose truth yet we have no certain knowledge. And here we shall have occasion to examine the reasons and degrees of ASSENT.

4. Useful to know the Extent of our Comprehension.

If by this inquiry into the nature of the understanding, I can discover the powers thereof; how far they reach; to what things they are in any degree proportionate; and where they fail us, I suppose it may be of use to prevail with the busy mind of man to be more cautious in meddling with things exceeding its comprehension; to stop when it is at the utmost extent of its tether; and to sit down in a quiet ignorance of those things which, upon examination, are found to be beyond the reach of our capacities. We should not then perhaps be so forward, out of an affectation of an universal knowledge, to raise questions, and perplex ourselves and others with disputes about things to which our understandings are not suited; and of which we cannot frame in our minds any clear or distinct perceptions, or whereof (as it has perhaps too often happened) we have not any notions at all. If we can find out how far the understanding can extend its view; how far it has faculties to attain certainty; and in what cases it can only judge and guess, we may learn to content ourselves with what is attainable by us in this state.

5. Our Capacity suited to our State and Concerns.

For though the comprehension of our understandings comes exceeding short of the vast extent of things, yet we shall have cause enough to magnify the bountiful Author of our being, for that proportion and degree of knowledge he has bestowed on us, so far above all the rest of the inhabitants of this our mansion. Men have reason to be well satisfied with what God hath thought fit for them, since he hath given them (as St. Peter says) [words in Greek], whatsoever is necessary for the conveniences of life and information of virtue; and has put within the reach of their discovery, the comfortable provision for this life, and the way that leads to a better. How short soever their knowledge may come of an universal or perfect comprehension of whatsoever is, it yet secures their great concernments, that they have light enough to lead them to the knowledge of their Maker, and the sight of their own duties. Men may find matter sufficient to busy their heads, and employ their hands with variety, delight, and satisfaction, if they will not boldly quarrel with their own constitution, and throw away the blessings their hands are filled with, because they are not big enough to grasp everything. We shall not have much reason to complain of the narrowness of our minds, if we will but employ them about what may be of use to us; for of that they are very capable. And it will be an unpardonable, as well as childish peevishness, if we undervalue the advantages of our knowledge, and neglect to improve it to the ends for which it was given us, because there are some things that are set out of the reach of it. It will be no excuse to an idle and untoward servant, who would not attend his business by candle light, to plead that he had not broad sunshine. The Candle that is set up in us shines bright enough for all our purposes. The discoveries we can make with this ought to satisfy us; and we shall then use our understandings right, when we entertain all objects in that way and proportion that they are suited to our faculties, and upon those grounds they are capable of being proposed to us; and not peremptorily or intemperately require demonstration, and demand certainty, where probability only is to be had, and which is sufficient to govern all our concernments. If we will disbelieve everything, because we cannot certainly know all things, we shall do much what as wisely as he who would not use his legs, but sit still and perish, because he had no wings to fly.

6. Knowledge of our Capacity a Cure of Scepticism and Idleness.

When we know our own strength, we shall the better know what to undertake with hopes of success; and when we have well surveyed the POWERS of our own minds, and made some estimate what we may expect from them, we shall not be inclined either to sit still, and not set our thoughts on work at all, in despair of knowing anything; nor on the other side, question everything, and disclaim all knowledge, because some things are not to be understood. It is of great use to the sailor to know the length of his line, though he cannot with it fathom all the depths of the ocean. It is well he knows that it is long enough to reach the bottom, at such places as are necessary to direct his voyage, and caution him against running upon shoals that may ruin him. Our business here is not to know all things, but those which concern our conduct. If we can find out those measures, whereby a rational creature, put in that state in which man is in this world, may and ought to govern his opinions, and actions depending thereon, we need not to be troubled that some other things escape our knowledge.

7. Occasion of this Essay.

This was that which gave the first rise to this Essay concerning the understanding. For I thought that the first step towards satisfying several inquiries the mind of man was very apt to run into, was, to take a survey of our own understandings, examine our own powers, and see to what things they were adapted. Till that was done I suspected we began at the wrong end, and in vain sought for satisfaction in a quiet and sure possession of truths that most concerned us, whilst we let loose our thoughts into the vast ocean of Being; as if all that boundless extent were the natural and undoubted possession of our understandings, wherein there was nothing exempt from its decisions, or that escaped its comprehension. Thus men, extending their inquiries beyond their capacities, and letting their thoughts wander into those depths where they can find no sure footing, it is no wonder that they raise questions and multiply disputes, which, never coming to any clear resolution, are proper only to continue and increase their doubts, and to confirm them at last in perfect scepticism. Whereas, were the capacities of our understandings well considered, the extent of our knowledge once discovered, and the horizon found which sets the bounds between the enlightened and dark parts of things;

between what is and what is not comprehensible by us, men would perhaps with less scruple acquiesce in the avowed ignorance of the one, and employ their thoughts and discourse with more advantage and satisfaction in the other.

CHAPTER XIV.

THE LIMITS OF PHILOSOPHICAL KNOWLEDGE

In all that we have said hitherto concerning philosophy, we have scarcely touched on many matters that occupy a great space in the writings of most philosophers. Most philosophers--or, at any rate, very many--profess to be able to prove, by *a priori* metaphysical reasoning, such things as the fundamental dogmas of religion, the essential rationality of the universe, the illusoriness of matter, the unreality of all evil, and so on. There can be no doubt that the hope of finding reason to believe such theses as these has been the chief inspiration of many life-long students of philosophy. This hope, I believe, is vain. It would seem that knowledge concerning the universe as a whole is not to be obtained by metaphysics, and that the proposed proofs that, in virtue of the laws of logic such and such things *must* exist and such and such others cannot, are not capable of surviving a critical scrutiny. In this chapter we shall briefly consider the kind of way in which such reasoning is attempted, with a view to discovering whether we can hope that it may be valid.

The great representative, in modern times, of the kind of view which we wish to examine, was Hegel (1770-1831). Hegel's philosophy is very difficult, and commentators differ as to the true interpretation of it. According to the interpretation I shall adopt, which is that of many, if not most, of the commentators and has the merit of giving an interesting and important type of philosophy, his main thesis is that everything short of the Whole is obviously fragmentary, and obviously incapable of existing without the complement supplied by the rest of the world. Just as a comparative anatomist, from a single bone, sees what kind of animal the whole must have been, so the metaphysician, according to Hegel, sees, from any one piece of reality, what the whole of reality must be--at least in its large outlines. Every apparently separate piece of reality has, as it were, hooks which grapple it to the next piece; the next piece, in turn, has fresh hooks, and so on, until the whole universe is reconstructed. This essential incompleteness appears, according to Hegel, equally in the world of thought and in the world of things. In the world of thought, if we take any idea which is abstract or incomplete, we find, on examination, that if we forget its incompleteness, we become involved in contradictions; these contradictions turn the idea in question into its opposite, or antithesis; and in order to escape, we have to find a new, less incomplete idea, which is the synthesis of our original idea and its antithesis. This new idea, though less incomplete than the idea we started with, will be found, nevertheless, to be still not wholly complete, but to pass into its antithesis, with which it must be combined in a new synthesis. In this way Hegel advances until he reaches the 'Absolute Idea', which, according to him, has no incompleteness, no opposite, and no need of further development. The Absolute Idea, therefore, is adequate to describe Absolute Reality; but all lower ideas only describe reality as it appears to a partial view, not as it is to one who simultaneously surveys the Whole. Thus Hegel reaches the conclusion that Absolute Reality forms one single harmonious system, not in space or time, not in any degree evil, wholly rational, and wholly spiritual. Any appearance to the contrary, in the world we know, can be proved logically--so he believes--to be entirely due to our fragmentary piecemeal view of the universe. If we saw the universe whole, as we may suppose God sees it, space and time and matter and evil and all striving and struggling would disappear, and we should see instead an eternal perfect unchanging spiritual unity. In this conception, there is undeniably something sublime, something to which we could wish to yield assent. Nevertheless, when the arguments in support of it are carefully examined, they appear to involve much confusion and many unwarrantable assumptions. The fundamental tenet upon which the system is built up is that what is incomplete must be not self-subsistent, but must need the support of other things before it can exist. It is held that whatever has relations to things outside itself must contain some reference to those outside things in its own nature, and could not, therefore, be what it is if those outside things did not exist. A man's nature, for example, is constituted by his memories and the rest of his knowledge, by his loves and hatreds, and so on; thus, but for the objects which he knows or loves or hates, he could not be what he is. He is essentially and obviously a fragment: taken as the sum-total of reality he would be self-contradictory.

This whole point of view, however, turns upon the notion of the 'nature' of a thing, which seems to mean 'all the truths about the thing'. It is of course the case that a truth which connects one thing with another thing could not subsist if the other thing did not subsist. But a truth about a thing is not part of the thing itself, although it must, according to the above usage, be part of the 'nature' of the thing. If we mean by a thing's 'nature' all the truths about the thing, then plainly we cannot know a thing's 'nature' unless we know all the thing's relations to all the other things in the universe. But if the word 'nature' is used in this sense, we shall have to hold that the thing may be known when its 'nature' is not known, or at any rate is not known completely. There is a confusion, when this use of the word 'nature' is employed, between knowledge of things and knowledge of truths. We may have knowledge of a thing by acquaintance even if we know very few propositions about it--theoretically we need not know any propositions about it. Thus, acquaintance with a thing does not involve knowledge of its 'nature' in the above sense. And although acquaintance with a thing is involved in our knowing any one proposition about a thing, knowledge of its 'nature', in the above sense, is not involved. Hence, (1) acquaintance with a thing does not logically involve a knowledge of its relations, and (2) a knowledge of some of its relations does not involve a knowledge of all of its relations nor a knowledge of its 'nature' in the above sense. I may be acquainted, for example, with my toothache, and this knowledge may be as complete as knowledge by acquaintance ever can be, without knowing all that the dentist (who is not acquainted with it) can tell me about its cause, and without therefore knowing its 'nature' in the above sense. Thus the fact that a thing has relations does not prove that its relations are logically necessary. That is to say, from the mere fact that it is the thing it is we cannot deduce that it must have the various relations which in fact it has. This only *seems* to follow because we know it already.

It follows that we cannot prove that the universe as a whole forms a single harmonious system such as Hegel believes that it forms. And if we cannot prove this, we also cannot prove the unreality of space and time and matter and evil, for this is deduced by Hegel from the fragmentary and relational character of these things. Thus we are left to the piecemeal investigation of the world, and are unable to know the characters of those parts of the universe that are remote from our experience. This result, disappointing as it is to those whose hopes have been raised by the systems of philosophers, is in harmony with the inductive and scientific temper of our age, and is borne out by the whole examination of human knowledge which has occupied our previous chapters. Most of the great ambitious attempts of metaphysicians have proceeded by the attempt to prove that such and such apparent features of the actual world were self-contradictory, and therefore could not be real. The whole tendency of modern thought, however, is more and more in the direction of showing that the supposed contradictions were illusory, and that very little can be proved *a priori* from considerations of what *must* be. A good illustration of this is afforded by space and time. Space and time appear to be infinite in extent, and infinitely divisible. If we travel along a straight line in either direction, it is difficult to believe that we shall finally reach a last point, beyond which there is nothing, not even empty space. Similarly, if in imagination we travel backwards or forwards in time, it is difficult to believe that we shall reach a first or last time, with not even empty time beyond it. Thus space and time appear to be infinite in extent.

Again, if we take any two points on a line, it seems evident that there must be other points between them however small the distance between them may be: every distance can be halved, and the halves can be halved again, and so on *ad infinitum*. In time, similarly, however little time may elapse between two moments, it seems evident that there will be other moments between them. Thus space and time appear to be infinitely divisible. But as against these apparent facts--infinite extent and infinite divisibility--philosophers have advanced arguments tending to show that there could be no infinite collections of things, and that therefore the number of points in space, or of instants in time, must be finite. Thus a contradiction emerged between the apparent nature of space and time and the supposed impossibility of infinite collections.

Kant, who first emphasized this contradiction, deduced the impossibility of space and time, which he declared to be merely subjective; and since his time very many philosophers have believed that space and time are mere appearance, not characteristic of the world as it really is. Now, however, owing to the labours of the mathematicians, notably Georg Cantor, it has appeared that the impossibility of infinite collections was a mistake. They are not in fact self-contradictory, but only contradictory of certain rather obstinate mental prejudices. Hence the reasons for regarding space and time as unreal have become inoperative, and one of the great sources of metaphysical constructions is dried up.

The mathematicians, however, have not been content with showing that space as it is commonly supposed to be is possible; they have shown also that many other forms of space are equally possible, so far as logic can show. Some of Euclid's axioms, which appear to common sense to be necessary, and were formerly supposed to be necessary by philosophers, are now known to derive their appearance of necessity from our mere familiarity with actual space, and not from any *a priori* logical foundation. By imagining worlds in which these axioms are false, the mathematicians have used logic to loosen the prejudices of common sense, and to show the possibility of spaces differing--some more, some less--from that in which we live. And some of these spaces differ so little from Euclidean space, where distances such as we can measure are concerned, that it is impossible to discover by observation whether our actual space is strictly Euclidean or of one of these other kinds. Thus the position is completely reversed. Formerly it appeared that experience left only one kind of space to logic, and logic showed this one kind to be impossible. Now, logic presents many kinds of space as possible apart from experience, and experience only partially decides between them. Thus, while our knowledge of what is has become less than it was formerly supposed to be, our knowledge of what may be is enormously increased. Instead of being shut in within narrow walls, of which every nook and cranny could be explored, we find ourselves in an open world of free possibilities, where much remains unknown because there is so much to know. What has happened in the case of space and time has happened, to some extent, in other directions as well. The attempt to prescribe to the universe by means of *a priori* principles has broken down; logic, instead of being, as formerly, the bar to possibilities, has become the great liberator of the imagination, presenting innumerable alternatives which are closed to unreflective common sense, and leaving to experience the task of deciding, where decision is possible, between the many worlds which logic offers for our choice. Thus knowledge as to what exists becomes limited to what we can learn from experience--not to what we can actually experience, for, as we have seen, there is much knowledge by description concerning things of which we have no direct experience. But in all cases of knowledge by description, we need some connexion of universals, enabling us, from such and such a datum, to infer an object of a certain sort as implied by our datum. Thus in regard to physical objects, for example, the principle that sense-data are signs of physical objects is itself a connexion of universals; and it is only in virtue of this principle that experience enables us to acquire knowledge concerning physical objects. The same applies to the law of causality, or, to descend to what is less general, to such principles as the law of gravitation.

Principles such as the law of gravitation are proved, or rather are rendered highly probable, by a combination of experience with some wholly *a priori* principle, such as the principle of induction. Thus our intuitive knowledge, which is the source of all our other knowledge of truths, is of two sorts: pure empirical knowledge, which tells us of the existence and some of the properties of particular things with which we are acquainted, and pure *a priori* knowledge, which gives us connexions between universals, and enables us to draw inferences from the particular facts given in empirical knowledge. Our derivative knowledge always depends upon some pure *a priori* knowledge and usually also depends upon some pure empirical knowledge.

Philosophical knowledge, if what has been said above is true, does not differ essentially from scientific knowledge; there is no special source of wisdom which is open to philosophy but not to science, and the results obtained by philosophy are not radically different from those obtained from science. The essential characteristic of philosophy, which makes it a study distinct from science, is criticism. It examines critically the principles employed in science and in daily life; it searches out any inconsistencies there may be in these principles, and it only accepts them when, as the result of a critical inquiry, no reason for rejecting them has appeared. If, as many philosophers have believed, the principles underlying the sciences were capable, when disengaged from irrelevant detail, of giving us knowledge concerning the universe as a whole, such knowledge would have the same claim on our belief as scientific knowledge has; but our inquiry has not revealed any such knowledge, and therefore, as regards the special doctrines of the bolder metaphysicians, has had a mainly negative result. But as regards what would be commonly accepted as knowledge, our result is in the main positive: we have seldom found reason to reject such knowledge as the result of our criticism, and we have seen no reason to suppose man incapable of the kind of knowledge which he is generally believed to possess. When, however, we speak of philosophy as a *criticism* of knowledge, it is necessary to impose a certain limitation. If we adopt the attitude of the complete sceptic, placing ourselves wholly outside all knowledge, and asking, from this outside position, to be compelled to return within the circle of knowledge, we are demanding what is impossible, and our scepticism can never be refuted. For all refutation must begin with some piece of knowledge which the disputants share; from blank doubt, no argument can begin. Hence the criticism of knowledge which philosophy employs must not be of this destructive kind, if any result is to be achieved. Against this absolute scepticism, no *logical* argument can be advanced. But it is not difficult to see that scepticism of this kind is unreasonable. Descartes' 'methodical doubt', with which modern philosophy began, is not of this kind, but is rather the kind of criticism which we are asserting to be the essence of philosophy. His 'methodical doubt' consisted in doubting whatever seemed doubtful; in pausing, with each apparent piece of knowledge, to ask himself whether, on reflection, he could feel certain that he really knew it. This is the kind of criticism which constitutes philosophy. Some knowledge, such as knowledge of the existence of our sense-data, appears quite indubitable, however calmly and thoroughly we reflect upon it. In regard to such knowledge, philosophical criticism does not require that we should abstain from belief. But there are beliefs--such, for example, as the belief that physical objects exactly resemble our sense-data--which are entertained until we begin to reflect, but are found to melt away when subjected to a close inquiry. Such beliefs philosophy will bid us reject, unless some new line of argument is found to support them. But to reject the beliefs which do not appear open to any objections, however closely we examine them, is not reasonable, and is not what philosophy advocates.

The criticism aimed at, in a word, is not that which, without reason, determines to reject, but that which considers each piece of apparent knowledge on its merits, and retains whatever still appears to be knowledge when this consideration is completed. That some risk of error remains must be admitted, since human beings are fallible. Philosophy may claim justly that it diminishes the risk of error, and that in some cases it renders the risk so small as to be practically negligible. To do more than this is not possible in a world where mistakes must occur; and more than this no prudent advocate of philosophy would claim to have performed.

G.W.F. Hegel (1770 – 1831) is notoriously difficult to understand. His style is very different than Russell's, even at the latter's most technical. Indeed, Hegel's philosophy was often dismissed by Russell and his disciple as obscurantist nonsense. Hegel's grasp of logic was a special target of Russell's derision. However, it is impossible to deny the influence that Hegel's so-called Absolute Idealism had on subsequent schools of thought. Marxism, British and American Idealism, Existentialism, all these owe an intellectual debt to Hegel.

While it is perhaps easy to dismiss Hegel as being obscure, it can be argued that the philosophical demand for certainty will not lead to "clear and distinct ideas" as Descartes claimed, but rather to exactly the sort of complex and opaque ideas that Hegel tried to express. If the truth were easy to obtain, we would have obtained it by now. Hegel is sensitive to the difficulty of the task, and especially aware that the mind which seeks to understand the universe is itself a part of the universe it tries to understand, and that this complicates matters.

Russell gives a reasonably sympathetic reading of Hegel in Chapter XIV, and the following selection gives s sense of Hegel's style as well as his philosophical concerns.

G.W.F. Hegel

from

INTRODUCTION TO THE PHILOSOPHY OF HISTORY

The subject of this course of lectures is the Philosophical History of the World. And by this must be understood, not a collection of general observations respecting it, suggested by the study of its records and proposed to be illustrated by its facts, but universal history itself. To gain a clear idea, at the outset, of the nature of our task, it seems necessary to begin with an examination of the other methods of treating history. The various methods may be ranged under three heads:

I. Original History. II. Reflective History. III. Philosophical History.

I. Of the first kind, the mention of one or two distinguished names will furnish a definite type. To this category belong Herodotus, Thucydides, and other historians of the same order, whose descriptions are for the most part limited to deeds, events, and states of society, which they had before their eyes and whose spirit they shared. They simply transferred what was passing in the world around them to the realm of re-presentative intellect; an external phenomenon was thus translated into an internal conception. In the same way the poet operates upon the material supplied him by his emotions, projecting it into an image for the conceptive faculty.

These original historians did, it is true, find statements and narratives of other men ready to hand; one person cannot be an eye-and-ear witness of everything. But, merely as an ingredient, they make use only of such aids as the poet does of that heritage of an already-formed language to which he owes so much; historiographers bind together the fleeting elements of story, and treasure them up for immortality in the temple of Mnemosyne. Legends, ballad-stories, and traditions must be excluded from such original history; they are but dim and hazy forms of historical apprehension, and therefore belong to nations whose intelligence is but half awakened. Here, on the contrary, we have to do with people fully conscious of what they were and what they were about. The domain of reality—actually seen, or capable of being so-affords a very different basis in point of firmness from that fugitive and shadowy element in which were engendered those legends and poetic dreams whose historical prestige vanishes as soon as nations have attained a mature individuality.

Such original historians, then, change the events, the deeds, and the states of society with which they are conversant, into an object for the conceptive faculty; the narratives they leave us cannot, therefore, be very comprehensive in their range. Herodotus, Thucydides, Guicciardini, may be taken as fair samples of the class in this respect. What is present and living in their environment is their proper material. The influences that have formed the writer are identical with those which have molded the events that constitute the matter of his story. The author's spirit and that of the actions he narrates are one and the same. He describes scenes in which he himself has been an actor, or at any rate an interested spectator. It is short periods of time, individual shapes of persons and occurrences, single, unreflected traits, of which he makes his picture. And his aim is nothing more than the presentation to posterity of an image of events as clear as that which he himself possessed in virtue of personal observation, or lifelike descriptions. Reflections are none of his business, for he lives in the spirit of his subject; he has not attained an elevation above it. If, as in Cæsar's case, he belongs to the exalted rank of generals or statesmen, it is the prosecution of his own aims that constitutes the history.

Such speeches as we find in Thucydides, for example, of which we can positively assert that they are not *bona fide* reports, would seem to make against our statement that a historian of his class presents us no reflected picture, that persons and people appear in his works in *propria persona* ... Granted that such orations as those of Pericles—that most profoundly accomplished, genuine, noble statesman—were elaborated by Thucydides, it must yet be maintained that they were not foreign to the character of the speaker. In the orations in question, these men proclaim the maxims adopted by their countrymen and formative of their own character; they record their views of their political relations and of their moral and spiritual nature, and publish the principles of their designs and conduct. What the historian puts into their mouths is no supposititious system of ideas, but an uncorrupted transcript of their intellectual and moral habitudes.

Of these historians whom we must make thoroughly our own, with whom we must linger long if we would live with their respective nations and enter deeply into their spirit—of these historians to whose pages we may turn, not for the purposes of erudition merely, but with a view to deep and genuine enjoyment, there are fewer than might be imagined. Herodotus, the Father, namely the Founder, of History, and Thucydides have been already mentioned. Xenophon's *Retreat of the Ten Thousand* is a work equally original. Cæsar's *Commentaries* are the simple masterpiece of a mighty spirit; among the ancients these annalists were necessarily great captains and statesmen. In the Middle Ages, if we except the bishops, who were placed in the very centre of the political world, the monks monopolize this category as naïve chroniclers who were as decidedly isolated from active life as those elder annalists had been connected with it. In modern times the relations are entirely altered. Our culture is essentially comprehensive, and immediately changes all events into historical representations. Belonging to the class in question, we have vivid, simple, clear narrations—especially of military transactions—which might fairly take their place with those of Cæsar. In richness of matter and fulness of detail as regards strategic appliances and attendant circumstances, they are even more instructive. The French "Memoirs" also fall under this category. In many cases these are written by men of mark, though relating to affairs of little note; they not unfrequently contain such a large amount of anecdotal matter that the ground they occupy is narrow and trivial. Yet they are often veritable masterpieces in history, as are those of Cardinal Retz, which, in fact, trench on a larger historical field. In Germany such masters are rare, Frederick the Great in his *Histoire de mon temps* being an illustrious exception. Writers of this order must occupy an elevated position, for only from such a position is it possible to take an extensive view of affairs—to see everything. This is out of the question for him who from below merely gets a glimpse of the great world through a miserable cranny.

II. The second kind of history we may call the *Reflective.* It is history whose mode of representation is not really confined by the limits of the time to which it relates, but whose spirit transcends the present. In this second order a strongly marked variety of species may be distinguished.

1. It is the aim of the investigator to gain a view of the entire history of a people, of a country, or of the world in short, what we call universal history. In this case the working up of the historical material is the main point. The workman approaches his task with his own spirit—a spirit distinct from that of the element he is to manipulate.

Here a very important consideration is the principles to which the author refers the bearing and motives of the actions and events which he describes, as well as those which determine the form of his narrative. Among us Germans this reflective treatment and the display of ingenuity which it affords assume a manifold variety of phases. Every writer of history proposes to himself an original method. The English and French confess to general principles of historical composition, their viewpoint being more nearly that of cosmopolitan or national culture. Among us, each labors to invent a purely individual point of view; instead of writing history, we are always beating our brains to discover how history ought to be written.

This first kind of Reflective history is most nearly akin to the preceding, when it has no further aim than to present the annals of a country complete. Such compilations (among which may be mentioned the works of Livy, Diodorus Siculus, Johannes von Müller's *History of Switzerland*) are, if well performed, highly meritorious. Among the best of the kind may be included such annalists as approach those of the first-class writers who give so vivid a transcript of events that the reader may well fancy himself listening to contemporaries and eye-witnesses. But it often happens that the individuality of tone which must characterize a writer belonging to a different culture is not modified in accordance with the periods which such a record must traverse. The spirit of the writer may be quite apart from that of the times of which he treats. Thus Livy puts into the mouths of the old Roman kings, consuls, and generals, such orations as would be delivered by an accomplished advocate of the Livian era, and which strikingly contrast with the genuine traditions of Roman antiquity—witness, for example, the fable of Menenius Agrippa. In the same way he gives us descriptions of battles as if he had been an actual spectator; but their salient points would serve well enough for battles in any period, for their distinctness contrasts, even in his treatment of chief points of interest, with the want of connection and the inconsistency that prevail elsewhere. The difference between such a compiler and an original historian may be best seen by comparing Polybius himself with the style in which Livy uses, expands, and abridges his annals in those periods of which Polybius' account has been preserved. Johannes von Müller, in the endeavor to remain faithful in his portraiture to the times he describes, has given a stiff, formal, pedantic aspect to his history. We much prefer the narratives we find in old Tschudi; all is more naïve and natural than when appearing in the garb of a fictitious and affected archaism.

A history which aspires to traverse long periods of time, or to be universal, must indeed forego the attempt to give individual representations of the past as it actually existed. It must foreshorten its pictures by abstractions, and this includes not merely the omission of events and deeds, but whatever is involved in the fact that Thought is, after all, the most trenchant epitomist. A battle, a great victory, a siege no longer maintains its original proportions, but is put off with a mere allusion. When Livy, for instance, tells us of the war with the Volsci, we sometimes have the brief announcement: "This year war was carried on with the Volsci."

1. A second species of Reflective history is what we may call the pragmatical. When we have to deal with the past and occupy ourselves with a remote world, a present rises into being for the mind—produced by its own activity, as the reward of its labor. The occurrences are, indeed, various; but the idea which pervades them-their deeper import and connection—is one. This takes the occurrence out of the category of the past and makes it virtually present. Pragmatical (didactic) reflections, though in their nature decidedly abstract, are truly and indefeasibly of the present, and quicken the annals of the dead past with the life of today. Whether, indeed, such reflections are truly interesting and enlivening depends on the writer's own spirit. Moral reflections must here be specially noticed—the moral teaching expected from history; the latter has not infrequently been treated with a direct view to the former. It may be allowed that examples of virtue elevate the soul and are applicable in the moral instruction of children for impressing excellence upon their minds. But the destinies of people and states, their interests, relations, and the complicated tissue of their affairs, present quite another field. Rulers, statesmen, nations, are wont to be emphatically commended to the teaching which experience offers in history; yet what experience and history teach is this-that peoples and governments have never learned anything from history, nor have they acted on principles deduced from it. Each period is involved in such peculiar circumstances, exhibits a condition of things so strictly idiosyncratic, that its conduct must be regulated by

considerations connected with itself, and itself alone. Amid the pressure of great events a general principle gives no help.

It is useless to revert to similar circumstances in the past. The pallid shades of memory struggle in vain with the life and freedom of the present. Looked at in this light nothing can be shallower than the oft-repeated appeal to Greek and Roman examples during the French Revolution; nothing is more diverse than the genius of those nations and that of our times. Johannes von Müller, in his *Universal History* as also in his *History of Switzerland*, had such moral aims in view. He designed to prepare a body of political doctrines for the instruction of princes, governments, and peoples (he formed a special collection of doctrines and reflections, frequently giving us in his correspondence the exact number of apothegms which he had compiled in a week); but he cannot assert that this part of his labor was among the best he accomplished. It is only a thorough, liberal, comprehensive view of historical relations (such for instance, as we find in Montesquieu's *L'Esprit des Lois*) that can give truth and interest to reflections of this order. One Reflective history, therefore, supersedes another. The materials are patent to every writer; each is prone to believe himself capable of arranging and manipulating them, and we may expect that each will insist upon his own spirit as that of the age in question. Disgusted by such reflective histories, readers have often returned with pleasure to narratives adopting no particular point of view—which certainly have their value, although, for the most part, they offer only material for history. We Germans are content with such; but the French, on the other hand, display great genius in reanimating bygone times and in bringing the past to bear upon the present condition of things.

2. The third form of Reflective history is the *Critical*. This deserves mention as preeminently the mode, now current in Germany, of treating history. It is not history itself that is here presented. We might more properly designate it as a History of History—a criticism of historical narratives and an investigation

of their truth and credibility. Its peculiarity, in point of fact as well as intention, consists in the acuteness with which the writer extorts from the records something which was not in the matters recorded. The French have given us much that is profound and judicious in this class of composition, but have not endeavored to make a merely critical procedure pass for substantial history; their judgments have been duly presented in the form of critical treatises. Among us, the so-called "higher criticism," which reigns supreme in the domain of philology, has also taken possession of our historical literature; it has been the pretext for introducing all the anti-historical monstrosities that a vain imagination could suggest. Here we have the other method of making the past a living reality; for historical data subjective fancies are substituted, whose merit is measured by their boldness—that is, the scantiness of the particulars on which they are based and the peremptoriness with which they contravene the best established facts of history.

3. The last species of Reflective history announces its fragmentary character on its very face. It adopts an abstract position; yet, since it takes general points of view (such, for instance, as the History of Art, of Law, of Religion), it forms a transition to the Philosophical History of the World. In our time this form of the history of ideas has been especially developed and made prominent. Such branches of national life stand in close relation to the entire complex of a people's annals; and the question of chief importance in relation to our subject is, whether the connection of the whole is exhibited in its truth and reality, or is referred to merely external relations. In the latter case, these important phenomena (art, law, religion, etc.), appear as purely accidental national peculiarities. It must be remarked, if the position taken is a true one, that when Reflective history has advanced to the adoption of general points of view, these are found to constitute not a merely external thread, a superficial series, but are the inward guiding soul of the occurrences and actions that occupy a nation's annals. For, like the soul-conductor, Mercury, the Idea is, in truth, the leader of peoples and of the world; and Spirit, the rational and necessitated will of that

conductor, is and has been the director of the events of the world's history. To become acquainted with Spirit in this, its office of guidance, is the object of our present undertaking.

III. The third kind of history is the *Philosophical*. No explanation was needed of the two previous classes; their nature was self-evident. It is otherwise with the last, which certainly seems to require an exposition or justification. The most general definition that can be given is, that the philosophy of history means nothing but the thoughtful consideration of it. Thought is, indeed, essential to humanity. It is this that distinguishes us from the brutes. In sensation, cognition, and intellection, in our instincts and volitions, as far as they are truly human, thought is a constant element. To insist upon thought in this connection with history may, however, appear unsatisfactory. In this science it would seem as if thought must be subordinate to what is given, to the realities of fact—that this is its basis and guide; while philosophy dwells in the region of self-produced ideas, without reference to actuality. Approaching history thus prepossessed, speculation might be supposed to treat it as a mere passive material, and, so far from leaving it in its native truth, to force it into conformity with a tyrannous idea, and to construe it, as the phrase is, *a priori*. But as it is the business of history simply to adopt into its records what is and has been-actual occurrences and transactions; and since it remains true to its character in proportion as it strictly adheres to its data, we seem to have in philosophy a process diametrically opposed to that of the historiographer. This contradiction, and the charge consequently brought against speculation, shall be explained and confuted. We do not, however, propose to correct the innumerable special misrepresentations, whether trite or novel, that are current respecting the aims, the interests, and the modes of treating history and its relation to philosophy.

The only thought which philosophy brings with it to the contemplation of history, is the simple conception of Reason; that Reason is the sovereign of the world; that the history of the world, therefore, presents us with a rational process. This conviction and intuition is a hypothesis in the domain of history as such; in that of philosophy it is no hypothesis. It is there proved by speculative cognition that Reason—and this term may here suffice us, without investigating the relation sustained by the universe to the Divine Being—is substance, as well as Infinite Power; its own Infinite Material is that underlying all the natural and spiritual life which it originates, as also the Infinite Form—that which sets this material in motion. On the one hand, Reason is the substance of the universe—viz., that by which and in which all reality has its being and subsistence. On the other hand, it is the infinite energy of the universe; since Reason is not so powerless as to be incapable of producing anything but a mere ideal, a mere intention—having its place outside reality, nobody knows where; something separate and abstract in the heads of certain human beings. It is the *infinite complex of things*, their entire essence and truth. It is its own material which it commits to its own active energy to work up—not needing, as finite action does, the conditions of an external material of given means from which it may obtain its support and the objects of its activity. It supplies its own nourishment and is the object of its own operations. While it is exclusively its own basis of existence and absolute final aim, it is also the energizing power realizing this aim, developing it not only in the phenomena of the natural, but also of the spiritual universe—the history of the world. That this "Idea" or "Reason" is the *true*, the *eternal*, the absolutely *powerful* essence; that it reveals itself in the world, and that in that world nothing else is revealed but this and its honor and glory—is the thesis which, as we have said, has been proved in philosophy and is here regarded as demonstrated.

In entering upon this course of lectures, I may fairly presume, at least, the existence in those of my hearers who are not acquainted with philosophy, of a belief in Reason, a desire, a thirst for acquaintance with it. It is, in fact, the wish for rational insight, not the ambition to amass a mere heap of acquirements, that should be presupposed in every case as possessing the mind of the learner in the study of science. If the clear idea of Reason is not already developed in our minds, in beginning the study of universal history, we should at least have the firm, unconquerable faith that Reason does exist there, and that the world of intelligence and conscious volition is not abandoned to chance, but must show itself in the light of the self-cognizant Idea. Yet I am not obliged to make such a preliminary demand upon your faith. What I have said thus provisionally, and what I shall have further to say, is, even in reference to our branch of science, not to be regarded as hypothetical, but as a summary view of the whole, the result of the investigation we are about to pursue—a result which happens to be known to *me*, because I have traversed the entire field. It is only an inference from the history of the world that its development has been a rational process, that the history in question has constituted the rational necessary course of the World-Spirit—that Spirit whose nature is always one and the same, but which unfolds this, its one nature, in the phenomena of the world's existence. This must, as before stated, present itself as the ultimate result of history; but we have to take the latter as it is. We must proceed historically—empirically. Among other precautions we must take care not to be misled by professed historians who (especially among the Germans, and those enjoying a considerable authority) are chargeable with the very procedure of which they accuse the philosopher—introducing *a priori* inventions of their own into the records of the past. It is, for example, a widely current fiction that there was an original primeval people, taught directly by God, endowed with perfect insight and wisdom, possessing a thorough knowledge of all natural laws and spiritual truth; that there have been such or such sacerdotal peoples; or, to mention a more specific claim, that there was a Roman Epos, from which the Roman historians derived the early annals of their city, etc....

CHAPTER XV.

THE VALUE OF PHILOSOPHY

Having now come to the end of our brief and very incomplete review of the problems of philosophy, it will be well to consider, in conclusion, what is the value of philosophy and why it ought to be studied. It is the more necessary to consider this question, in view of the fact that many men, under the influence of science or of practical affairs, are inclined to doubt whether philosophy is anything better than innocent but useless trifling, hair-splitting distinctions, and controversies on matters concerning which knowledge is impossible. This view of philosophy appears to result, partly from a wrong conception of the ends of life, partly from a wrong conception of the kind of goods which philosophy strives to achieve. Physical science, through the medium of inventions, is useful to innumerable people who are wholly ignorant of it; thus the study of physical science is to be recommended, not only, or primarily, because of the effect on the student, but rather because of the effect on mankind in general. Thus utility does not belong to philosophy. If the study of philosophy has any value at all for others than students of philosophy, it must be only indirectly, through its effects upon the lives of those who study it. It is in these effects, therefore, if anywhere, that the value of philosophy must be primarily sought.

But further, if we are not to fail in our endeavour to determine the value of philosophy, we must first free our minds from the prejudices of what are wrongly called 'practical' men. The 'practical' man, as this word is often used, is one who recognizes only material needs, who realizes that men must have food for the body, but is oblivious of the necessity of providing food for the mind. If all men were well off, if poverty and disease had been reduced to their lowest possible point, there would still remain much to be done to produce a valuable society; and even in the existing world the goods of the mind are at least as important as the goods of the body. It is exclusively among the goods of the mind that the value of philosophy is to be found; and only those who are not indifferent to these goods can be persuaded that the study of philosophy is not a waste of time.

Philosophy, like all other studies, aims primarily at knowledge. The knowledge it aims at is the kind of knowledge which gives unity and system to the body of the sciences, and the kind which results from a critical examination of the grounds of our convictions, prejudices, and beliefs. But it cannot be maintained that philosophy has had any very great measure of success in its attempts to provide definite answers to its questions. If you ask a mathematician, a mineralogist, a historian, or any other man of learning, what definite body of truths has been ascertained by his science, his answer will last as long as you are willing to listen. But if you put the same question to a philosopher, he will, if he is candid, have to confess that his study has not achieved positive results such as have been achieved by other sciences. It is true that this is partly accounted for by the fact that, as soon as definite knowledge concerning any subject becomes possible, this subject ceases to be called philosophy, and becomes a separate science. The whole study of the heavens, which now belongs to astronomy, was once included in philosophy; Newton's great work was called 'the mathematical principles of natural philosophy'. Similarly, the study of the human mind, which was a part of philosophy, has now been separated from philosophy and has become the science of psychology. Thus, to a great extent, the uncertainty of philosophy is more apparent than real: those questions which are already capable of definite answers are placed in the sciences, while those only to which, at present, no definite answer can be given, remain to form the residue which is called philosophy. This is, however, only a part of the truth concerning the uncertainty of philosophy. There are many questions--and among them those that are of the profoundest interest to our spiritual life--which, so far as we can see, must remain insoluble to the human intellect unless its powers become of quite a different order from what they are now. Has the universe any unity of plan or purpose, or is it a fortuitous concourse of atoms? Is consciousness a permanent part of the universe, giving hope of indefinite growth in wisdom, or is it a transitory accident on a small planet on which life must ultimately become impossible? Are good and evil of importance to the universe or only to man? Such questions are asked by philosophy, and variously answered by various philosophers. But it would seem that, whether answers be otherwise discoverable or not, the answers suggested by philosophy are none of them demonstrably true. Yet, however slight may be the hope of discovering an answer, it is part of the business of philosophy to continue the consideration of such questions, to make us aware of their importance, to examine all the approaches to them, and to keep alive that speculative interest in the universe which is apt to be killed by confining ourselves to definitely ascertainable knowledge.

Many philosophers, it is true, have held that philosophy could establish the truth of certain answers to such fundamental questions. They have supposed that what is of most importance in religious beliefs could be proved by strict demonstration to be true. In order to judge of such attempts, it is necessary to take a survey of human knowledge, and to form an opinion as to its methods and its limitations. On such a subject it would be unwise to pronounce dogmatically; but if the investigations of our previous chapters have not led us astray, we shall be compelled to renounce the hope of finding philosophical proofs of religious beliefs. We cannot, therefore, include as part of the value of philosophy any definite set of answers to such questions. Hence, once more, the value of philosophy must not depend upon any supposed body of definitely ascertainable knowledge to be acquired by those who study it.

The value of philosophy is, in fact, to be sought largely in its very uncertainty. The man who has no tincture of philosophy goes through life imprisoned in the prejudices derived from common sense, from the habitual beliefs of his age or his nation, and from convictions which have grown up in his mind without the co-operation or consent of his deliberate reason. To such a man the world tends to become definite, finite, obvious; common objects rouse no questions, and unfamiliar possibilities are contemptuously rejected. As soon as we begin to philosophize, on the contrary, we find, as we saw in our opening chapters, that even the most everyday things lead to problems to which only very incomplete answers can be given. Philosophy, though unable to tell us with certainty what is the true answer to the doubts which it raises, is able to suggest many possibilities which enlarge our thoughts and free them from the tyranny of custom. Thus, while diminishing our feeling of certainty as to what things are, it greatly increases our knowledge as to what they may be; it removes the somewhat arrogant dogmatism of those who have never travelled into the region of liberating doubt, and it keeps alive our sense of wonder by showing familiar things in an unfamiliar aspect. Apart from its utility in showing unsuspected possibilities, philosophy has a value--perhaps its chief value--through the greatness of the objects which it contemplates, and the freedom from narrow and personal aims resulting from this contemplation. The life of the instinctive man is shut up within the circle of his private interests: family and friends may be included, but the outer world is not regarded except as it may help or hinder what comes within the circle of instinctive wishes. In such a life there is something feverish and confined, in comparison with which the philosophic life is calm and free. The private world of instinctive interests is a small one, set in the midst of a great and powerful world which must, sooner or later, lay our private world in ruins. Unless we can so enlarge our interests as to include the whole outer world, we remain like a garrison in a beleaguered fortress, knowing that the enemy prevents escape and that ultimate surrender is inevitable. In such a life there is no peace, but a constant strife between the insistence of desire and the powerlessness of will. In one way or another, if our life is to be great and free, we must escape this prison and this strife.

One way of escape is by philosophic contemplation. Philosophic contemplation does not, in its widest survey, divide the universe into two hostile camps--friends and foes, helpful and hostile, good and bad--it views the whole impartially. Philosophic contemplation, when it is unalloyed, does not aim at proving that the rest of the universe is akin to man. All acquisition of knowledge is an enlargement of the Self, but this enlargement is best attained when it is not directly sought. It is obtained when the desire for knowledge is alone operative, by a study which does not wish in advance that its objects should have this or that character, but adapts the Self to the characters which it finds in its objects. This enlargement of Self is not obtained when, taking the Self as it is, we try to show that the world is so similar to this Self that knowledge of it is possible without any admission of what seems alien. The desire to prove this is a form of self-assertion and, like all self-assertion, it is an obstacle to the growth of Self which it desires, and of which the Self knows that it is capable. Self-assertion, in philosophic speculation as elsewhere, views the world as a means to its own ends; thus it makes the world of less account than Self, and the Self sets bounds to the greatness of its goods. In contemplation, on the contrary, we start from the not-Self, and through its greatness the boundaries of Self are enlarged; through the infinity of the universe the mind which contemplates it achieves some share in infinity.

For this reason greatness of soul is not fostered by those philosophies which assimilate the universe to Man. Knowledge is a form of union of Self and not-Self; like all union, it is impaired by dominion, and therefore by any attempt to force the universe into conformity with what we find in ourselves. There is a widespread philosophical tendency towards the view which tells us that Man is the measure of all things, that truth is man-made, that space and time and the world of universals are properties of the mind, and that, if there be anything not created by the mind, it is unknowable and of no account for us. This view, if our previous discussions were correct, is untrue; but in addition to being untrue, it has the effect of robbing philosophic contemplation of all that gives it value, since it fetters contemplation to Self. What it calls knowledge is not a union with the not-Self, but a set of prejudices, habits, and desires, making an impenetrable veil between us and the world beyond. The man who finds pleasure in such a theory of knowledge is like the man who never leaves the domestic circle for fear his word might not be law. The true philosophic contemplation, on the contrary, finds its satisfaction in every enlargement of the not-Self, in everything that magnifies the objects contemplated, and thereby the subject contemplating. Everything, in contemplation, that is personal or private, everything that depends upon habit, self-interest, or desire, distorts the object, and hence impairs the union which the intellect seeks. By thus making a barrier between subject and object, such personal and private things become a prison to the intellect. The free intellect will see as God might see, without a *here* and *now*, without hopes and fears, without the trammels of customary beliefs and traditional prejudices, calmly, dispassionately, in the sole and exclusive desire of knowledge--knowledge as impersonal, as purely contemplative, as it is possible for man to attain. Hence also the free intellect will value more the abstract and universal knowledge into which the accidents of private history do not enter, than the knowledge brought by the senses, and dependent, as such knowledge must be, upon an exclusive and personal point of view and a body whose sense-organs distort as much as they reveal.

The mind which has become accustomed to the freedom and impartiality of philosophic contemplation will preserve something of the same freedom and impartiality in the world of action and emotion. It will view its purposes and desires as parts of the whole, with the absence of insistence that results from seeing them as infinitesimal fragments in a world of which all the rest is unaffected by any one man's deeds. The impartiality which, in contemplation, is the unalloyed desire for truth, is the very same quality of mind which, in action, is justice, and in emotion is that universal love which can be given to all, and not only to those who are judged useful or admirable. Thus contemplation enlarges not only the objects of our thoughts, but also the objects of our actions and our affections: it makes us citizens of the universe, not only of one walled city at war with all the rest. In this citizenship of the universe consists man's true freedom, and his liberation from the thralldom of narrow hopes and fears.

Thus, to sum up our discussion of the value of philosophy; Philosophy is to be studied, not for the sake of any definite answers to its questions, since no definite answers can, as a rule, be known to be true, but rather for the sake of the questions themselves; because these questions enlarge our conception of what is possible, enrich our intellectual imagination and diminish the dogmatic assurance which closes the mind against speculation; but above all because, through the greatness of the universe which philosophy contemplates, the mind also is rendered great, and becomes capable of that union with the universe which constitutes its highest good.

22280230R00158

Printed in Great Britain
by Amazon